Tusker

Dougie Arnold

Published by Clink Street Publishing 2020

First edition.

ISBN: 978-1-912850-88-4 (paperback)
ISBN: 978-1-912850-89-1 (ebook)

Author's note

As a young man working in Kenya in the 1980's I fell in love with the country and its amazing wildlife. I have a vivid memory of trying to count the number of elephants in a herd as they passed us one evening, there were certainly over seventy. Amongst them was one whose tusks were so long they were close to touching the ground. I was awe struck! Such elephants are traditionally called "tuskers". Today there are probably fewer than thirty of these giants left in the whole of Africa.

Elephants remain under a constant threat, mostly as a result of intensified poaching for ivory. In the Great Elephant Census, the results of which were released in 2016, experts estimated that their population in Africa had dropped by over 110,000 in a decade. That means that only 415,000 remain across the whole continent. When I was born there were thought to be around 5 million!

This book is dedicated to all those remarkable men and women who devote their lives, not just to the protection of elephants but of all our precious wildlife in every corner of the world.

The rest of us owe you a huge debt of gratitude.

Dougie Arnold

Chapter One

It had never occurred to Harry that this was a day on which he might die.

He kicked the log further towards the dying embers and looked into the silent faces of the men who shared this night with him, each lost in his own thoughts. There was murder in the air and unless they had extreme good fortune, there wasn't a thing they could do about it.

He had forgotten just how dark African nights were. Of course the stars were like nothing he saw back home, here they filled the sky, but they were too distant to help. The moon was the problem, just a slither, and that is what made it such a dangerous time.

His uncle Jim had posted their most trusted trackers at the vulnerable entry and exit points but it was a vast area and they were so thinly spread. In past years they could have counted on the help of the Kenya Wildlife Services to spare some rangers but not now. This was war and there were more important priorities than the Uwingoni Reserve. They were on their own.

That morning Harry had watched the small herd, the rugged matriarch in the lead, her head swaying gently from side to side, as she climbed up the steep northern escarpment. The others dutifully followed, some of last year's youngsters struggling with their footing on the loose rocks. He had willed them to turn back, anywhere was better than their northern border. One of the largest, the last into the tree line, had turned briefly, the early morning sun catching the whiteness of her tusks, and then she was gone.

The walkie talkie crackled into life. "Base, this is Mike."

Harry snatched the set off the table. "Go ahead."

"They're here, about eight of them I think, but it's difficult to tell, and they're on foot."

"Are you still up by the northern spur?"

"Yes and they're following baboon stream east. My guess is they are heading for the watering hole."

"Bastards," muttered Harry as everyone who had been listening round the fire sprinted through the camp entrance towards the two waiting Land Rovers. There was a single treacherous track to the waterhole, dangerous at the best of times but on a dark night…

The wheel spun easily in Bethwell's hands as he took the sharp right-hand fork. It was pointless to drive quietly; the engine noise would carry a long way on a night like this. Anyway, he wanted the poachers to know they were coming, wanted them to feel the fear of being caught but above all else he wanted them to turn away from their target.

Harry willed the Land Rover on. Startled waterbuck sprang back from the side of the track, the white ring of their rumps briefly highlighted in the darkness. Despite his youth he had bonded well with the others. He had such respect for them and they in turn had learnt to trust him. He hoped he would be worthy. The adrenalin coursed through his body but strangely he felt no fear, just an overwhelming urge to reach the waterhole in time.

He was plotting the route in his head, he had always been fortunate to have that knack of being able to remember terrain well. Some people had photographic memories of what they read, for him it was almost as though there was a virtual map in his mind. Bethwell was an experienced driver but he would just stay to the main track, worried perhaps about the consequences of damaging the vehicle for which he was responsible.

"Take the next left. If we go through the water splash and up the old buffalo track we can cut off a whole corner and perhaps save ten minutes."

Bethwell looked doubtful. "That's a treacherous route Harry. It takes us right on the edge of the escarpment and the heavy rains last month washed it away in places. Are you sure?"

Harry had to admit that he had his doubts but he had been hiking up there only five days ago and it had been dry since. "I'm sure we'll manage and we couldn't be in better hands." Harry had this easy way with them, his uncle was a lovely guy but compliments to anyone were pretty few and far between.

Bethwell smiled despite himself, "The buffalo track it is then. Hang on in the back this is going to be a bumpy ride." He stopped momentarily before the turn, pressing down the small coloured gear stick that engaged four-wheel drive. There was no way they would make it otherwise.

The wardens in the back braced themselves, sitting only on canvas webbing; they had an idea of what lay ahead. They were sideways on, facing each other, the rather ancient 303 Lee–Enfield rifles, relics from a bygone age, clamped firmly between their knees.

Harry heard the loose stones clattering away under their wheels as the steepness of the track increased. Bethwell kept them to a middle course, quickly making corrections when he felt them slipping sideways. To their right was thick forest, and every so often the headlights caught the sudden movement of dark shapes as animals, ever cautious, distanced themselves from the oncoming noise and light.

To their left the tree line had thinned out and all but disappeared, replaced instead by an almost sheer drop already some five hundred feet to the valley floor. Harry tried not to look down, he wasn't bad with heights but it didn't take a great imagination to picture what would happen if Bethwell misjudged one of the sharp bends. Even as the image played through his mind his senses were aware of some sort of burning smell. He glanced across at the temperature gauge, the needle hovering dangerously on red, hardly surprising after the gradient of the climb and the age of the vehicle. Almost everything in Uwingoni was a little tired and out of date he thought.

"We should make it to the top of the ridge," shouted Bethwell above the clatter of the engine. "When we level out she should start to cool down."

"I think you love this old lady more than your girlfriends," smiled Harry, trying to inject some humour into the situation.

Bethwell grimaced, but whether at the thought of his girlfriends or the damage he might be doing to his precious Land Rover, Harry was unsure.

They took a final sharp right hander, the outside rear wheel almost biting on clean air and then they were there, and the thin line of the escarpment top lay before them.

Harry glanced back at the four men behind him. In the reflected light from the headlights he could make out the sheen of sweat across their faces. He wasn't aware of any of them even speaking during the treacherous climb and they were only too happy to scramble out and stand on solid ground again. He didn't blame them.

This was as far as they could go by vehicle; the track simply petered out by the densely packed trees ahead. The waterhole was about another fifteen minutes on foot through weaving forest paths. They couldn't wait for the others. He could see their headlights below. They had taken the safer route so they were still ten minutes away and time was far too precious. They would have to risk the waterhole by themselves; the others would just have to catch up as soon as they could.

Kilifi took the lead; he didn't need anyone to tell him. His normal cheerfulness suppressed, he moved with quiet purpose, often just speaking with his hands. If there was a better tracker in East Africa, thought Harry, he would be surprised.

What was already a dark night became even more shadowy as the trees closed in around them. There was no obvious path but there were animal tracks that crisscrossed one another and Kilifi silently signalled for them to halt every few minutes while he examined the ground and then unfalteringly moved on again. The only sounds they were aware of, apart from each other, were animals scampering away from them deeper into the night.

"The waterhole can't be that far up ahead," whispered Harry to Kilifi. He was not conscious of the sound of elephants or indeed other larger animals, but of course they might be in the clearing itself which radiated for about two hundred feet in a circle from the water.

Far more concerning was the exact whereabouts of the poachers. They would have known the rangers were coming, simply from the sound of the Land Rovers. Mike had said he thought there were about eight of them which would make sense because they would physically have to carry any tusks back from an area like this. Their vehicles would almost definitely be beyond the northern boundary of the reserve. Worryingly he hadn't heard from Mike since that transmission. However, communication signals were poor up here anyway and if he was following them closely he might well have his radio turned off.

Kilifi had his right hand raised and everyone stopped, standing as motionless as possible. Had he seen something? Harry was now in the middle of the group, the only one without a weapon as was to be expected, the others had spent years in the bush honing their skills. He couldn't come along and pick up a gun like some comic hero. Real life didn't work like that. They were all crack shots and old though their rifles were, that was a comforting thought.

Harry moved cautiously to the front of the line. Kilifi pointed to an area ahead where it seemed a little lighter and he realised that must be the waterhole; with no trees above he could start to make things out a little more clearly. Before they moved any closer he thought he would try Mike again. He pressed the side of the walkie talkie and the red transmission light glowed unnaturally bright.

"Mike are you there? Come in." Harry kept his voice as hushed as possible and tried again. "Mike, can you hear me?" Nothing, the silence was almost overpowering. Without details of the poachers, an already dangerous situation became potentially much more lethal.

Some poachers were quite inexperienced, men who were desperate to risk anything to earn money in hard times. Others, however, were hardened, callous men who thought nothing of the slaughter they were carrying out and anyone or anything that stood in their way would be removed without hesitation. The wardens may be hunting them but the tables could easily turn and the hunters become the hunted.

They edged cautiously towards the clearing, careful not to make a sudden movement, trying to blend with the tree trunks, breathing quietly and watching both ahead and where their footfall landed, intent on not giving away their position.

The trees thinned out and they were able to see the waterhole itself. The first and most obvious thing was that there wasn't an elephant in sight. Harry assumed they must have already had their evening drink. If they were on their way they were far too large to move quietly through the trees and undergrowth.

There was surprisingly little activity at the waterhole. A family of warthogs were lapping noisily at the surface, their father keeping a close watch, his large tusks a reminder that, despite his size, he was to be treated with respect.

Harry was aware of moving shadows behind the trees on the far side. He nudged Kilifi gently but he simply shook his head, indicating this was nothing to be concerned about. The shadows came slowly into focus as they moved very cautiously from cover into the open space. Despite their circumstances, Harry found himself transfixed. Moving with easy elegance towards the water were two greater kudu, large woodland antelope. Even in the half-light he could make out the reddish brown of their coats and the contrasting thin vertical white stripes that that gave them a touching beauty. Sniffing the air they stepped gently forward.

Without warning the night erupted. White spurts of light on the far side of the water and the sound of bullets smacking into the branches and tree trunks just to their left, had everyone leaping for cover.

"Flatten yourself behind a trunk," shouted Kilifi, pushing Harry behind a large cedar tree. A second burst of fire a little more to the left. "They know we are here," continued Kilifi, "but they certainly haven't got a proper fix on us. Just stay still and quiet." On the word quiet there were some very raucous bird calls and two large black and white hornbills, their peace shattered, flapped noisily out of the tree tops, their huge bills pulling them down before they rose once more in their rather ungainly flight. Again the guns on the far side blazed away.

Bethwell joined them. "These guys are much more heavily

armed than us but they are very raw, firing at any movement. That's the good news. We could retreat out of harm's way but then they would simply retrace their steps and be back again another night. Our rifles are worse than useless unless they are going to show themselves, which I doubt. Looks like they are using the old favourite, the AK-47, and we have no answer in this gloom to that sort of firepower."

Harry hadn't said a word since that first burst. His heart was pounding and his hands sweaty. He was actually being shot at. This wasn't a film where some heroic deed saves the day; this was the reality of the war against poaching. Perhaps when you are young you never think about dying, you feel somehow immortal, well he certainly didn't feel that now.

Despite or perhaps because of the threat his mind raced. Last time he had been at the waterhole, it had been exciting, dangerous he supposed, but in an entirely different way. He had come up with two of the younger men from camp to look for wild honey. One of them, Bear, the others called him, climbed trees with an ease that they could only marvel at. It had been a fruitless morning and so they had headed off to see whether there was any interesting game at the waterhole when Bear became very excited about a small greeny, brown bird no more than five inches long. It was a honey guide and he explained to Harry that often they led them to the hives of wild bees. Unbelievably they had followed it directly to this clearing and there fifty feet off the ground in an aging podo tree was a huge nest.

Bear had shinned up using a large piece of leather that he wrapped round the trunk to help him a step at a time. When he had got level with the hive he lit some large foul smelling, smoky leaves which he had waved about vigorously to calm down the bees while he cut off a small part of the grey structure. Despite a few stings he had returned in one piece and they had enjoyed the wonderful delights of wild honey, making sure to leave a small piece as a present for the honey guide.

Harry recognised the podo tree now as it stood out from the others around it. The plan formulating in his head seemed crazy but it might just work.

Kilifi and Bethwell listened as he explained his idea. "The nest in that tree was huge; there must be thousands of bees in there. Can you imagine what would happen if we could bring part of it down near the poachers?" They had all been stung at one time or another by African bees and even hardened men jumped about with the pain. "Imagine hundreds swarming round you because their broken nest was suddenly at your feet."

"Interesting idea Harry but what about us?" inquired Bethwell. "They will be spreading out attacking anything that moves."

"I had thought about that," he replied. "Jim told me a story about when he was attacked by wild bees; I suppose that is why I thought of it. He escaped the worst of their attention by diving into a nearby stream. Water is bee proof! And what do we have just behind us, the stream that feeds the waterhole."

He could see their minds analysing what he had just suggested and the slow smiles spreading across their faces gave him the answer he wanted.

"Who are your best marksmen?" Harry asked. "I suggest we use two as that will double our chances of taking part of the nest down. The rest of us will already be back by the deepest parts of the stream that we can find. As soon as they have fired they will have given away our position and will have to make a run back to the safety of the water as fast as they can."

The plan was explained to everyone. It seemed

straightforward and Harry hoped there wasn't something he'd forgotten. He took the two marksmen up to the cover of the last trees before the clearing and pointed out the large dark shapes of the nest some fifty feet up. The bees were sleeping, if you didn't have some prior knowledge you would never have guessed they were even there. The men drew back the bolt action of their old rifles, the bullets sliding comfortingly into the firing chambers and raised their weapons to their shoulders.

Harry had done what he could so he moved back to the stream. The water was inky black in the shade of the trees and he eased himself slowly into its protection, with just his head sticking out. Four clear shots rang out in quick succession, followed immediately by the clatter of the poachers' AK-47s. Then the gunfire stopped as quickly as it had begun.

Harry heard the most dreadful yelling and screaming and despite being some way from the podo tree he was aware of an increasingly loud, angry buzzing. Two dark shapes crashed through the undergrowth as the marksmen retreated to the comparative safety of the stream. They splashed unceremoniously into the water and all of them ducked their heads under the surface holding their breath for as long as they could.

As he felt his lungs about to burst Harry raised his head, took a huge gulp of air and retreated under the surface again. The others were doing the same, nobody stupid enough to even risk a quick glance around. They repeated this for what seemed ages but in reality was about seven or eight minutes.

Then very slowly Harry raised just his head out of the water and tried to work out what was going on. Occasional bees flickered overhead and there was still an angry buzzing on the far side of the waterhole but no sound of voices.

He was suddenly alerted to the radio set he had left on

the bank and eased himself out a little further to grab it.

"Harry come in, are you there?" Before he could respond Samson's urgent voice was crackling through the speaker again. "Harry what's going on, over?"

"Samson, whatever you do just stay away from the water-hole area. We are safe for the moment."

"But we heard gunfire and then nothing and that already seems ages ago!"

"I'll explain but not now..." He suddenly felt a searing pain in his left ear, threw the radio back on the bank and plunged his throbbing head below the surface. Harry had been stung before but not on his head or by an especially angry bee. He couldn't believe the needle like pain that now seemed the only sensation in his body.

He peered cautiously above the surface again, alert to any sound or movement that might indicate another attack. The others were still in the water up to their necks; Bethwell, much to the amusement of the others, had been stung twice but they had escaped.

Slowly they pulled themselves up onto the bank and took stock of the situation. The sound of the bees had almost died away.

Harry picked up the radio and explained to Samson what had happened. There was no sign of human movement under the podo tree but that meant nothing, they still needed to take great care. Harry gave Samson their position and they waited for those from the other vehicle to join them.

It was a while before they arrived, silent but recognizable shadows moving easily through the trees. Occasional bees came their way but seemed to show little interest in them now. Nevertheless, everyone agreed it was still too dangerous to move towards the area where they had last seen the poachers. They posted sentries to watch and then simply waited.

Harry was delighted that for the moment at least the threat of the poachers seemed to have disappeared but his ear felt twice the size of normal, his head pounded and he realised how cold he felt from being immersed in the water for so long.

It was agreed that Kilifi should take a closer look. He disappeared silently into the trees, working his way cautiously round to the far side of the waterhole. Ever alert but silent, the others waited for his return.

After what seemed an age he reappeared, a grim smile on his face.

"Come," he said. "There is a sight that will make your heart glad, but take care."

Cautiously they crossed the clearing, aware of a slight lightening of the sky in the east. Dawn could not be far away. A few bees buzzed unthreateningly near the ground and the broken nest but that was not what drew their attention.

Five men lay motionless on the forest floor, their bodies curled up in a defensive position with hands over their faces. Every inch of visible skin was covered by large, angry lumps, the green camouflage trousers and tops they were wearing would definitely be hiding similar evidence of a frenzied attack. They would have had little chance, vastly outnumbered and having nothing to fight back with they had literally been stung to death.

"Serves them right," said Samson. "That's another five poachers who won't be after our elephants. I hope their deaths were as painful as they look."

Kilifi nodded his wise head. "I have known men to die from bee stings but never like this. Then again who has a bees' nest falling on them in the night?"

"Down here, come and see," shouted Bethwell. They ran down the slope away from the waterhole where two further bodies were splayed out on the ground, their AK-47s, which for once had offered no protection, by their sides.

"Looks like they might almost have escaped," said Harry, "but hard to move faster than a swarm of bees! That makes seven. Mike said he thought there were eight, let's search more widely."

He tried to make contact with both Mike and his uncle again but frustratingly with no success. The radios themselves were old, ex-military, but their range was also very limited and worked on line of sight, so frequently people were uncontactable in this steep terrain. Harry had tried to persuade Jim to build a repeater mast near the top of the escarpment but had been informed that funds weren't available.

Despite the increased visibility with the early morning light they couldn't find any other bodies. However, Kilifi had been examining the ground carefully. "Look," he said, "you can see where they came up along the ridge but the stony ground makes it difficult to be sure of their numbers. There are prints of boots but the sole markings are so similar it isn't easy to get a clear picture."

Suddenly he stiffened as though he had somehow picked up the scent of his prey. The others gathered round and peered at the ground. "Here," he said, his face alive with excitement, "there is a single set of prints heading back towards the northern border and they are easy to follow because they belong to someone with a bad right leg."

Harry was always amazed by Kilifi's remarkable tracking skills. He looked at the ground and at first saw nothing and then he made out the marks of a left footed boot print and to its right a very different mark as though something was being dragged. This was repeated over and over again and it became obvious, even to a novice like Harry, that they were following the tracks of someone moving away from the bodies and heading north.

"These are very recent," said Kilifi. "There is often a morning wind up here that would soon blow away these print marks. The person we are following is moving with difficulty, the left print is deep because he is putting most of his weight on it and the dragging mark on the other side is the toe of his right boot which obviously can't take too much load. Whoever he is, there is a fifty-fifty chance we can catch up with him before he reaches our border."

"Samson why don't you stay here with your crew and try to make contact with Jim to tell him what has happened and we will follow the tracks."

Samson looked disappointed but saw the sense in what Harry said. "Good luck, hope you get to him in time."

Kilifi needed no encouragement. If they managed to catch the eighth man the chances were they would have the whole poaching team and importantly he might well be able to tell them crucial information that could lead to those higher up the poaching chain.

The sun was getting up and with the heat and the chase; Harry's clothes were almost dry already. Kilifi rarely paused, knowing how vital it was not to let this individual escape. The tree line was thinning, giving them a much better view of the land ahead. Apart from some large rocks there was nowhere to hide.

Almost instantly they saw their man. Despite the distance they could make out his lopsided movement. "I could almost have a good shot at him from here," said Kilifi but Harry was reluctant to take that course of action. His uncle had warned him that they weren't the police or KWS and so shooting someone, despite all they might have tried to do, was the very last option.

They increased the pace. There was no need for Kilifi's tracking skills now they just needed to get to him before Uwingoni's border with the outside world.

They scrambled down the loose rock screed, finding it hard to keep their balance with the constant movement under their feet.

Their quarry had looked behind him and despite the obviously damaged leg increased his speed.

Harry could make out a vehicle on the other side of the fence. It was an open four-wheel drive and he could see there was nobody in it but there was no doubt where their man was heading. That must be what the poachers came in thought Harry and if he has the keys he might well be away before they could reach him. That spurred him on. Despite the experience of the African bush that the others had, he was younger and faster than them. He was really closing the gap but he needed to, it would be a close-run thing.

His lungs were working overtime, screaming for more oxygen but he was almost on his man, just one final push. As he launched himself, arms outstretched, shoulder aiming just above the poacher's knees, he felt certain he would bring him down.

They fell together in a crunching, jarring crash, rolling over several times on the rock-strewn surface.

As Harry looked into the other man's face for the first time, he instinctively felt himself recoil. Not surprisingly there were a number of angry bee stings strewn across his skin, although nothing as extreme as the others, but it was his eyes that held Harry. They radiated pure evil, red rimmed with dark swirling centres that seemed to draw him in and repulse him at the same time.

A fist slammed into his chin and he instinctively threw up his hands to protect his face. His sole purpose had been to catch his man and strangely he realised that he had thought no further than that or what might follow.

The early sunlight caught the blade in his opponent's right hand and Harry leapt back. A curse in a language he didn't recognise screamed from the dark hole that was his mouth. Harry was prepared for the lunge and scrabbled out of the way but recognised that he was in trouble and out of his league.

Again he retreated, this time catching his heel on a large rock, putting him off balance. The look of triumph on the poacher's face told him all he needed to know as he fell clattering onto the hard surface.

He curled into a protective ball and closed his eyes but the blow never came. Instead he heard a loud crunch and the crash of another body hitting the rocks. When he looked up a concerned Bethwell was standing over him. Harry smiled nervously back and saw the body of his would-be assassin sprawled to his side.

"He'll have a headache for a few days," smiled Bethwell. "The butts of these old rifles come in handy sometimes."

The others arrived all out of breath but their obvious pleasure at seeing that Harry was uninjured was evident. Kilifi aimed a kick at the body's ribs and looked suitably pleased when it emitted a loud groan.

"Somali scum," he sneered. "I might have guessed they would be up to their necks in poaching. They don't care for anyone or anything except themselves. No doubt the ivory would have paid for more weapons for whichever war lord or crazy religious group he works for."

They hauled him roughly to his feet and bound his hands behind his back. His hatred and arrogance were so visible as he glared at Harry, cursing once again in his native tongue, but the others took no notice as they made him crouch down by the boundary ditch.

The distant sound of an engine caused everyone to tense and as they looked west they could see a large dust cloud, indicating a vehicle heading their way at high speed. Rifles were unslung as the small group waited to see whether it was friend or foe.

Kilifi raised his worn binoculars and squinted towards the rising sun. With his smile came a visible relaxation of the others.

The battered, sand-coloured 110 Land Rover with a worn elephant image that could clearly be seen on the door announced it as belonging to Uwingoni. It skidded to a halt in front of them and out jumped the driver, a small, strongly built man with piercing blue eyes who took in the scene in an instant.

As Jim strode towards them everyone smiled. He may not have been full of compliments to his men but they liked and respected him and the feeling was mutual.

"What have we here Bethwell?" he inquired as he looked down at the scowling Somali. The events of the last couple of hours were recounted as quickly and simply as possible. Jim enjoyed a long tale round a campfire in the evening but when it was a matter that concerned his beloved Uwingoni he wanted things short and precise and they all knew that.

When they recounted Harry's idea about the bees, half a smile crossed his face but he said nothing.

"You were lucky with this one Harry. Just as well. What would I have told your father if that knife had moved a little quicker than it did?" Harry didn't need reminding, he had already played everything back in his mind several times.

The other door of the Land Rover opened and out limped Mike, his uncle's trusted lieutenant, tall and lanky with a slow, slightly awkward way of speaking. He was in many ways everything Jim was not but they had been friends since school and both shared a passion for preserving African wildlife.

"Useless radios," he grumbled. "With the escarpment in the way we were always going to struggle to stay in touch."

"I know," replied Harry, "but at least we knew to look for an eighth man before we lost contact. We really must try to update our communications though."

"We must do lots of things Harry," interrupted Jim, "but unfortunately they all cost money."

Harry knew that money was a constant problem, but he couldn't understand why things were quite so bad; Aziz, his uncle's finance manager, was always full of doom and gloom.

"Bethwell get the Somali in the back of the Land Rover with a couple of your chaps and take him to the local police station. It's quite a trek but I know Inspector Mwitu well and I am sure he has ways of finding out more about who is behind this from our friend over there. Mike you deal with the police, I'm going up to the waterhole. We will see you back at camp later."

Chapter Two

The mood round the campfire could not have been more different from when they were last there. Everyone was smiling and the chatter was more like that of a family of preening superb starlings, as each man told the part he had played during the previous hours.

Nearly everyone held tin mugs brimming with sweet, milky chai but Harry couldn't get his taste buds round that and he had his hands cupped round his favourite Kenyan coffee. The smell of bacon sizzling on a huge pan on the fire was almost better than the taste that was to follow. Sweet potatoes cooked in the ashes round the side made an odd combination, but a truly tasty breakfast.

Jim had smiled with grim satisfaction when they returned to the waterhole and the bodies of the poachers were slung like sacks of grain into the back of one of the Land Rovers. They would be handed over to the authorities later.

When he heard the story in full he turned his gaze a little more intently on Harry as though he was looking at something he had not seen before. "Glad you remember some of my old stories." Harry had shrugged; that was about as close to praise as he would get.

After the meal Jim had summoned them all to a meeting. He was a great believer in keeping everyone in the know.

"We are like a chain holding back this evil," he said, "and of course that means we are only as strong as our weakest link." Harry had heard this before, as had everyone else. His uncle was a little unimaginative with words but nevertheless, there was truth in what he said. There wasn't a man there who wouldn't give his all for the reserve and the precious wildlife in it.

Before he had arrived in Kenya it had been lions and leopards that Harry had really wanted to see. Of course, he always relished the magic of watching them; the leopards solitary and beautiful but so secretive; the lions much easier, more open, majestic but lazy, rousing themselves only when their tummies grumbled. However, it was the elephants that had won a special place in his heart.

On his second day at Uwingoni, Bethwell had taken him out for an early drive. It had been a shock to Harry's system to get up before the sun but he had soon come to appreciate the pre-dawn magic.

There had been a surprising chill in the air but that was almost instantly forgotten once they had splashed across the little stream near camp.

"This week Harry I will take you up to see the spring where this water begins. It comes bubbling out of the volcanic ground with the gentlest of sounds. I have never tasted anything so pure. Forget all the promises made on the bottles in the supermarket, this is so special. Even here, further down-stream it is good to drink, only a bit of baboon shit to spoil the taste." Harry turned up his nose and Bethwell laughed. He felt instantly at ease, the pupil and the teacher, but Bethwell was unlike any teacher he had had before. Harry soon began to realise how amazing his knowledge was, but this wasn't something learnt from books, rather from a life out in the African bush.

Equally well Harry soon found that he did not need the

facts repeated as he had done at school, rather he craved more; there wasn't anything he didn't want to know.

Then there had been that special moment, one that he almost felt he had been waiting for all his life. Ironically he had been looking in the other direction when Bethwell had stopped the Land Rover and cut the engine, his hand moving to signify the need for quiet.

Moving slowly out of the valley floor was a group of elephants; the sun throwing its new light across the far hills caught them as they made their way peacefully towards them. There were seven of them, one of the largest and the smallest together as the mother protected a calf in her shadow as they moved. There were two other larger elephants, their ears flapping gently as they walked and then three assorted youngsters that followed on behind. He couldn't believe how close they were coming to the vehicle; he could actually hear the rumbling of their breathing and the calm swish of their legs against the long grass as they moved unhurriedly up the slope.

The matriarch almost paused on the track no more than fifty meters from where they were, gave an inquisitive glance in their direction and without a break in her stride continued up the gentle incline, the others in tow, until they were swallowed by the trees and dense vegetation. Harry could play the whole thing back in his mind but what he remembered was that, for what seemed an age, neither of them spoke, simply lost in the moment.

"Harry," his uncle's voice cut into daydream. "I was asking what you thought we might have done differently last night."

"Well, one of my main concerns was our lack of reliability in talking to each other on the radio. If we could only find the funds to update, it would make a huge difference."

His uncle grunted, "What do you think Aziz? Harry does have a point; can't we find the money from somewhere?"

Aziz clasped his hands together as if in prayer, smiling in that rather concerned manner that he always seemed to have. "Well, I'll re-examine next month's accounts but I'm not very hopeful..."

"That's all I ever hear," groaned Jim. "Harry is the youngest person here but he's right. We were lucky last night. Poor radio contact gave the poachers a real advantage over us and we just can't afford to let this keep happening."

Harry was watching Aziz as his uncle spoke and noticed not just the tightening of his knuckles as his hands bunched into fists but something in his eyes that he had never spotted before, a hardness perhaps, but it seemed so quick that he wasn't quite sure.

He was the only person in Uwingoni that Harry hadn't taken to, perhaps he reminded him too much of some of his past teachers, facts, figures, little personality and always wanting to be in control.

As he looked again, the permanent smile was there and the silky voice purred as usual. "I'll see what I can do Jim."

Harry dismissed his thoughts. It had just been the briefest of moments after all.

"I know it's been quite a night and you must feel ready for a good sleep but you'll have to put that on hold," Jim instructed. "We have guests coming in soon, a family of six and one extra which I will brief you about later. Bethwell, just check the four-wheel drive on your Land Rover please. I drove it the other day and it was really difficult to engage when I was at the top of the escarpment road. If you came down that track just on your brakes, you would probably burn them out."

"Harry, I'd like you to go down to the airstrip. My pilot friend Ollie is kindly dropping off some fresh food supplies from Nairobi on his way north to another job. He's not much older than you, I think you'll get along well. As for everyone else, get that chai down your throats and crack on. You must all have a dozen things to do before the morning is out."

Within a few minutes only Harry and his uncle were by the campfire, even Aziz had retreated to his office to trawl through more bills and papers.

"You are growing into Africa well Harry but make sure you always respect it, despite its beauty, it can be wild and unforgiving. Now off to the airstrip. Take Bluebird, she's had a new clutch so should be fine."

Harry trotted over to the garage at the back of the camp where Ken the mechanic had his head under the bonnet as usual.

"I'm taking Bluebird down to the airstrip. Is she all ready to go?"

"All sorted Harry but look after her, she is very special."

Harry knew Ken treated the vehicles like his children but Bluebird was the oldest and had a special place in his heart. He had listened to the life history, made way back in 1975, smaller than the others, short wheel base as he had discovered they called it, and the only vehicle that was not green or sand coloured in the reserve.

Harry had always loved cars and had been out driving on the day of his seventeenth birthday, new licence in his pocket. Nothing here could be further removed from the streets of London, he thought. He took handfuls of the old steering wheel as Bluebird bumped round the sharp left-hand bend below the garages, the yellowing dust from the track already billowing out behind him.

The strip was only about a mile from camp and as he approached through the low shrub he startled several Thompson's gazelle that had been peacefully grazing and swiftly darted off, their tails swishing from side to side like windscreen wipers. He had been amazed to learn from Kilifi recently that they slept only for five minute bursts and then only for a total of about an hour a day. How on earth did they survive on so little sleep he wondered.

Sitting quietly and still trying to identify certain bird-song, he was aware of the distant sound of an engine. The small Cessna plane with its distinctive high wings above the cockpit was soon clearly visible but as it came in it didn't attempt to land, instead it came in low only about thirty feet off the ground driving away the Tommies who had chosen another bad spot for their morning graze. Harry had learnt that this was a common thing for pilots to do in order to make their landing that much safer. The plane banked and came in again, impressively landing without a bounce. It taxied up to the Land Rover, the engine cut and a young pilot in a crisp white shirt with gold captain's bars on his shoulders jumped to the ground. With an open, cheerful face and arm outstretched he bounded up to Harry.

"I'm Ollie," he smiled. "I've got some boxes of fresh supplies for you. Bit of a squeeze, I had to use this old 150 today, only two seats and not much space behind."

"Harry," he replied, shaking hands. "This really is a small plane, barely room for two big people."

Ollie passed down the boxes of supplies, chatting as he went. "She's a bit like a little car I suppose; you are so at one with her once you are up, every subtle movement of the stick or bit of turbulence is something you feel straight away. Pretty slow, flies at about eighty knots generally but you can push her to just over a hundred even though she is pretty old."

"Can I jump in?" enquired Harry. "I have always dreamed of taking the controls one day and learning to fly but it's expensive and in England the weather is pretty rubbish much of the time but out here …"

"Well this is probably the best plane in the world to learn on. In fact it is the fifth most produced plane of all time, which tells you something."

"I can't believe how few controls there are!"

"You really don't need many," replied Ollie. "Look, you have dials for your air speed and altitude which is pretty basic. Another shows you how steep your turns are then of course you have a compass and direction indicator so you know where you are going and the main stick is a bit like a steering wheel on a car, only it makes you go up and down too and finally that extended black knob is the throttle. Of course there are other things but if you get your head round those then you can fly."

Harry could actually feel his heart racing. "How long did it take you to learn?"

"I went solo pretty quickly," Ollie laughed. "One of the most exciting ten minutes of my life! The instructor got out and told me to go it alone. It was only a circuit of the airport but to be up there with nobody sitting next to me was something else, and no lay-by to pull into if something went wrong! Expensive too. I had to buy everyone at the Aero Club a drink afterwards. Tradition."

Harry instantly liked him. It's strange he thought, sometimes it just takes minutes to know that you are going to be good friends with someone.

"Look Harry, I'm afraid I have to go; some important Chinese engineer who is working on that new dam project needs to be picked up. Better not be late but I should be here again in a few days. I'm sure we could go up together for a short flight over the reserve then you could get a real feel about the excitement of flying a small plane."

"That would be amazing Ollie. Can't wait."

The young pilot was back in his cockpit in an instant, shutting the flimsy door behind him. The single propeller spun into life, as the plane turned back onto the strip. The engine noise increased and she trundled forward, bumping over the uneven surface of the grass. Within only a few hundred metres the wheels lifted off and the plane soon became a distant speck in the vastness of the African sky.

Harry jolted himself back to reality, jumped back in Bluebird and headed for the kitchen to deliver the supplies.

Raymond, the camp cook, who could work wonders with the simplest of ingredients grinned broadly as Harry put the boxes inside the kitchen door. His face glistened in the heat of the cooker which had several bubbling pans on it, the old blue and white apron stretched dangerously over his stomach.

"Just working on something new for our guests. Think they will really enjoy it; hope you will have a chance to try some too. Won't find it in any of those smart recipe books."

He moved back to stirring the pots, the wooden spoon tiny in his large hand.

The morning flew by and at lunch Mike was back from the police station.

"How did you get on?" inquired Harry.

"I was lucky. Inspector Mwitu was there himself. He said he would be having a chat with our Somali friend this afternoon and thought he would soon have some answers for us. The prisoner didn't seem so arrogant as they led him off to the cells. Rather him than me, Mwitu has a reputation for getting the answers he wants!"

Harry inwardly shuddered at the thought of just what a question session in the police station would involve. Nevertheless, sometimes the rules needed to be pushed to the limits. They were effectively at war with the poachers and had to be one step ahead, otherwise there would soon be no elephants left.

The remainder of the day passed in a whirl with everyone involved in preparing the camp for the arrival of the visiting tourists.

It seemed to be dark even earlier than normal and Harry just wanted to get to his tent, even the thought of a tasty evening meal had lost its appeal. This had been one of the most exhausting but exhilarating days he could ever remember.

Chapter Three

"Harry come quickly." It was Kilifi's voice intruding on his dreams. "If you don't move now we will have to leave you behind and believe me that's something you would regret more than you know."

Harry opened his eyes, propping himself up on one elbow. He recognised the early morning birdsong but he could see through the flap that it wasn't quite light.

"It's Mara," Kilifi's normally calm voice was mixed with both urgency and excitement. "I have been hearing the elephants trumpeting on and off for the last two hours and they are close to camp, less than a mile down the track I would guess. They are not concerned about danger, it is not that sort of noise and I don't feel they have really moved. Jim asked me to come and get you; he is already behind the wheel by the camp entrance. Be quick or he'll leave us behind.

Harry was instantly alert. Still in his clothes from the previous day he was out of the tent running in socks and carrying his boots. The little stones on the path barely registered as he sprinted as fast as he could to the waiting Land Rover.

Jim acknowledged him with a grunt as he squeezed into the front bench seat next to Kilifi and they set off down the track. They drove slowly, experienced eyes picking out the track in the half light.

"We might be about to witness something so special that it will live with us forever. But don't get your hopes up too much; this is an event I have seen just twice before in my life."

They could hear the elephants much more clearly now, their sounds breaking the stillness of the dawn, making everything else seem insignificant.

As they came up over the rise in the hill there they were, actually on the track itself. They looked at the vehicle and its occupants, their intelligent eyes taking in the new arrivals. They had seen them on numerous occasions and there were more important things to concern them than a few onlookers.

They were a close-knit family group, three sisters, three youngsters who were about six or seven years old and still learning much about life and one younger calf.

Everyone's attention was on the largest of the elephants in the middle of the group and very much its leader. They had named her Mara after the most famous reserve in the country and she was easily to distinguish because her left side tusk had broken about a third of the way up.

Harry knew she was heavily pregnant and they had hoped to see her with a new baby any day. He was aware that elephants nearly always give birth at night. There was less chance of being interrupted and it would give the calf an opportunity literally to find its feet. It generally took about an hour to stand up properly and perhaps the same again before it could take any meaningful steps. He knew too that hardly any animal would risk taking on even a partly grown elephant, but a baby, despite the protection of the herd, was always at risk.

Jim brought the Land Rover to a halt surprisingly close to them, cut the engine and remained motionless in his seat.

Mara was the one who was trumpeting and the others kept circling her, flicking their trunks about and snorting onto the track, blowing up small clouds of fine dust. It was clear she was close to that magic moment.

"Look, look," whispered Kilifi. "You can already see a shiny grey sack appearing between her back legs. Well inside that is her calf. She has been pregnant for just less than two years and I really can't believe the luck that has brought us here right now."

They watched in silence, no attempts to take photographs or even talk. It was all absorbing.

Mara's back legs flexed and as the grey sack lengthened they were amazed to see her gently kicking it with the inside of her feet, first to one side and then the other. The rest of the family moved closer and closer, their bodies partly obscuring her. Then she let out a trumpeting call far louder than before and the sack hit the track splitting as it did so to reveal her baby.

"It isn't moving!" whispered Harry, the emotion of the moment catching in his throat.

"Just wait and watch," urged Jim, his own feelings betrayed by his voice.

Mara and her sisters were gently pacing noisily round the baby knocking the little body softly with their feet and then it started to move; the back legs first, wriggling from side to side, its tiny trunk flopping about in the dust.

Even the youngsters were trying to do their bit, copying their mothers, using their trunks and feet to give support to the newest member of their family as it tried yet again to stand up.

Eventually after what seemed an age and with Mara's trunk partly wrapped round its body, the calf was off his knees and standing, all be it in a very wobbly way. It swayed forward where there was no support onto its knees again but was soon up, back legs splayed out, not trying to walk, just to stand and take stock of this new world of which he was the latest member.

Harry realised tears were rolling down his cheeks but as he looked across at the other two hardened veterans of the African bush, he saw too that they were similarly moved. He knew he had witnessed something few would ever see and it was a lesson in how the power of nature can evoke such strong feelings even in those who have spent a lifetime trying to protect it.

Now that the calf was standing, Harry pulled out his camera and started to take shots. Who else would have anything as sensational as this in their album?

"I know there is a lot to do back in camp," whispered Jim, "but it goes without saying that everything will have to be on hold for a while. Within the next hour he should be up to walking, even if only quite a small distance. They will want to head off into the bush where they'll feel safer. It always amazes me that animals as large as these can hide themselves so easily."

"I know you named Mara because she is such a special elephant and that you have names for some of the others. Do you think we could name the new calf too?"

"Did you have something in mind?"

"Well uncle, I had thought of Meru. It is a fantastic game park and the name has a rugged feel about it, like the park itself. Meru and Mara sound quite good together too. What do you think Kilifi?"

"It's a powerful name for a young calf. Perhaps it will bring him luck and help him to grow into a strong and wise bull."

Harry looked across at his uncle. As usual he gave little away but a broad grin spread across his face. It was as though the magic of the morning's events had weakened the normal stern mask. "Meru it is then. Let's hope we can do all we can to make sure his days are long and healthy."

At that moment, as if on cue, Meru took his first unsteady steps and surrounded by his new family he was gently led off into the bush and undergrowth on the side of the track and in a remarkably short time they had all disappeared from sight."

"Time for breakfast," grinned Kilifi. "I can't wait to tell the others about this morning. They will be so happy, but jealous of course that they weren't here too."

As they sped back to camp they had little idea how much Meru was to play a part in their lives in the months to come.

Over eggs and bacon Kilifi took on the role of storyteller and obviously relished the part. Anyone who could be there was, listening with amazement as the tale of the morning's events unfolded.

Harry sat in silence. He found it hard to believe how lucky and privileged he was to have witnessed something so wonderful. As he played the birth back in his head he marvelled at the way the other elephants had behaved, how supportive and protective they had been; one close-knit family. If only more humans could be like that he thought.

He left the others and wandered up to the small rather ramshackle admin block. There were a couple of things he needed to sort out before their guests arrived the following morning.

As he passed Aziz's door, which was slightly ajar, he heard a somewhat different tone to the usual smooth voice, there was an urgency in it he wasn't used to.

"Yes that's right, the big female has finally given birth so with him in tow they will not be able to move fast and will be much easier to track…"

Harry was suddenly aware that his shadow must be showing through the gap in the door.

"Who's that? I'm busy on a call. Is it something important?"

"It's just me," said Harry quickly. "Don't worry, it can wait."

"Oh Harry, come in, come in. I was just on a call to a friend. It can wait," smiled Aziz as he closed a file on his desk.

"Thanks Aziz. I was wondering whether we had any spare solar lights. There seems to be something the matter with the panels of one in a guest tent, it's not recharging and they will be here early tomorrow." With pretty much guaranteed sunshine the solar lamps had been a great addition to camp. They just had to be left upside down in a sunny spot during part of the day and they gave up to four hours light each evening. The only other source of electricity was a rather old and noisy camp generator which they liked to switch off not long after dinner each night so that everyone could enjoy the sounds of the African night, rather than the distant throb of a diesel engine.

"I think there are a couple of spares. I will get someone to check in the store. Anything else?"

Harry felt he was keen to get him out of the office. "Well," he said, "I know your feelings about the finances for improving our communications in the reserve. Of course, mobile phones work in some places where there is a good signal but it's very hit and miss. I have been doing some research and have a promising idea for my uncle when we next meet."

Aziz's eyes seemed to narrow. "Well that sounds interesting," he commented with little enthusiasm. "Now I must get on."

As Harry wandered off, he played back the end of Aziz's phone conversation in his head. Who had he been speaking to and why was he suddenly interested in the wildlife of the reserve, the elephants, in particular?

Aziz was not what he appeared to be, his gut instinct told

him that, and yet he had no proof, just his sixth sense. He could hardly go to his uncle and express his thoughts. Much though he liked so many of the others who worked in the reserve he did not know them well enough to confide in, and what would they do once he had told them anyway? He decided the best thing was to be quiet for the moment but keep a close eye on Aziz whenever possible.

That evening Jim briefed them on the guests who were due the following day. There was a family of six. Luckily the youngest of the children was ten; much younger than that and they got bored very easily. They just wanted to tick animals off on a list to say they had seen them and move on to the next one.

To be fair he thought many adults were the same. It was all too easy to be like that when you were only on safari for a few days. You wanted to cram in as much as possible, take endless photos and then relive the experiences when you were back in your own home, dull but safe!

"Before you head off to bed Harry there is something important I want to talk to you about. You know there is an extra guest arriving in the morning. Well, she isn't just any guest; she is the daughter of one of my oldest friends Patrick Gogan. When your grandparents sent your dad and me to boarding school it was pretty tough. On the outside that is what we all had to be too, you couldn't show any weakness and if you did there were always those who would pounce on it and use it to get at you. There was no cosy home to escape to at the end of the day, just cold, bleak dormitories. In a way your close friends became like your family and Patrick was the one who saw me through some dark days. He was bigger than the rest of us and always seemed to know exactly what to say and when. The bullies never took him on and because we were close mates I generally got left alone too. Well, it's Ana, his daughter who is coming tomorrow."

Harry looked at Jim in a new light. His rather distant behaviour and reluctance to show his feelings too much or let others get close to him suddenly made so much more sense. Although he was in his fifties, in many ways he had been moulded into the person he was all those years ago in some grim country boarding school.

"I don't know how long she will be here. I have told Patrick she is welcome for as long as she likes, it's the least I can do. You see she is suffering from something they call PTSD, Post Traumatic Stress Disorder. I don't know much about it except that it affects some people when they have experienced or witnessed dreadful things that somehow they cannot get it out of their minds."

Harry had heard it mentioned sometimes in the news but never really given it a second thought.

"You see Harry she is a really talented young journalist, won several awards. I know Patrick is so proud of her. Anyway she pushed and pushed her editor to be sent to Syria. She is only in her early twenties and she wanted to tell the story of what was happening to other young people out there and how they were coping with an endless war. She wrote some amazing articles, I will show you later. She felt the world wasn't listening and that these stories might make a difference. Anyway something dreadful happened, I don't even know what it was and it isn't something she is prepared to talk about. She returned to the UK a different person. He has tried everything to help and eventually she saw an especially understanding specialist who confirmed that she was suffering from PTSD and recommended she went somewhere peaceful and remote in the hope that it will help her to get better."

"So you suggested Uwingoni," said Harry. "What a great idea."

"Well we'll see about that, only time will tell, I suppose. I haven't seen her since she was a girl but I certainly remember her being very strong willed, even then, and more adventurous than any boys I knew of the same age!"

"How do we go about helping her?" asked Harry. "None of us knows anything about PTSD."

"We just have to be ourselves Patrick says. I have told Mike the same as I have just told you but I am not going to inform anyone else unless the need arises. As you are only a few years younger than her I thought you would be the ideal person to take her under your wing. Just let her enjoy the beauty of Uwingoni. If she wants to tell you things then she will, but the advice I have is not to ask questions about her time in Syria.

"That is a big responsibility uncle. Thank you for the trust you place in me, I feel very humbled."

"Just be yourself Harry and if you need to chat you know where to find me. Oh, and one more thing, I really don't think you need to call me uncle any more, Jim will do just fine."

Before Harry had a chance to reply he had turned on his heels and was marching off towards the kitchen. New instructions for the day ahead no doubt. His restless energy would shame people half his age.

Harry was in a thoughtful mood as he headed for his tent. What would Ana be like he wondered, what sort of things must she have seen in Syria and would he be able to help her?

Outwardly he knew he had grown so much in confidence since arriving in Kenya. He wasn't sure that people had valued the sort of person he was back in London. He had a close-knit group of friends, most of whom he had known since he was nine or ten when they had started to play sport together in the school teams. Much to his own surprise he had been a natural goal and try scorer. He just put it down to being fast rather than skilful and that too he now realised was typical of him. To others he was always confident and easy going but inside there were endless doubts and uncertainty, but of course that was the sort of thing you never discussed.

His mates were either at university now, a couple had even started working and yet he had been unsure of what to do and that was certainly a part of why he was out here in this remote corner of Africa. Even in the few months since his arrival he realised how much he had changed. This was a life he could never even have imagined. How was it possible to fall in love with a place like this, but he knew he had. It was wild but striking and apart from their camp and the rough tracks, pretty much the same as it must have been hundreds of years ago. In a world that never seemed to stand still that was special and of course they shared it with the most wonderful creatures. From the graceful speed of the cheetah to the industry of the dung beetle, they all had a part to play, everyone belonged. And strangely he felt that he did too, in a way that he had never experienced in his life before. He was part of this and he knew in his heart that he would do all he could to protect it.

Chapter Four

Harry gasped as a powerful spray of cold water instantly burnt the sleep out of his system. He still hadn't got used to the fact that his shower only had a cold tap. The water came directly from the stream, fresh and pure and until very recently lying hundreds of feet under the volcanic rock that Uwingoni was perched on.

It wasn't yet dawn and he had planned to drive out with Kilifi to one of the waterholes to see what game was up and about and near the camp. When visitors first arrived it was important to have a good idea of what animals were in the immediate area so that they could take their guests out to places where they had a good chance of sighting something interesting.

He wrapped himself in a warm coat. Tourists always found it strange just how chilly the African bush could be before the sun came up. Despite that he was still wearing shorts, a habit he had copied from many of the others when he had first arrived.

He stopped by the kitchen to grab a thermos of tea and some of Raymond's delicious homemade biscuits, something to keep the two of them going for a couple of hours.

Kilifi was already waiting for him by Bluebird. Harry

turned the key in the ignition and the old engine spluttered into life.

"Hope you slept well Kilifi. What do you think the chances are of seeing Mara and Meru this morning?"

"If I have learnt one thing over the years, it's the difficulty of guessing just what animals might or might not do," replied the old tracker. His face split into that customary grin that Harry had come to associate with him. He could almost predict the words that would come next. "We will see what we will see."

Harry smiled to himself at the familiar phrase which was so often the answer to the host of questions that he always seemed to have.

They bumped over the uneven track throwing up barely any dust as the dampness from the night air was yet to burn off.

They spotted a few zebra in the undergrowth and on one bend a tiny dik-dik startled by the lights of the Land Rover sped across the track in the rather frantic zigzag pattern they used when they were frightened.

"Just turn off the engine and listen," said Kilifi. Harry was used to these sudden stops. They always formed part of his daily lessons.

In the silence they could hear the tiny antelope's call.

"When you whistle it's through your mouth but the dik-dik makes that noise through his nose. Look he is still watching us."

Harry studied the little face, its eyes looking unnaturally large. It licked its lips in the way that animals often do when they are frightened and then its nose seemed to extend and out through the two black nostrils came the warning call which sounded something similar to dik-dik.

"He's a quick little guy," said Kilifi. "Almost as fast as Usain Bolt, which isn't bad when you are not much taller than a ruler on end and weigh about the same as a large cat. The other animals like their calls too because it warns them that danger might be near. Clever creatures."

He was joined by his mate. Harry had noticed that they were nearly always in pairs. With a single bounce they moved behind the trunk of a tree and were gone.

They didn't see anything else as they made their way down to the clearing where the largest of the waterholes was, and then stopped where there was still cover for Bluebird.

Harry was always amazed at the different animals he came across. You would expect the same ones to be there at a similar time each day but this was rarely the case.

His first sight was of a small family of giraffe drinking. Kilifi had taught him the difference between the various types they might come across and he saw straight away that these were reticulated. They had much whiter lines between the brown patches on their coats which were quite smooth whereas their cousins the Masai giraffes had more jagged edges. He knew there was a third kind in Kenya called Rothschild which had cream coloured legs, almost as though he was wearing long socks, but the chances of seeing one of them was very slight. In fact he had read somewhere that they were rarer than mountain gorillas and pandas put together.

Whenever Harry's mind started wandering into thoughts like this he could feel that strange blend of sadness and anger inside. He knew that he had developed a special love for elephants but there were so many other animals out there that were in serious danger too. Yes, there were amazing people who did all they could to protect them and inform the world through wonderful and often moving films, but sometimes he felt that when those powerful enough to do anything about it actually woke up, it would be too late.

He brought his thoughts back to what was in front of

him. The four giraffe were positioned close together their front legs splayed out so that they could get their tongues to the water's surface. A long neck was just what was needed for feeding off the leaves at the top of acacia trees but he marvelled at how they managed to suck water up through a neck that was about eight feet in length. He wasn't even sure whether Kilifi knew either; it couldn't really work like an eight-foot straw. He made a mental note to do some research.

Apart from a small family of Thomson's gazelle, that was it, no sign of elephants or any of the big cats that often stalked areas like waterholes. It was a positively gentle scene with the animals drinking peacefully with each other.

They sat silently watching them just getting on with life. After a while Kilifi suggested moving on to check another couple of spots where the elephant might be.

They spent another half hour going down some of the narrower tracks looking for signs of the small elephant herd. As they rounded a bend Harry thought their luck was in as there was some elephant dung on the road.

Kilifi opened the door and wandered up to the dung, signalling for Harry to join him. As he looked at the large pile he reached down and pulled the surface apart, pushing his hand deep inside.

Harry wrinkled his nose and Kilifi grinned. "Although this looks very recent it is over a day old."

"How on earth do you know that?" asked Harry.

"Well, elephant dung keeps its heat quite well after it has come out of the elephant. By pushing my hand into the middle of the pile I can get an idea of how long ago it was that the elephant decided to relieve itself here. The warmer it is the more recent, quite simple really. It is not something I can really teach but over the years it has proved quite an accurate indicator of when it last walked this way."

"That's amazing," replied Harry, "but I'm not so keen on learning all the details of that!"

There was a sudden crashing noise in the thick undergrowth behind them. As Harry turned to face the sound his worst fears were realised. Bursting through the dense bush was a very large, dark shape.

"Run for Bluebird," ordered Kilifi. "Don't look back, just get in that cab."

Harry didn't need any further encouragement. The Land Rover was only a short distance away but somehow his normally quick legs seemed to lack power.

He heard the tearing of the vegetation and then the distinctive hoof beat behind him. It was as though everything was in slow motion.

His right hand reached the handle of the passenger door and he could sense how close the buffalo was. It was as though he could feel the snorting breath on the back of his neck.

The door flew open and he flung himself through the opening, his left knee crashing onto the bare metal of the foot well as he grabbed for the gear slick to haul himself in.

There was a thunderous crash just behind him and the whole vehicle shuddered. Harry scrabbled to shut the door properly and there was a second grinding thud. He pulled the door violently shut as the buffalo hit Bluebird for the third time.

Harry was conscious of the pounding of his heart which seemed magnified in his eardrums. His mouth was dry and he just lay there, half on the seat half on the floor, replaying the last brief moments in his head.

His first thought was that he had made it and apart from a few scrapes and bruises he was alright. He realised that the buffalo had charged the rear of Bluebird rather than the flimsier doors which was a bit of luck. It must simply have gone for the nearest thing. Even though it was a Land Rover it would certainly have done some damage. Kilifi had told him that the biggest of them could weigh as much as nine hundred kilos and charge at around fifty kph.

With a sickening jolt Harry realised that he hadn't got a clue what had happened to Kilifi. He had done exactly what he had been told, running and not looking back.

He pulled himself up into a sitting position in the passenger seat and looked round.

The buffalo had found a new target, a nearby tree and then Harry saw why, for clinging on desperately to the trunk around ten feet off the ground was Kilifi. He shouted and banged the door to try and distract the animal but to no effect.

The buffalo took another charge at the trunk, smashing the area between its horns against the base of the tree.

Instinct told Harry that Kilifi wouldn't be able to hang on much longer.

He leapt over to the driver's seat and was relieved when the engine fired straight away. Thank goodness the attack had been at the rear of the Land Rover, not the front.

He swung off the track heading directly for the large tree. The buffalo seemed totally unaffected by the approaching vehicle and was stepping back to have another crack.

"Get as close as you can" shouted Kilifi. "I should be able to jump onto the roof but make it quick my grip is already weakening."

Harry nudged Bluebird forward trying to get the opposite side of the trunk to the buffalo without causing any more damage.

"I could open the game hatch," he suggested, thinking that would be easier and Kilifi could land on the seat.

"No, there isn't enough time and I would rather have a whole roof to jump on."

Harry moved the last few yards towards the tree. The buffalo was now eying the Land Rover up again. Harry had never sensed such rage in a creature before.

"That's as close as I can get."

There was suddenly a loud crash on the roof. "I'm all right but let's get out of here, not too fast though, there isn't much to grip onto up here."

The buffalo gave them another glance and stepped back suddenly looking disinterested. As Harry drove slowly back onto the track it simply turned away and headed into the undergrowth, almost as though nothing had happened.

Once they were a safe distance away Harry pulled up and Kilifi got down onto the bonnet, then clambering over the spare tyre, jumped nimbly onto the ground.

As he got into the front seat he was grinning as usual.

"Well that was a close call. What a way that would have been to go, gored by a buffalo before I have even had breakfast."

Harry marvelled at his ability to make light of things. Jim had told him that buffalos killed or gored at least two hundred people a year, although he thought the true figure was probably much more.

"It's always the old males Harry," continued Kilifi. "When they are no longer top dog and some youngster takes over the females they are booted out of the herd. Then they have to spend the rest of their life wandering through the bush on their own, hardly surprising they are so bad tempered, think I would be if I was them. All this excitement has made me hungry and our visitors will be coming in soon. Let's head back to camp."

Harry didn't need further prompting. He checked the time on his watch and was amazed that what had been a near-death experience had probably lasted under five minutes. It was a lesson he was learning fast in Kenya. In the routine and comparative monotony of his life in London most things were fairly predictable but out here in the wild there were no rules to play by. Nature was beautiful but there was often a sting in the tail and to survive you had to learn fast. Despite the obvious fear he had felt such a short time ago there was a realisation that each of these experiences made him a stronger person inside. Already he was hard put to recognise where he had come from in a comparatively short period of time. Despite feeling that his thoughts might be rather over dramatic, he knew that he was fast becoming a man, and a man he hoped those closest to him would look at and respect.

After checking in back at camp and giving a warning about the buffalo, Harry went off to find Bethwell. He had just finished washing down the two smartest of the Land Rovers they used for game viewing when they had visitors, or clients as Aziz liked to call them. Unlike Bluebird they were long wheel base vehicles which provided more room and comfort for those inside. They had beautifully made local blankets for early morning and late evening drives and cold boxes at the back containing an array of snacks and refreshments.

He greeted Harry with a huge smile and a pat on the back. "How is the buffalo hunter?" he laughed. The news of their early morning encounter had spread quickly and Harry was in no doubt that Kilifi would be the butt of many a joke. He had already heard one of the others talking about his tree climbing ability.

"Fine thanks, hope I don't get that bad tempered in my old age!"

"Jim told me that the plane was due to land in about fifteen minutes so I think we should make our way down to the landing strip pretty soon," suggested Bethwell.

They headed off at an easy pace, trying not to throw up

too much dust and undo Bethwell's hard cleaning work of the morning.

Harry wondered whether Ollie would be the pilot. He imagined that they would be flying in a large Cessna, probably a Caravan which could seat nine passengers despite the fact that it still just had one single propeller at the front.

They sat waiting by the side of the strip. It was a perfect morning. The ka'ka, ka'ka sound of the red-billed hornbill filled the air and the sky was that amazing blue that seemed to go on forever, with not a cloud in sight. For once there was no sign of any animals nearby. Harry looked east where he expected the plane to come from and sure enough he could just make it out in the vastness of blue. He picked up the binoculars that he always kept by his side when he was out driving and focused on the sky. It was getting closer and starting to drop in height so was obviously destined for Uwingoni.

Soon the sound of the engine became dominant and the plane, the largest type to land on this fairly short strip touched down within the first fifty meters to give it enough space to slow to a halt. It then did a tight turn and bumped its way back to the waiting vehicles over the somewhat uneven surface.

The pilot cut the engine and remarkably after what seemed like only a few seconds the morning birdsong was back, seeming louder than ever.

Harry was surprised to see that the pilot was a young woman he had not seen before.

"Hi I'm Charlie," she smiled. "Ollie asked me to send you his best. He has had to fly some UN medical supplies up to Southern Sudan this morning, rather him than me. I hear it's fast becoming one of the most dangerous places in Africa."

"Good to meet you Charlie," said Harry. "Let's get your passengers and their baggage off and into the Land Rovers."

The family of six were the first off. The parents looked so young thought Harry, amazed that they could have four children, the oldest obviously in their mid-teens. Introductions were made. They were all pleasant, fresh faced and eager to get into safari mode straight away.

"Bethwell will take you all up to camp in one vehicle. It will be fun for you to keep together and who knows, you might see something interesting on the way. I will take the luggage to give you the room you need."

Harry turned his attention back to the plane. A young woman wearing a simple white top and faded blue jeans was walking from under the wing. She carried a somewhat battered suit case and a well-used khaki rucksack dangled comfortably from her shoulder.

"Hi, you must be Ana," he said stepping forward. "I'm Harry. Let me help you with your case."

She smiled gently at him, a tanned face under fairly short cut dark hair but it was her eyes that held his attention, they were the deepest of blue and as she looked at him Harry felt as though she could see right into him.

"I'm fine thanks, pretty used to carrying my own stuff but I'll give you a hand with all these others. They seemed a nice family but it looks as though they have packed for a month."

Before Harry could reply the beat of the engine increased and as he looked up at the cockpit, Charlie gave him a thumbs up out of the window.

The bags were loaded in no time, despite his protests that he could manage by himself. Although Ana was slimly built he couldn't help noticing how easily she moved even the heavier things into the back of the Land Rover.

"So Harry, what's your role here?" she asked as they drove back up the track to camp, her arm resting lazily out of the window but her gaze endlessly moving to the thick bush on either side as if she was afraid she would miss something.

"Good question," he replied. "It seems to be evolving all the time which is exciting but a little scary too. Until I came here I had never really taken responsibility for anything much in my life. My dad is Jim's brother and so it was suggested I take a gap year and help out here in Uwingoni. I gather both of them go back a long way with your dad too."

"Yes. I don't know all the ins and outs. They were at school together and have remained close since. It is good of your uncle to invite me out here for a while."

There was no further explanation as to why she had come out and Harry certainly wasn't going to start asking.

They drove on in silence but it wasn't awkward and the time slipped easily by.

Harry pulled up outside the main camp entrance. "I'm just going to drop the other bags off here then I'll take you to your tent. You stay there; one of the guys will help me get them out of the back."

Harry then drove them round to the back of the camp, passed the kitchen where the smell of lunch being prepared wafted invitingly through the windows until they reached a small group of tents, dotted about twenty yards apart, each under the shade of some fairly squat trees.

He stopped at one furthest from the main camp. "I thought you might like this one. Mine's down here too away from the bustle of camp life. You will find it gives you a real feel of being in the wild. Often at night you can hear animals quite close and during the day the sound of insects seems almost constant."

Ana pushed the tent flap back and walked inside, past the single bed and into the wash area at the back.

"It's all a bit basic I'm afraid but everything works and we have a little modern technology with the solar light but that's about it. No hot water but if you want a decent shower there are a couple you can use in the main area of the camp."

That easy smile crossed her face again. "I love it. Give me simplicity every time. I used to be a bit of a city girl, keen for the latest of whatever was going around, but I tired of it. Everything seemed so comfortable but you know Harry, people just want more and more. Somehow they think their stuff defines them, sad really. This is just perfect."

"I have realised that myself, well since being here anyway." Harry felt almost embarrassed that he was talking so easily to someone he had just met. "Look I'll give you a while to freshen up then I'll take you up to meet Jim. He has asked me if I would show you the ropes."

"That sounds great. Thanks for the warm welcome. I'll catch up with you in a bit."

Harry walked back to the Land Rover. It was good to have someone else young in camp he thought and yet already he could detect sides of her that were far older than her age.

Forty-five minutes later found the two of them sitting round part of a small circle, on green canvas directors chairs. They were in the main guest area of the camp but the family group had already headed off with a driver to see if they could spot any interesting game before lunch.

Jim had greeted Ana with a broad smile and a rather formal handshake in the slightly awkward style he had, and she was given brief introductions to the others.

Mike was there, and Harry realised he had hardly seen him since he had taken the Somali to the police station. Kilifi and Bethwell sat next to each other and slightly apart from the others was Aziz.

"Good morning everyone," began Jim, "and thanks for making this rather hastily convened meeting but I wanted to update you on one or two things. By the way I have asked Ana to join us as she is likely to be here for a while and you never know what a new perspective might bring to things. Now over to Mike for the latest from Inspector Mwitu."

Mike stood up, his face slightly flushed. Harry knew he was a shy individual who never liked being put on the spot. He only really became talkative when he had drunk a few White Caps, the favoured beer in camp.

"Well," he began in his slightly nasal voice, "Inspector Mwitu didn't get much out of the Somali and he is being sent for further questioning in Nairobi. However, they found some interesting things in his vehicle. There were several cartons of Baisha cigarettes with a white crane on the front. They were unfamiliar, but due to the labelling obviously Chinese. There were also several bottles of cheap Chinese spirit under the back seat. Despite some, let's say fairly forcible questioning, our Somali friend said he could not explain this.

"There are a lot of Chinese working in Kenya now so I suppose they could have come from any of them," remarked Jim, as ever not keen to jump to conclusions.

"There is something that might be more telling than that," continued Mike. "The AK-47s that the poaching party were carrying had ammunition with some form of far eastern writing on the bullet casings. Mwitu has sent those to Nairobi too for closer examination."

"My bet is that it will be something to do with that Chinese engineering group building the dam twenty miles up the road." said Bethwell. "I've got relations working in other reserves in the country and generally these guys are bad news."

Harry knew there were serious issues with a number of Chinese projects. What he heard was of course only gossip but it had a sad ring of truth about it. Many of the projects they were involved in were hugely expensive and the need for some of them was questionable too. But of course they also involved senior politicians who were rumoured to receive huge kickbacks for their support. In theory the dam sounded great, fresh water and a hydroelectric plant to usher in the modern world, but that is not how many saw it.

"I have a couple of friends who farm just below this new project," said Kilifi, "and nobody has even asked them what they think. They are so worried that the whole supply of water will either change direction or be drastically reduced and without water they are finished. Their animals and crops will die and their farms will be worth nothing. And they are just two, there are hundreds of other small farmers further downstream and the chances are the same thing will happen to all of them. So hardly what you would call progress!"

"I don't feel the Chinese are so bad," said Aziz. "I have met some of them and they seem decent, hardworking people."

"I don't feel anyone will argue with that point," stated Jim, "but that is not really what we are talking about here. Someone seems to be targeting Uwingoni. The Somali and his mates are just the troops on the ground. There have to be some individuals with power and influence behind all this and Chinese clues are one of the few leads the police have."

"Well," said Aziz, "that strikes me as pretty flimsy evidence and what's more China has only just banned the import of ivory, for those of you who look at the news."

Harry was conscious of a worsening atmosphere amongst the small circle. Aziz was not popular at the best of times.

"Look," he said, "why don't we wait for inspector Mwitu to get back to us and then we might have something more definite to go on. While we are here I wanted to mention something else." He took a big breath, knowing the opposition from some individuals around what he had to say. "If we can improve our communication system I am sure it would make a big difference. As we know there are many areas of Uwingoni where there is no phone signal and the radios seem unable to contact each other properly. That is such a huge disadvantage for us so I have an idea."

The others all seemed focused on what he was about to say. "I know you think I have this thing about us being old-fashioned, well we are and if we are going to save the elephants, in particular, we have to move with the times. I have been doing some research into special repeater masts."

"We have gone into radio masts before Harry," said Jim, with a heavy sigh, "and I am afraid they are just too expensive. Isn't that what your research showed Aziz?"

"I'm afraid that is right, it would be wonderful but you see the cost…"

"Is much better than you think," interrupted Harry. "And I believe I have come up with just the thing. Portable masts. We don't need great big things dug into the hillsides. We can buy portable antenna tripods. They weigh less than five pounds and extend to over nine feet, together with the antenna itself and a simple battery pack, the cost is less than $US600."

The others were silent, even Aziz couldn't come up with a reason why they couldn't afford this. "I reckon if we had even three we could make a huge difference to our radio coverage in the reserve. They are made by several companies but I thought the best was Lite-Link. I looked at all the online reviews and they were really positive."

"If I may just say something," said Ana. Everyone's eyes turned to her and Harry saw that confident smile again. "I know I have just arrived and what little I know about Kenya game reserves I have only read in books but I do know about communication."

"Please," said Jim, "Everything we learn can be useful."

"As some of you know I am a journalist and have found myself in remote areas where just trying to communicate with the outside world is extremely difficult. The sort of masts that Harry mentioned are a fantastic link. They fit in a simple bag that goes over your shoulder and are easy to put up, take down and move. All they need to work is a small solar battery. You are obviously having problems here in Uwingoni and they would seem a straightforward solution."

Aziz was about to speak but Jim put up his hand to silence him. "What better recommendation could we have," he smiled. "I suggest we look at buying three straight away. Thank you, Ana, oh and Harry for bringing it up. No Aziz I don't want to hear another word, get on the case straight away please."

Everyone else in the circle smiled broadly. They then discussed some rather necessary but uninteresting sides of the camp, from vehicles that needed repair to the purchase of a new freezer enabling the kitchen to have much greater flexibility with meals.

"Finally," said Jim turning to Kilifi, "what news of young Meru and his mother?"

"I was out with Harry yesterday but we didn't come across them. I imagine they have gone deep into the bush for safety as I have had no reports of sightings today either."

"I don't suppose that's anything too much to worry about just yet but keep me posted as soon as you hear anything."

As the meeting broke up and everyone went their separate ways Harry found himself walking back to the tents with Ana.

"I don't know how you did it," he said, "but that smile of yours seemed to win Jim over. I have never known him to agree to spending money so quickly."

"Do I have some special smile, that's good to know."

"I only said that as a bit of a joke. I am sure it was your knowledge as a journalist that won the day. You must tell me about a few of your experiences sometime."

"Perhaps," replied Ana with little enthusiasm.

Harry couldn't believe his own stupidity. The one thing he had been determined not to bring up was her recent past and yet he had just blurted out the question. He could feel his face going a little red.

"I'm not interested in lunch. It has been quite a journey getting here, I think I'm just going to put my head down and have a sleep."

"I could pick you up about five o'clock if you feel up to it and we could go for a bit of a game drive before it gets dark if you like," said Harry, desperate to change the subject.

She stopped by the little veranda in front of her tent as if summing up her options. As she turned towards him it was almost as though the tension seemed to leave her face and shoulders. "That sounds fun. See you later then."

Before he could reply, she was through the flap into the comparative gloom of the tent.

He strolled back up the track, kicking the dust absent-mindedly as he went. It seemed to hang in the stillness of the air, there wasn't a breath of wind and he was conscious of the harshness of the sun's rays on the back of his neck. Even the birdsong sounded muted as though it was too much effort in the midday heat.

His thoughts turned to Meru. It was strange but even baby elephants could get sunburnt he had learnt. Their skin was still quite soft in places, which is why they often spent time directly under their mother's great bodies, even when walking along. It was the shadiest place around.

Chapter Five

It had been an afternoon full of little bits and pieces for Harry; in the supply store checking things off on rather dull lists and then with the mechanics trying to gain more of an understanding of what was under the bonnet of the Land Rover and how it worked. He was amazed about how much he had learnt in such a short time. There was something he particularly liked about practical knowledge and he had already developed real respect for the crew who kept everything mechanical working in the camp.

He was still buzzing about the decision to buy the repeater aerials and had already given a rather grumpy Aziz internet details for their purchase. However, the image that kept jumping into his brain was of Mara, and how safe she and her family were. Harry had talked to Kilifi about where he thought they might be and now had a few good ideas of where to look.

Five o'clock came round surprisingly quickly and he wandered down to Ana's tent where he had fully expected to find her still asleep but she was sitting in the shaded canvas porch writing in what seemed to be rather a large book.

"You're spot on time Harry; just give me a couple of minutes while I finish up my journal. He sat down in the other rather rickety chair, trying not to let his enthusiasm to be up and going show too much. He could see the page of closely packed neat script and thought how unusual it was to see someone writing by hand in this way.

As if to answer his question Ana looked up and said, "I expect you are wondering just what I write in this journal of mine."

"The day's events I imagine, I have thought about doing something like that myself, since being here anyway, but somehow I never seem to get round to it, too tired at the end of the day I suppose." He thought that a pretty lame excuse, even as the words came out.

"That's part of it I suppose but it goes much deeper than that. I am aware you will know something of why I am here and a little of my immediate past." She put up her hand to prevent Harry saying anything. "I don't expect you to understand, indeed I am only beginning to get my head round some of it myself but one of the doctors who has been keeping an eye on me suggested I keep a daily record, not just of what I have done but importantly what I have been thinking about. I am a journalist and writing has always come easily to me but this is something very raw and personal and involves lots about my thoughts. Getting them down rather than having them flying round my head really seems to help and writing by hand rather than on a computer has become important, it becomes much more a part of me. In a way the journal has become one of my closest friends and when I try to make sense of things, rereading it helps me to understand stuff. We are going to be seeing a great deal of each other. Don't expect me to go into detail about the past but I feel we will become friends and it's important that you learn a little, at least, of what makes me tick."

"Thank you for sharing that with me." There was a time when he would have said much more, questions tumbling out of his mouth but he remained silent.

"Now what about trying to find those elephants?"

It was just the two of them, as Kilifi was busy, so Harry had taken Bluebird. It was odd, he thought, that he should have developed so much affection for the oldest vehicle in Uwingoni. Everything seemed to rattle, the canvas seats were positively uncomfortable, especially on hot sweaty days, the gears often grated unless he got the change just right and with no power steering, he already thought he had built up new muscle strength, just through turning the large, old-fashioned steering wheel. Harry had grown to love her, oddly for all the reasons that many would consider negatives.

He drove a little faster than normal. Being so close to the equator the light slipped away quickly, at six-thirty everything was clear and well defined, yet by seven it was dark with little chance of spotting or tracking much. They had an hour and a half if they were lucky.

They were heading for Twiga waterhole, as the Swahili name implied, this was somewhere favoured by giraffe. It was a little off the main drag and Bluebird's suspension was struggling with the endless line of ruts that ran horizontally directly in front of them, the product of the last heavy rains.

Harry stopped to inspect some animal tracks. Kilifi would have been proud of his pupil. He identified two sets of hyena prints moving from right to left in front of them and several tell-tale indications that giraffe had passed this way fairly recently, but there was no hint of elephants.

"Are we heading in the right direction?" asked Ana. "I am afraid you could write my knowledge of wild Africa on a postage stamp so I won't be much help."

"That's exactly what I was like a few months back," he smiled, "but there are some great teachers here and because I really want to learn I have found that I only need to be told things once. Sometimes I need a little clarification but because I show a real interest everyone is keen to tell me what they have spent years discovering. I have such a long way to go but already my head is bursting with information I could never have imagined."

"Where are we heading then?"

"Well at this time of day, particularly when it has been so hot and dusty many of the animals pay a visit to one of the waterholes before the darkness really settles in. The larger elephants can drink up to fifty gallons of water in a day. That's as much as you could fit into your bath if you filled it up. They can go up to four days without a drink but always quench their thirst when they can. Amazingly they can actually smell it from more than two miles away."

He could see the look of surprise on Ana's face.

"They are incredible animals but until they come close you don't really appreciate just how huge they can get. Bethwell told me that the average weight is around twelve thousand pounds. I am not very good with metric I'm afraid but I think that is getting on for five times as much as the average small car. They usually spend over half the day just eating; grass, leaves and bark from the trees and any other vegetation they think is tasty. A large bull elephant might eat as much as six hundred pounds."

"In one day?" said Ana, almost a look of disbelief on her face. "Your facts are staggering, I simply had no idea."

"As I said I am only just learning myself but when I sit and listen to some of the older rangers I feel like a kid again, listening to some magical bedtime story I never want to end."

Harry took the right fork, stopping briefly to put Bluebird into four-wheel drive. "This is a steep track down to the waterhole and if I only used the brakes they would be red hot before the bottom, so it's first gear and slowly does it."

Below them was a thick patch of greenery with a thin line of shrubs and bushes leading to it.

"You can see where the stream usually feeds the water-hole," Harry pointed out. "Although there is only a trickle in there at the moment there is a surprising amount just below the surface so the Twiga watering hole nearly always has something in it, even in the very dry season."

Bluebird bucked and jolted over the rocky track, the thorns from the acacias scraping against the worn paint-work and the engine protesting loudly at the steepness of the descent.

After what seemed an age the track levelled out and wound its way towards the shade of the trees.

"There will be little, if anything drinking now. We have made enough noise to startle even the boldest of animals."

"This might sound a rather stupid question Harry, but what's the next step?"

"Simple," he replied. "We find a good viewing spot, turn off the engine and just sit and wait. There is a lot of that out here."

"Perfect. I feel that is something so many people never do these days. They rush from one thing to the next, are rarely still, have their heads down outside so don't even notice their surroundings."

As soon as he turned the engine off, the chirp of crickets was almost deafening. A strong breeze that seemed to come like individual breaths threw up small cones of dust by the water as it rippled the surface, but there was no sign of any other movement.

Time ticked by but neither of them was aware of its passing.

It was getting near dusk and yet still there was no sign of life round the water. "This is very unusual," whispered Harry. "Something is up. There would usually be several different types of animal drinking round the hole by now."

"I am sure I caught some sort of movement just over there

in the bushes to the left of that large boulder, said Ana, "but what do I know, it just seemed briefly that the shadow of the bush was darker and…"

She caught a gasp in her throat and held it down. As if by magic two male lions were standing in front of the tree line. They appeared both unconcerned and unhurried. Their heads moved slowly scanning the far side. It seemed to Ana as though they were staring right at her. Although they must have been seventy or eighty yards away it was still possible to pick out some of the detail. The particular evening light seemed to emphasise the deep redness of their manes. The one on the left stretched his back in just the same way as their cat back home. Their large tummies swung gently beneath them as they moved easily towards the water.

Harry was reluctant to break the spell but whispered gently, "These are two young brothers; I have seen them before with Bethwell but never at this watering place. That would explain why there were no other animals around, they must have sensed them. But by the look of their tummies they need not have worried. The reason they are hanging down so much is that they must have killed and eaten fairly recently. They are beautiful but lazy and they won't be bothered by anything much until they are hungry again.

"If I was standing up I think my knees might have gone weak," replied Ana. "I know we came looking for elephant but this is unbelievably special." Even as she spoke the two brothers ambled to the water's edge, crouched down with their chins on the surface of the water, their large pink tongues delving repeatedly into the surface, their heads though remaining amazingly still and watchful.

Suddenly the spell was broken, a sound in the dusk, not even near but the brothers were off, a few quick strides and it was as though they had never been."

"That distant crackle sounds like gunfire," said Harry. "That's what spooked them!" He revved the engine into life.

"See if you can get the camp on the radio. I need both hands on the wheel over this surface."

"This is Ana in Bluebird," she shouted above the noise of the clattering on the track. "Can anyone hear me?" She took her finger off the send button waiting for a reply.

"Keep trying," said Harry. "This is such a steep valley we are probably still out of radio contact!"

"It is difficult to know where the shots came from. It felt as though it was over to the north but perhaps I am just jumping to conclusions because that has been the danger area for so long. Keep trying on the radio, someone should pick us up soon."

Harry suddenly turned right down an even narrower track. "I know this seems nuts heading back down again but I am sure I remember this route with Bethwell a few weeks ago although in this half-light I can't be sure."

Ana was still trying to get through on the radio. "These repeater masts can't come too soon," she said. "Just think what a difference it would make. All the decisions and actions would be joined up."

The hill seemed to be getting even more sheer if that was possible and Harry could actually feel some of the endless loose rocks that littered their way hitting the underneath of Bluebird. He knew he should have slowed down but in his mind, larger than any other thought was the image of Mara and Meru. Where were they? Were they and the other elephants safe and who was behind the gunfire?

"There is a crossing a little further down here. It is like a concrete ledge under the water of the stream which will take us up onto the far side and quickly to a major track."

The trail dipped even more steeply and they could actually see the line of the water below. Harry braked sharply but they didn't slow. He pumped the brake pedal but it went straight to the floor. If anything Bluebird was speeding up.

"We have lost the brakes Ana! Hang on to whatever you can."

She didn't say a word but braced her legs in the foot well as Harry gripped the wheel fiercely in a desperate attempt to keep them on the track. The trunks of large trees flashed past, almost close enough to touch. He didn't let himself dwell on what on what a mess it would make of Bluebird, and more importantly them, if they were to hit one straight on.

They took one final turn and there was the water, dark and uninviting baring their way. Strangely time seemed to slow down and the images played out in front of him. The trees cleared on either side, one last large boulder seemed determined to knock them off course. He knew how vital it was that he hit the narrow concrete wash-away as near centre as he could manage. He remembered Bethwell's tip, even though that was when they had been driving slowly! Always keep your eyes on where the track begins on the far side and aim for that like a target, forget if you can, what is under you.

He lined them up as well as he could and with his foot still on the accelerator, so that he at least had some control, they hit the water. It was better to have speed than nothing at all.

When Bluebird met the surface, neither of them could believe the amount of spray that erupted around them. It was obvious the stream was far deeper than they had realised. Harry fought the pressure and the wheel with all his strength staring with a fixed vision at the other side.

The engine stuttered a couple of times and with one final splutter died completely. They both sat there in the sudden silence, neither saying a word but being in no doubt how lucky they were.

"Well, I'll say one thing for you Harry you would make a great dodgems champ. You missed all those trees and the huge boulder at the end. Don't know how you did it. Think you have a special bond with old Bluebird here."

They both laughed somewhat nervously, aware of just how narrow the margins in life can be.

"I wouldn't normally say this in such odd circumstances but how happy I am to be sitting where we are! However, let's get out of here now."

Harry turned the key several times but the engine showed no sign of life. In frustration he kept trying, pumping the accelerator repeatedly.

"Just stop Harry. You will only make things worse."

He looked across at her, surprise written on his face. "What do you suggest then?" he inquired trying to keep his voice level.

"Well, something similar happened to me once in Jordan when I was out with a film cameraman. We hit a flooded road unexpectedly and our vehicle, also some old four-wheel drive, just ground to a stop. Luckily he just happened to be a good mechanic as well as being great with a camera. I remember it well because I had just the thing to fix the engine in my bag!"

Harry looked puzzled. "What on earth was that?"

Ana delved inside the large kiondo basket behind the seat, her hand emerging with a small pack of tissues. "These," she said with a chuckle.

Harry was none the wiser but avoided coming out with some stupid comment that would show his lack of knowledge.

"He showed me what to do, so let's see if I can remember. Of course I might be completely wrong but at the moment we are going nowhere and are still unable to get in touch with anyone else so let's give it a go."

She had a good point he thought so cautiously he opened the door. The water level was below the rim so fortunately nothing was getting inside. "Step out on your side but take care, I suspect you are pretty close to the concrete edge."

"About a tyre's width," she smiled. "Perfectly judged! Now get that bonnet up and let's have a look inside."

Harry pulled the lever inside the cab to release the bonnet and holding it up with a rusty, old metal rod they both peered into the comparative gloom of the engine compartment.

"My knowledge is pretty basic," he admitted. "I am learning from the guys at camp but have a long way to go."

"I know some bits and pieces that I have picked up over the last few years. In many of the remote places I've been there are no garages or mechanics for further than you can imagine so you have to look after yourself. Luckily I have rarely been on my own."

The water droplets were still dripping from parts of the engine. The force and speed of Bluebird as she entered the stream had been huge.

"My feeling is that as we stopped so suddenly it will be to do with the electrics getting wet." Ana flicked a catch on the side of the distributer, a control point that contained the leads that went to the four spark plugs. She checked a tiny pair of metal points she knew to be important and then ran her tissue round the inside of the cap. When it came out it was more than damp.

Handing another to Harry she said, "Now wipe down each of those cables that go to the spark plug caps and then the plugs themselves. Wetness in these areas means the plugs don't work properly, so no spark and without that nothing to ignite the fuel and so the engine cannot work, simple!"

Harry made a mental note of yet something else to study up on as soon as he was back in camp.

"Right then, hop back in and try starting her again and

remember gentle on the accelerator too, otherwise there will be more flooding, only petrol this time!"

Harry cautiously turned the starter a couple of times without success but on the third time after a brief hesitation the engine coughed once and then roared back into life as though there had never been a problem.

"You're a wonder," he exclaimed as she hopped back in. "There aren't many men who would have known what to do, let alone women!"

Ana raised one eyebrow. "There is almost nothing women can't do when they put their minds to it. If you meet the right women in life Harry, you will soon find that out!"

"All I meant…" he cut himself short. "Let's get out of this stream first." Slowly he headed for the far bank and drove until they found a fairly level area away from the stream. He kept the engine running and put the hand break on. He already knew that worked on a different system.

He got on his back and pushed himself under Bluebird checking round each of the wheels in turn. When he reached the back on the passenger side it became instantly obvious what had caused the brake failure. One of the small metal pipes that carried the fluid to the brakes to make them work was completely shattered.

"I've got lots to learn about engines," he shouted up, "but I understand enough about brakes to know this is nothing we can fix out here. One of those large rocks must have been flung up onto the pipe and just completely snapped it. As I was pressing the brakes near the end I was simply squirting all the brake fluid out of the system. In a funny way we were lucky the stream was there to stop us without any damage. It could have been much, much worse."

"Well then chauffer, as most of our journey will now be uphill, let's see whether you can get us back to camp in one piece without brakes."

The return journey was just as slow as you would expect. Harry drove with real respect for his surroundings. It was dark by the time they arrived on the main track and he used the gears to slow them down where needed.

Suddenly the radio crackled back into life, they must be in range again. "Bluebird report your position please." They both sensed a hint of concern in Jim's voice.

Ana picked up the radio. "We have had some trouble with Bluebird but are up and running and making our way back to camp. I must tell you that we are sure we heard gunfire earlier but radio contact has been useless."

"Glad you are safe. That's what's important. There has been an incident in the reserve but of course you have been out of touch for over an hour."

"We should be back fairly soon I think." She looked across to Harry for confirmation and he raised the fingers of his left hand three times. "About fifteen minutes providing there are no more mishaps."

"OK," came Jim's reply. "Just come straight to the main dining area. There are a few of us there and I will give you the latest about what's been going on."

Harry resisted the urge to drive faster and it wasn't long before they saw the distant glow of lights from the camp.

He didn't even bother to take Bluebird to the mechanics workshop; they wouldn't be working this late anyway.

Seated round the main table were, Jim, Mike, Bethwell, Kilifi and a grim-faced man he had never seen before.

"Sit down and I will tell you as much as I can. This by the way is Sergeant Odika from KWS." Odika nodded briefly in their direction, strongly built and with a slight air of menace about him, Harry thought he was not a man he would care to cross.

"He and a small crack group of rangers have been following some suspected poachers for several days now. Just before dusk this evening they found three of them on our eastern border. In a brief exchange of gunfire all three were shot and killed. That's the good news."

Jim paused, "Sadly they were carrying a pair of tusks still wet with blood." He put up his hand to silence Harry. "At this stage we don't know any more than you. They looked as though they came from a youngish elephant but we will have to wait until first light before we can piece everything together.

Harry could feel the fury rising up inside him. Which elephant was it? He didn't know them all yet. Was it from the small herd they had hoped to see at the waterhole that evening? Only dawn would give them some answers.

Chapter Six

Harry supposed he must have slept on and off but it hadn't come easily, his mind had been racing with endless images of elephants being shot. As the poachers advanced towards the dying creatures he found himself awake again, almost as though he couldn't allow his dreams to let him see what happened next.

He was up and ready to go way before sunrise and as he made his way up to the main camp he passed Ana's tent. He almost missed her sitting unmoving in the darkness of the veranda.

She greeted him with a "Good morning," and he tried to smile in return but it was obvious the prospect of what lay ahead dwelt heavily in both their minds.

She fell in beside him as they made their way towards the kitchen for an early cup of strong coffee to sustain them for the next few hours. The thought of anything to eat was very unappealing.

Harry had both his hands round the welcome warmth of the mug and he asked the question that had been jiggling round his mind since the previous evening.

"Ana are you sure you want to come this morning? I have only witnessed what we are about to see once and to say it was one of the grimmest sights of my life would be an understatement. I know you will have seen the most dreadful things as a reporter but in many ways you are here to try and forget what you can of that."

Ana was silent, the steam coming off her coffee in the pre-dawn chill, as she seemed lost in her own thoughts.

"I don't think I can ever forget the horrors of war and perhaps it would almost be an insult to those who suffered so much for me to allow myself to do that. I know you only mean well and you are right in some ways. I certainly have to learn how to manage those dreadful memories but cutting myself off from reality isn't the way to do that. I know I'll hate what I see but controlling the anger and channelling it in a positive way is a crucial part of what makes me the person I am."

Harry stood awkwardly by the embers of the previous night's campfire, their dull warmth failing to raise his spirits.

She moved across and squeezed his shoulder gently, "But thank you anyway."

Five minutes later and they were in the back of Jim's Land Cruiser heading off pretty much due east, still searching for the first rays of the sun on the horizon.

Odika sat in the front seat and his men were in the other vehicle with Mike and Kilifi. Nobody really talked and somehow the silence was comforting.

There was little evidence of game on the way and the only sound they were really conscious of was the rattling of the vehicles on the rough track.

The plan was simple and obvious, to head to where the KWS rangers had first come across the poachers the previous evening and to use Kilifi's wonderful skills to track their movements back until they found the dead elephant.

The miles ticked by. Harry was glad of his fleece as the heater did little to throw any warmth onto the rear seats.

Odika sat passively, the cold steel of his gun resting

gently in his palm as though it was always meant to be there. Harry had learnt through brief snippets of conversation before he went to bed that he was very highly thought of. He was one of a relatively small group of rangers who had been selected to train with instructors from the British army special forces, arguably the toughest soldiers in the world. Various Western governments were helping where they could to provide support to a number of African countries whose wildlife was threatened. It was a small step but anything helped.

Jim bought the Land Cruiser to a halt in a clearing just to the side of the track. The headlights picked out several inquisitive pairs of eyes in the thick scrub in front of them. As he flicked them off Harry was aware of a very early light beginning to give their surroundings a faint touch of colour.

Jim had timed the journey just right, there would be enough for Kilifi to pick out the tracks and other tell-tale signs that would point the way.

"This is where we nailed those vermin last night," said Odika, his voice devoid of any feeling. There seemed little sign of where the poachers met their end but as Kilifi examined the ground to the right-hand side even Harry was able to pick out the darker areas where their blood still stained the dirt.

"This should be easy going to start with," he explained as the others gathered round. "The ground here is fairly soft so if you look you can see three distinct sets of footprints. They weren't walking abreast so it makes it a little trickier. Although the soles of their shoes do make slightly different patterns the easiest sign to follow is the depth the prints go into the sand."

The others peered down at the surface waiting for further explanation. "You see," he continued, "on this set the right-side foot makes a deeper indent than the left and the one next door is the complete opposite."

Now that he had pointed it out it seemed obvious even to Ana and Harry who had no experience.

"My guess," said Kilifi is that the first set belong to the poacher who was carrying the elephant tusk on his right shoulder so the extra weight causes his right foot to sink in that much deeper. The other is the exact opposite so I imagine he was left-handed. The third set is quite well balanced so that man isn't weighed down by anything much. Our experience shows us that poachers tend to travel light apart from their weapons so this would make complete sense."

"OK," said Odika, "let's follow Kilifi and see where they lead back to. But keep on the alert, the bush is a dangerous place as you know. We have assumed there are no other poachers in the area but wherever there are elephants you can never be too sure."

As Odika took the lead behind Kilifi, Harry noted that he clicked the safety switch on his weapon to off. He suddenly felt very inexperienced and vulnerable.

The bush was thick and the shade above did its best to keep out the brightness of the early morning light. There were occasional noises deeper in, the snapping of twigs and rustling of leaves but Kilifi paid them no attention. A life time in these sorts of surroundings enabled him to tell where true danger lay.

The tracks were surprisingly easy to follow at first but then the terrain became much rockier and to Harry's eye the prints seemed to disappear completely but Kilifi hardly broke his stride. Occasionally he would pause, looking for signs that only he could see and then the little group were off again. Two of Odika's men brought up the rear with Mike, displaying the same easy, alert confidence as their leader.

They reached a small stream and miraculously the same prints appeared again in the soft, wet earth of the bank. Kilifi asked everybody to stay where they were as he waded through the water to the other side. He examined the ground to left and right and then summoned the others across.

"There are no signs of them here so my guess is that they walked through the water for a while, perhaps trying to throw people off their scent. I suggest we split up with some of us going upstream and the others downstream. Their prints on the bank should be easy to spot and radio coverage is traditionally quite good in this area."

Harry and Ana stayed with Odika and Jim and headed upstream. The others made their way in the opposite direction, trying their best to avoid the thick vegetation that came almost down to the water's edge.

"The stream isn't deep," said Jim, "so I suggest it would be much easier if we wade through it. We'll get a far better view of the bank and will only get our feet wet."

"Good thinking," replied Odika as his large military boots splashed in.

It turned out to be more difficult than anticipated. They had to watch where they were going as the bottom proved rather uneven and rocky and yet at the same time four pairs of eyes were scanning the bank for signs of the poachers. After fifteen minutes and several radio conversations with the other group, who were using the same tactics, frustration was beginning to set in. There was a feeling that they must have missed something camouflaged by the boulders and fallen tree trunks by the water's edge.

They splashed on for a little longer and Jim was just about to suggest they retraced their steps when Ana shouted an alert and moved towards the bank. It was less steep here and there were signs where various animals had used this trail to take them to the water more easily.

"Look at this," she shouted with excitement. "Not right by the water, there are too many animal tracks there but up near the top of the bank."

As the others followed where she was pointing they too could see the distinct mark of human prints. They all climbed out, careful not to disturb her find. As they looked down with the advantage of being above the tracks, rather than in the stream, it was instantly obvious that these belonged to the same three individuals. The deeper right and left prints of those carrying the tusks really stood out.

"You have done well," said Odika with a new respect in his voice. "Let's call the other group up here straight away."

"Well done," smiled Jim. "I don't know how you spotted them in amongst all the animal tracks. You must have amazing vision."

"Oh, just a bit of luck," shrugged Ana.

It took about twenty minutes for the other group to reach them, enough time to wring out their socks as the increasing heat of the morning sun began to dry off everything else.

As they moved along the bank their surroundings seemed surprisingly quiet. Harry wasn't even aware of the brief flashes of smaller animals that they so often glanced when they were walking through thick vegetation like this.

Suddenly Kilifi put his hand up and everyone stopped, staying as motionless as they could.

"I know the kill was only yesterday," he said, "but I can actually sense death in the air. Take care."

They moved on, more cautiously now, the rangers with fingers on their trigger guards. The bush was thinning out and they knew that up ahead would be a clearing.

Stopping once more, Odika signalled to the other members of his squad to come forward.

"Kilifi is right," he said. "The killing ground must be just up ahead. You are to remain here while my men and I check it out. You never know what or who might be lurking in the shadows."

The three of them moved silently ahead and were almost instantly hidden from view. Harry looked at the others in the small group and could sense each person's tension. It wasn't so much for their own safety but rather what they might find up ahead. The hands of his watch seemed stationary and he tried to resist checking how long they had been away. It seemed ages but in reality was probably no more than five minutes.

Suddenly there was a movement behind a tree to their right and one of the rangers materialised, his camouflage uniform hiding him amazingly effectively until the last few seconds.

"The sergeant asks for you to come forward. The clearing appears to be safe."

There was no mention of the elephant and nobody asked. The small group made its way into the opening with a sense of dread.

There almost in the centre was the elephant. It appeared to be kneeling on the ground, its back legs tucked under its body, its head facing away from them. A strange, unpleasant smell clung to their nostrils.

"Be prepared," warned Odika, who stood by the side of the body, "this is especially unpleasant."

As Harry moved round to the front of the victim he could instantly feel the sickness rising in his throat. On the only other occasion he had witnessed a poached elephant it had been unbelievably upsetting and they had seen immediately where axes had been used to chop out the tusks, but this was something on a totally different scale.

The whole of the front of the elephant's head was missing. There was simply a gaping pink mass of flesh where it had been. Already innumerable flies buzzed and danced over the flesh. Some twenty yards in front of the body was the trunk lying alone in the dust, twisted and distorted, in a large sticky pool where it had been hacked off and discarded like so much rubbish.

Harry was unable to control himself; he took several paces towards the trees but started retching violently before he got there. As the residue dribbled down his chin Ana moved towards him calmly putting some tissues in his hand.

"I'm sorry this is so embarrassing," he muttered.

"Don't be silly. You are surrounded by people hardened by such sights and I bet even some of them felt their stomachs churn, mine certainly did. What sort of mentality sinks to such depths? It is only when you see the aftermath of the crime and that is exactly what it is, vile, repulsive and literally sickening, that you realise the evil we are up against."

"The poachers who carried this out were totally ruthless," said Odika. "They see elephants as nothing more than the bearers of ivory and the fact that they left behind such a horrible scene would hardly have crossed their minds. We had been tracking them for a while and feared they had made a kill when we heard the shots. It is not unknown for some poachers to empty half a magazine of an AK-47 into an elephant. In all honesty we were somewhat lucky to ambush them so soon after the kill. Their ruthlessness showed then too. Although we had the element of surprise, there was no way they were going to surrender to us. They went down fighting and we were lucky to escape without a scratch."

"We cannot thank you enough," said Jim. "A group like this operating in Uwingoni would have been very tough for us to deal with. Of course the missing part of the equation is where they were taking the tusks to."

"Well," replied Odika, "KWS and a special police unit are working closely together at the moment and the finger points to the Chinese who are building the dam up here but of course trying to prove it will be really tough. It's no secret that they will have corrupt officials in their pocket and although we have men keeping an eye on the dam project there are a lot of lorries coming and going all the time and we would have to be really sure before we stopped and searched one. There is too much at stake to get this wrong."

"Look at these," interrupted Kilifi. "I've just been having a good skirt round the body and over by the trunk this is what I found."

In his hand were two cigarette ends. "If you look more closely you will see the same Chinese symbol on these that was on the outside of the packets of cigarettes we found in that Somali's vehicle."

"Good work," said Odika. "Let me have those and I will make sure they get added to the evidence that is being put together. It's small stuff but it all helps. I suggest you head back to camp now. There is nothing more you can do here. We will take some photos and write up an account of what happened. That will end up back in Nairobi HQ with the tusks. We should be in this area again soon but we have an operation in Tsavo National Park, starting in two days. Keep us posted with any news."

After brief handshakes and goodbyes they left the rangers with Mike who would drive them down to the airstrip later in the morning. Men as skilled as Odika and his team were highly valued.

There wasn't much appetite for breakfast but the delicious crispy bacon and perfectly fried eggs soon disappeared from their plates.

Aziz, who had joined them half way through the meal, announced that the repeater radio masts were arriving on the same plane that was picking up the rangers.

"You youngsters are more technical than the rest of us about these sorts of things. Why don't you experiment with finding the best positions for them this morning." suggested Jim.

"Oh, I'm not sure they know enough," scowled Aziz.

"We know a lot more than you think, about all kinds of stuff," replied Harry.

"Just what is that supposed to mean?" said Aziz, his hands clasped fist-like again.

"That's enough bickering!" Jim tried hard to mask his irritation. "We're here for the animals and Uwingoni; there is no place for personal squabbles. Harry and Ana are more than capable."

Aziz shrugged, "I've got important things to be getting on with. I'll be in the stores if anyone needs me."

"Take Bethwell and one of the mechanics with you. Let's hope these masts are as good as you suggest. That will be the best way to keep Aziz quiet."

Ana and Harry made their way down to the garage area to find Bethwell.

Kamau, one of the most experienced mechanics appeared from under Bluebird which was jacked up at the back. "You did well to break a pipe like that," he laughed. "Anyway I have taken a replacement from that old Land Rover wreck we use for spares. It is almost a perfect fit but still leaks a little brake fluid. However, I've got just the thing to fix that."

They both watched as Kamau pulled a large thread out of the collar of his somewhat frayed shirt. He coiled it tightly around the little aluminium nipple at the end of the break pipe. "This should make the perfect seal," he smiled. He disappeared under the back wheel again.

"Now try that brake pedal Harry. Pump it a couple of times and hold your foot down until I tell you. Now let it up slowly."

He reappeared from under the wheel clapping his hands

with delight. "Perfect. They don't teach you that in mechanics school," he grinned, "but that won't be leaking in a hurry!"

They were all laughing as Bethwell came round the side of the garage. "Kamau been teaching you some tricks of the trade?"

"You could say that," beamed Harry. "Now we're off with you to work out where to site these masts."

"Mike has just returned from the airstrip. They are in the back of the Land Cruiser already. Let's see what a little new technology can do for Uwingoni."

"I thought it made sense to start on the eastern end," suggested Harry. The ground rises when we drive along the escarpment but then drops away quite suddenly. I am sure a well-placed mast somewhere there would make a real difference."

"Are you thinking of having someone on the far boundary with a radio and Bethwell and one of us with the vehicle and the mast trying different positions?" asked Ana.

"That is pretty much it. It isn't some complicated experiment, just a lot of trial and error till we have got the best signal and coverage possible."

"Sounds good to me. If we take the placing of the masts in turn it should help keep us focused. It's going to be a long day!"

Ana's prediction was more accurate than any of them had imagined. As the sun rose higher they experimented with locations, trying where possible for the higher ground where there was fairly clear access below so that the signal could be repeated as easily as possible without being interrupted.

So unblemished was the sky that the sun acted as a clock even more than usual. By mid-afternoon they had two of the three really well positioned and it was exciting to be in touch with base from what had previously been dead areas.

The third was taking longer than expected but for the best

of reasons. In an area where they wouldn't have expected them they came across the small herd of elephants that they had come to know so well and there right in the centre as if protected by the others was Meru. Through the binoculars they could make out his little face as he sheltered from the direct rays of the sun under Mara's tummy. He was trying to feed from her milk every so often.

"Look at that," whispered Harry as he handed the binoculars to Ana.

She watched closely as Meru raised his tiny trunk, not to get the milk but up on her side behind her front, left leg to keep it out of the way. He was then able to drink his mother's milk directly with his mouth.

"Oh, that's amazing," she said, "for some reason I had thought he would use his trunk. I don't know why, probably because it's what I most associate with elephants."

"I had thought that too but I feel when you are that small a trunk takes a bit of getting used to. I have certainly heard of very young calves actually tripping over theirs. One of the loveliest things that I have seen a few times is that they actually suck them just as we used to suck our thumbs when we were young."

"Speak for yourself!" she laughed. "We could easily be here for the rest of the day but we must get this last mast sorted."

They retraced their steps to the area above where they had the break failure only the day before and after several attempts found an ideal spot just before a large rocky outcrop. When they experimented by moving down near the stream they still had a strong enough signal to reach back to camp.

"Well," said Bethwell, "I can't remember moving the Land Cruiser back and forwards as much as I have done today but it looks like you have done a great job."

"We have all done a great job," interrupted Harry. "Without your incredible knowledge of Uwingoni and your endless patience and skill we would never have achieved so much today."

"I think we should head back now. See what cook has got for us, that bacon and eggs seems a lifetime ago. I don't know about you but all I need to do now is eat and sleep."

That seemed to get everyone's vote and they headed back to camp, little knowing how important their day's work was to prove in the near future.

After supper the conversation turned to the events of the day.

"Well, Harry and Ana," said Jim, "we all owe you a huge vote of thanks for the faith you had in your portable repeater masts. I really find it hard to believe we have got such great coverage almost everywhere in Uwingoni now. This is going to make such a huge difference to us all."

"Thanks Jim," smiled Harry. "I just want to leave you with one more thought before we all hit the sack."

"What's that?" joked Mike. "Our own helicopter I suppose?"

"Well you're not so far off but you can't buy one of those for under £3000!"

"I don't understand," Mike, suddenly looked serious.

"What I am talking about," said Harry, "is a drone."

Jim frowned, "Those are just playthings; I have read about them in the papers."

"What you need is to read up the details properly online Jim. I know you don't use the computer in your office that much but I am going to give you a website to look at. Just promise me you will keep an open mind."

"I always try to do that," came the slightly gruff response.

"Oh, I know you do. That's why we have great radio reception now," said Harry in his most flattering voice.

"They are using them in some game parks in South Africa in anti-poaching exercises. They have cameras on board and are amazing. Anyway, enough from me. Please check it out and let's discuss it when you have time."

Surprisingly Jim smiled. "Well, you were right about the masts so I should learn to trust your ideas a little more."

"Thank you."

As Harry and Ana headed back towards their tents, their heads were buzzing with ideas about how they could use their knowledge and skills to protect their beloved elephants.

"I shall never forget how I felt when I saw the poachers work for the first time this morning. You know Harry, as a journalist, you do your best through words and images to convey to people the reality of situations but in the end little comes close to what you witness first hand."

"I have read some great pieces on poaching but do wonder how much difference that actually makes to reducing the horror of what is going on."

"That's just the point Harry. Much of it is read by people who would agree with you anyway, so how do we really make our writing count? Well, I have the germ of an idea that still needs working on."

"I don't want to sound rude but could we talk about it in the morning? I can just about drag one foot in front of the other and the moment I collapse on that bed I will be out like a light."

Of course," she smiled. "See you tomorrow."

Chapter Seven

Ana followed her usual routine once in bed, something she had learnt way back in her teenage years.

She called it mind ordering. Everything that was important at the time had to be placed in a particular compartment in her thoughts and as each little door closed the activity became less and she slowly relaxed. At last the final major thought was put to rest, usually with a plan of action for the following day.

The activity in her head was the busiest it had been since leaving Syria yet somehow she felt at peace with herself. Importantly she had found a new purpose and she was always happiest when she had a cause to follow.

With her mind made up, she gratefully embraced the release and comfort of sleep.

She woke early. It was that half-light between the night and the new day. Outside seemed unusually peaceful as she searched for flaws in the plan she had hatched the night before.

She knew there would be risks, but that was always the trade off when you want something. Risks, yes but not danger; that was something different.

She threw on some fresh clothes and splashed her face with the delightful coolness of the stream water. No makeup, she had dispensed with that some time ago, perhaps a little something round her eyes when she was back in a city but that was about it.

She wanted to share her thoughts with Harry but had to control her impatience. Switching on the solar light, she sat at the rickety veranda table and wrote up her journal.

As she slipped it back in the bottom of her case she wondered with a smile what those who had been helping her with PTSD would make of her current ideas.

Arriving outside Harry's tent she considered how best to announce her arrival with no door to knock on.

She called his name quietly a couple of times without luck. Stooping down she unzipped the front of the tent and peered into the gloom. Harry was sprawled out on the bed. He had managed to kick his shoes off but had obviously been too tired even to get under the blanket.

She gently shook his shoulder and something like a groan escaped from his lips. With a second shake he opened his eyes.

"Good morning Harry," she chirped brightly. "Looks like you might need one of those nice cold showers to bring you into the land of the living today."

"Look at the state of me," he groaned.

"Oh you'll be fine. I'm going to get some coffee on the go. I'll see you up in the main camp in about ten minutes or so."

"What's the rush?"

"No rush, but I have had a great idea and I think you are probably the only one I can share it with."

"OK, OK. You are too full of life this early in the morning. What time is it anyway?"

"Almost 5.45."

"What?" He tried to put the pillow over his head. "Nobody else is likely to be awake."

"So much the better. Do you want a biscuit with your coffee?"

Ana was gone before Harry could even answer, a lightly swaying tent flap the only visible sign she had even been there.

She was right, the shower washed away any sleep in an instant. He threw on something cleanish and marched off, marvelling at how a few simple things can transform you in a matter of minutes. Coffee was the final part of the morning jigsaw.

The pot was bubbling away and the smell was just perfect. The coffee he had become used to since being away from the UK was coarser yet more natural, grown and roasted on farms not a hundred miles from where they stood and he loved it.

"Sit down Harry and promise you won't interrupt until I have given you an outline of this idea that has been screaming to get out of my head for almost twenty-four hours."

"Of course, as long as you don't go on for too long," he joked.

"Well, in view of what Odika was telling us yesterday, I feel we should pay a visit to the Chinese dam project and see what we can find out."

Harry had already put his coffee back on the table and resisted the urge to break his promise after just a single sentence.

"Before you say it, I know we cannot just walk in there, we need to have a reason and this is what I thought. I am still an accredited journalist and my experience is that people love to talk about themselves and their work. It is simply a side of human nature. If you are ever stuck for a conversation at a party just ask the person you want to speak to what they do. It is the one subject everyone is an expert on."

"I propose that we contact Ching Pang, the company building the dam, and tell them we are interested in an interview about the fantastic progress the dam will bring to the area. I know there are those who will think it is the worst idea possible, but if we promise to tell the company's story they might just go for it."

Harry pondered the idea. "And then what?"

"How do you mean?"

"Well, you gain your interview, we have a brief tour of the areas they want us to see and write your piece on. Where does that get us?"

Ana could feel her impatience rise. "Harry I don't have a clue. Obviously they aren't going to ask us whether we want to see their collection of elephant tusks but who knows what we might see or hear. It's a start. Ching Pang appear to be involved but because they aren't Kenyan nobody seems to know how to deal with them."

"You're so right, too much politics of course. Actually Ana, if you can get through the front gate, I think it's a great idea."

Her face split into a large smile, "Why thanks Harry."

"There is a but. We have to get the all clear from Jim. If anything goes wrong he could be in a very difficult position. We're just passing through but Uwingoni is his life's work. If he doesn't want us to go then that's it."

"That's a fair point Harry. Let's see how persuasive I really am."

When everyone else had eaten and headed off for the morning they tracked Jim down to his rather pokey little office and Ana put forward her idea. His response was certainly not what either of them had expected.

"I certainly think it has merit and as long as you are cautious and perhaps more importantly respectful, as that is such an important part of Chinese culture, I am happy for you to go ahead. In fact you might be surprised to know that I can probably gain you an invitation," he grinned.

"You're a man of many parts," said Ana, "but this was certainly something I hadn't expected to be within your powers."

Jim seemed pleased with himself. "Well, Mr Pang, one of the owners of the company, actually spent a few days on safari here about eighteen months ago."

"How did that come about?" asked Harry. "It is not every day you have a Chinese millionaire wanting to spend time in Uwingoni."

"Strangely it was through Mike. He had gone on one of his rare trips to Nairobi and during his last night there had decided to risk a little of his hard-earned cash at one of the big casinos, up by the museum of Kenya I think. I'm not sure; it is not really my scene."

They were all ears, quiet, conservative Mike in some plush casino. "I didn't know he even possessed long trousers and shoes other than his old desert boots," grinned Harry.

"Well, he has always liked a little bet ever since I have known him. Nothing big of course and more often than not he loses! But on this night he was playing roulette and doing very nicely for a change and Mr Pang just happened to be playing at the same table. They got chatting over a beer and discovered how close his dam was to us, Mike told him he must pop by sometime."

"And?" prompted Ana.

"His secretary contacted me the following week and asked whether he could come on a short safari before heading back to China. Mike said he hadn't really meant the invite that seriously but I could hardly say no, could I?"

"And what was Mr Pang like?" asked Harry, a little surprised that nobody had even mentioned his visit before.

"Not what I expected at all, although I haven't really met

any Chinese, apart from the wonderful people who run the Tin Tin restaurant in Nairobi. Hardly in the same league! Actually he was a pleasure, interested in all we did, polite and charming with a very beautiful wife." Jim suddenly seemed a little flustered. He rarely spoke with such enthusiasm about people.

"The point is, we got on and I am pretty sure if we contact the company they will let you up onto the dam site to meet the chief engineer and write your article. The one thing I am sure about is that if there is any poaching link with the Chinese then Mr Pang will know nothing about it."

"Thank you Jim," said Ana. "I feel I have hardly been here but there is something so magical about this place that draws you in. If I can help in any way it would be great and I promise to behave."

"Leave the Chinese to me and I will keep you posted. Now the morning is ticking by Harry, I'm sure you have lots to do."

"Gosh, I hadn't realised the time. I said I would help some of the guys replace the old wood on one of the small bridges. Catch you later."

"Before you shoot off Ana, I haven't seen you on your own and I was wondering how you are doing? I can see the outward signs of you, which seem really positive but inside with all of us can be a different matter."

"That's kind of you to ask. PTSD is a difficult thing to explain and personal experiences that brought it on even tougher to talk about if I am honest." She offered him rather a sad smile. "The wonder of being here is that I am so far away from the place that triggered it all off. That is a massive help. You are all so lovely and although I have tended to detach myself from others your warmth definitely heals. I am also the sort of person who loves having something to believe in, I need to be busy and if I can help in any small way to protect Uwingoni, that is wonderful for me; there is the selfish bit, but hopefully useful for you too. I am afraid at the moment that is about all you will get from me. Sorry."

"Thank you. I don't want to probe into people's lives, not really my scene but your dad was such a friend to me so anything I can do please ask, no matter how daft it might sound." He got up from his desk and gave her a hug, surprising himself almost more than her. "If I had a daughter I would have wanted her to be like you. Now off you go and find something useful to do."

Ana returned to her tent, added quite a long passage in her journal and no sooner had she closed it than she shut her eyes and went into a blissfully dreamless sleep.

She was woken by a gentle coughing and saw Harry standing there, the sun behind him already high in the sky.

"You have been asleep for ages but I left you to it, obviously something you needed."

She smiled groggily up at him. "As a correspondent in some pretty out of the way places you develop the habit of sleeping when you can as you never know when the next chance will come. I suppose old habits die hard."

"Let's hope those journalistic skills of yours are sharp because tomorrow first thing we are off to the dam!"

"Already!" she exclaimed. "That's amazing."

"That's what I thought too but Mr Pang got back to Jim almost straight away and everything is sorted. You have to have a driver of course and Bethwell is busy in the morning so it will be you, me and old Bluebird again."

"That will be great. You had better be on your best behaviour too," she chuckled.

After yet another early start they reached the eastern gate of Uwingoni sooner than expected and before long Bluebird was enjoying the experience of driving on tarmac again.

Despite her age she was like an old thoroughbred horse suddenly discovering terrain that gave her the will to gallop again. The road surface was wonderful after what they had been used to. Harry had discovered from Bethwell that there used to be more potholes than tarred surface until a few years back, so much so that it was far worse than driving on the rough tracks in the bush. However, with the building of the dam had come a new road too, also part of the deal with the Chinese. Most roads in the country were notoriously bad and he knew the accident rate was dreadful. It had been drilled into him – assume the other drivers have never passed a driving test, expect the worst and you will probably be fine!

There was little else on the road except a number of matatu mini buses transporting people and their goods to the local market.

"Anyone who complains about London commuting in the rush hour should try a ride in one of these," he laughed as a bright orange matatu with the words, *Jesus Saves*, emblazoned in electric blue down the side, roared past. Stacked high on the roof rack were baskets of vegetables and wooden cages full of chickens.

"I am always amazed," said Ana, "just how high things can get stacked. Vehicles like this are the same in almost every corner of the Third World I have been to. There are so many little farmers everywhere who work all hours their particular god brings. I have such respect for them."

"Sadly those are just the sort of people whose whole way of life is at risk from projects like the dam. Anyway we are almost there so we should be able to see for ourselves very soon."

Bluebird pulled up in front of a large yellow barrier, stopping with ease thanks to Kamau's recent magic with the brake repairs.

There were sentry huts in the same colour either side of the barrier. A burly looking guard came up to the window.

"We are here to see Mr Zhang Wei. He is expecting us."

There was no attempt to be welcoming. "Names please."

The guard disappeared back to his hut and Harry could see him on the radio. The barrier opened and they were directed to a small car park where there was one solitary vehicle.

"You must wait for company transport. No private cars are allowed to drive in the restricted area."

Ana got out, adjusting her sunglasses to the sharp glare. There was little or no vegetation, just large bleached rocks and a gravelled road heading off in a straight line towards some distant buildings.

"Hardly very inviting," said Harry. "The people as well as the landscape!"

"Nothing negative, remember," scolded Ana. "The more pleasant we are the more we are likely to get something useful out of the visit."

A cloud of dust suddenly appeared as a vehicle of some sort headed up the track in their direction. They could soon make out a yellow jeep with a single occupant at the wheel.

"Seems to be a bit of a favourite colour," commented Harry.

It stopped just feet away and a young man bounded from behind the wheel. He held out his hand inviting a polite handshake.

"Good morning. We have been expecting you. My name is Michael Cheng, one of the assistants to our wonderful chief engineer Mr Zhang Wei. He is looking forward to receiving you."

He opened the passenger door for Ana and Harry clambered in the back.

As they drew up at the collection of huts their earnest young driver was equally swift to open Ana's door for her again and as he ushered them in to the largest of the buildings, Harry almost began to feel himself invisible.

When they entered a pristine office the first thing that struck him was how sparse it was. One enormous desk dominated the room with an open laptop placed exactly in the centre. There were no books or papers or anything resembling clutter. A large picture of a monstrous dam holding back a sea of water filled much of a spotless wall. Behind the desk, glass doors gave a panoramic view and silhouetted in front of them was a diminutive figure, hands behind his back, intent on something the other side of the glass.

"Forgive my manners," said Mr Zhang Wei, as he turned to greet them. "I was lost for a moment in thought. Please sit down. Michael, have you offered our guests refreshment?"

Michael looked crestfallen, even though they had been in the office only a matter of seconds.

"That's fine thank you," smiled Ana. "I don't feel we need anything just at the moment."

Mr Zhang Wei moved briskly round the desk, hand outstretched. "You must be Ana. Mr Pang told me to expect you. And you…?" his gaze rested briefly on Harry but seemed to instantly dismiss him.

"I'm Harry," he replied with an unaccustomed nervousness. "My uncle Jim runs Uwingoni," he added, almost as though he needed to assert a certain status.

"Indeed," expressionless eyes swivelled back in his direction, peering slightly over the top of rimless glasses. "I am pleased to make your acquaintance. I trust your uncle is well?"

"Yes thank you," responded Harry, almost taking on the same formality in his speech.

"Welcome to Prosperity Dam. Our directors in China have recently selected this title which they hope will reflect what it will bring to the people of this region. Water and power from the hydroelectric plant for the growing towns, which in time might resemble those of our wonderful Chinese Republic itself. Ching Pang is bringing progress."

"Absolutely," said Ana, "and that is something I am keen to write about, so it's kind of you to allow me access. I would like to highlight the benefits of the partnership that has grown up between China and Kenya in this project. I hope it is in order for Harry to accompany me, he is a talented photographer and spectacular images will only enhance what I write."

"That will be in order but please check either with Michael or our head of security who will also be accompanying you on the visit to our site, before photographs are taken. Some parts of our work might be a little sensitive, for example new technology that I wouldn't want our competitors to know about. I am sure you understand."

As if on cue there was a firm knock at the door and a large unsmiling man joined them. He bowed slightly from the waist to his boss and inclined his head to the others in the room.

"I have meetings in Nairobi, indeed the helicopter should be here very soon, so I fear I won't see you later but I am sure you will have an informative trip. Oh and Mr Hu here will make sure you come to no harm. Building sites can be dangerous places."

Michael showed them out of the office and as Harry glanced back Zhang Wei had taken up his position by the window again, a frown on his face and a phone already in his left hand.

Michael seemed rather subdued at the wheel now that Mr Hu was sitting next to him. Ana and Harry looked eagerly about as they headed down to the gorge, searching for any clues that might indicate a suspicious area that had nothing to do with building a dam.

Mr Hu remained grimly silent but as they approached the dam site itself Michael became genuinely excited, talking of the problems they had encountered and how they had solved them.

As agreed Ana had a recorder on, the days of jotting in a notebook, long gone.

When they arrived at the crest of the gorge it became apparent why they had hardly seen any signs of activity so far. Everything seemed to be happening beneath them, it was almost as though they had stumbled on a giant ants' nest. Countless figures moved with a sense of purpose in various directions. Huge plumes of dust trailed lorries as they crisscrossed tracks. Everything seemed dry and barren and the only relief in the desert-like landscape was the river itself which gently twisted and turned its way, water glinting in the sunshine, its banks lush with vegetation.

As they drove on it was obvious that this was a much bigger project than either of them had imagined.

"May I take some photographs from up here?" asked Harry.

"That is permitted," came Mr Hu's terse reply.

As he looked through the lens he could see even more clearly how the gorge narrowed and the rocky cliffs on either side converged to something almost like the tip of a V.

"I can see all these men at work at the base but where has the water gone?"

Michael smiled with pleasure. "That was a particularly clever piece of Chinese engineering. If you look carefully you will see there is a large opening, like a huge cave on the left-hand side. They blasted an underground channel which takes the water round where the dam is being built and allows it to feed back into the river on the other side. You will get a much better idea when we move closer but we will have to do that on foot now."

As they made their way down a gravel track the heat became progressively more oppressive. There was no shade, light glanced off the rock surfaces and thick dust clung to everything.

"These are tough conditions for your workers," commented Ana. There were a mixture of Kenyan and Chinese toiling away in what almost felt like the bowels of the earth. Concrete was being poured into vast square containers as they passed. "These will dry and become the main building blocks of the dam," said Michael.

Harry raised his camera. "No photographs of the men working here! Mr Hu waved his hand in front of the camera. Good opportunity coming up on the dam itself. It will display the skill of Ching Pang."

Although the dam was effectively only an excuse for them to be there it was impossible not to marvel at the skill and scale of the project. As they looked down from the walkway on top of it, the wall curved outwards on either side and even the huge slabs of concrete looked small from where they were.

"When we are finished," said Michael, "we will stop the flow to the side and the river behind will rise and rise until we have a fantastic lake here in the middle of what is almost a desert. We will feed the towns with fresh piped water and the rest that flows through the middle below us will drive turbines to provide electricity for all here. Truly it is well named Prosperity Dam."

Ana was distracted and noticed that Mr Hu had been talking rapidly into his phone and his lips seemed more turned down than ever.

"Something important has come up. It will be necessary for you to depart now. I am sure Michael will fill you in with additional information on the way back to the main gate. I must leave you." With the smallest of nods he was gone, summoning other security men to him while he strode away towards the far side of the dam.

As they walked towards the jeep Michael seemed visibly more relaxed. "So Harry I was interested to hear you are helping out your uncle. Mr Pang is my mother's brother, which is why I am out here this year to learn more about our business. There is nothing stronger than family, don't you agree?"

That explained a lot about Michael's easy-going manner, thought Harry, certainly not the hard-nosed company man, well not yet anyway.

As they headed away from the gorge he talked enthusiastically to them. Ana thought he was highly unlikely to have anything to do with poaching or indeed anything else that the company might do which was illegal.

He took a left-hand fork and she realised they were on a different track to the one they came on. Soon he pulled up at a small building with a neat line of old shipping containers next to it.

"Let me show you something else while you are here." Harry was keen to see what this place was. Any piece of information might come in useful.

He opened the door for Ana, beating Michael to it. "Come on let's see what this is about."

He looked up at her. Just a few minutes ago she had been chatting animatedly but she didn't say a word. She looked very pale and even her eyes had a glazed faraway look about them.

"Ana are you OK. Ana?" he shook her arm gently.

She gave a start, her eyes coming back into focus. "Welcome back, you were miles away," he smiled. "Come on let's see what he's got to show us."

"You go. I'm not feeling so great."

"Probably just the heat and the ride on this rocky surface. You'll be fine and stretching your legs will be good for you."

Reluctantly she stepped out and they walked slowly across to the hut.

"I just wanted to show you something else that might turn out to be important," said Michael. He didn't go into the hut but instead made his way to the nearest container and with a grunt released the bolt and opened the large doors at the end.

"There is no light but you can see perfectly well once the doors are open. Come inside."

Harry followed Michael in. The heat was even more oppressive. It was after all just a metal box with no ventilation. As his eyes adjusted from the glare outside he saw that the whole of one side had an enormous shelving system running the length of the wall but somewhat disappointingly all it contained was rocks. As he looked more closely he saw that each one had a label underneath it.

"We have taken rock samples from every place where we have been digging or boring holes. The information underneath tells exactly where it was found and a large grid map allows us to trace the sample back to a precise area. Most of them are just boring old rocks but we hope a few will have precious metals or stones inside and then we can explore those areas more carefully. Who knows what wealth might be under the ground. We have a team of geologists coming over from China next week. All very exciting! A small amount of gold and even rubies have been found not far from here and that was without any serious mining."

"What do you think Ana?" As he turned round he realised that it was only him and Harry in the container. He could see her silhouette framed in the door, her hands hanging loosely by her side, unmoving.

"Oh my goodness Ana, what's the matter? You look as though you have seen a ghost!"

She looked vaguely in his direction as though registering

the question but not much else. "That's closer to the truth than you might realise. I'd like to move on now if you wouldn't mind."

"Of course." Michael smiled weakly, not really knowing what else to say.

As they set off again she sat impassively in the front, listening to the conversation of the other two but taking no part.

Just before they got onto the flat surface above the gorge the jeep passed one more familiar yellow barrier. Unusually there was a sentry hut and a bored looking individual stood up straight and saluted.

"What's up there?" inquired Harry, intrigued to see a guard but wanting to sound as casual as possible.

"That's Mr Hu's security headquarters. Nobody really goes there except for him and some of his senior assistants and Mr Zhang Wei, of course. I haven't been invited yet, but I can't imagine it's particularly interesting."

The rest of their journey to the main gate seemed to pass in a flash.

They shook hands with Michael. "Whatever it was that caused you to feel unwell during the end of your stay Ana, I can only say how sorry I am and sincerely hope it was nothing I have said or done."

"Please don't worry Michael you have been a caring host. We will see you again I'm sure. You and Harry have got along famously it would be lovely for you to visit us in Uwingoni."

"What a good idea," said Harry. "I will sort something out with my uncle."

"That would be fantastic. I have a real love of wildlife and sadly absolutely nothing seems to come anywhere near here. Safe journey."

Once they were back on the tarmac and away from

Prosperity Dam Harry assumed that Ana would start chatting but she sat in silence and as the miles slipped by he began to feel more and more awkward. He searched his mind for something that had brought about such a change.

"I am sorry if I have done something to upset you," he said at last.

She glanced across at him. "Would you stop at the next lay-by Harry?"

"Sure."

Some five minutes later he pulled off the road onto a small area with a large sign stating *Viewpoint* which partly obscured the view if you didn't park in the right place.

They sat in silence, the vastness of Africa stretching out before them. A few tiny settlements dotted the landscape but they were insignificant. Harry still couldn't get over the fact that he could see until his eyesight ran out in a haze of far distant hills. No photograph or film could get close to depicting this. He had tried to explain to a couple of friends back in London but words simply weren't enough. It almost felt as though this was where the world was created.

"Well you certainly know how to choose your spot Harry."

"We stopped here when I first came out to Uwingoni," he replied. "Jim told me not to speak but just to sit, think and enjoy what I could see. I cannot really remember ever doing anything in my life like that before. There was a wild sea on a beach in Cornwall once and a rainbow in some hills above Aberdeen but they were pretty insignificant." He remained silent.

Time slipped by. "You must wonder what kind of nutter you have hitched up with," said Ana, with a reluctant smile.

He kept his jaw clamped shut, letting the view wash through him. It was almost as though it was speaking, reminding him that time and space were essential gifts in life.

"Do you believe in fate Harry? I used to think it was rubbish but these days I'm not so sure. The fact that you stopped at this spot with a view that most people couldn't even dream of is no coincidence. Under an hour ago walls of darkness and despair were pressing in on me, suffocating, chilling, equally difficult to imagine, even in your most vivid nightmares. Now I see light, feel hope. It's a different world."

A pair of eagles crossed their vision, twisting and turning as though in play.

"One day my knowledge of birds will be enough for me to tell you just what kind of eagles they are. All I see at the moment is their beauty and freedom."

"I suppose in some ways I feel freedom sitting here and that is a rarity for me, despite what you might think from the outside. I am going to try to tell you something which might help you to understand me. It won't be easy and if you don't want the responsibility of listening and need me to stop just say so."

She sat quietly for a short time, her gaze lost in the distance. "I know Jim will have told you a little of my immediate past, what he knows anyway, but I am going to tell you a part that nobody else really knows."

Harry turned to look at her but didn't speak.

"I have always wanted to be a journalist, to tell stories that others might like to hear but also those that they won't, but crucially are crying out to be told. I suppose that's why I ended up in Syria. I don't know what your idea of hell is but believe me it can't be worse than what I found there. If you can imagine vast areas of the London you know as piles of rubble but with people trying to live by it or in cellars under it with little food, water or medication you wouldn't be close. Those are facts but that doesn't tell you just how frightening it was or the despair and hopelessness felt by normal people who were simply trying to survive. It is on the world's TV screens week in and week out; so much so that I think watchers almost become indifferent about it."

Ana paused, taking a long gulp of warm water from the bottle by her side.

"I was writing a particular piece about a group of amazing women. The men in their lives had either been killed, forced to serve in the army or joined one of the various rebel groups. I spent days with them really trying to get an understanding of what made them so strong, resourceful and protective. Then one morning soldiers appeared at the top of the steps to the cellar in which everyone was sheltering. We were herded out at gunpoint and then the older women were separated from the younger ones. You cannot imagine what it was like for mothers seeing their daughters being marched away. I have never heard such distress in people's voices in all my life."

Harry could see the dreadful anguish written on her face as she relived the story in its telling.

"I was taken with the younger women. I protested that I was a British journalist but I might as well have been shouting at the wind. The streets were deserted except for other groups of soldiers and after half an hour or so of walking we were halted by two rusting shipping containers. A door was opened and we were thrust in like animals, kicked and shoved by gun barrels and then it clanged shut behind us. There was the faintest light from round the rim of the opening but it was oppressively dark and unbelievably hot. There was no food or water. We sat on the metal floor, the older ones doing their best to be strong, trying to console the youngsters, some of whom were only eleven or twelve years old."

"Oh my God Ana. I have read enough to have an idea of what happened next." Harry could feel the heartbeat in his ears, sense the anger boiling up inside him.

"Whatever you have read doesn't touch the surface of what it was really like. Every so often soldiers reappeared, some rotting food and rancid water would be thrown in and two or three of the girls removed, at first fighting and scrabbling, young women against grown men. Then hours later they were dumped back like so much dead meat and others taken in their place. They curled up in the hot metal floor and sobbed or sometimes just lay there unmoving."

She sat, her chest heaving deeply, staring out of the window but seeing nothing. Her hands grasped the coarseness of Bluebird's ancient canvas seat as if to reassure her of the reality of the present.

"They took me out on several occasions but obviously didn't quite know what to do with me. My ID cards were taken away and I was roughly handled. Lewd remarks were made about me, that was obvious though I couldn't understand what they said, just the nature of it. I waited my turn but despite being shouted at, kicked and knocked about by rifle butts, nothing else happened to me. After each session I was returned to the container. Some of the original women never reappeared but others took their place. What staggers me is that these men had wives, girlfriends and daughters and yet their behaviour was totally inhuman. They didn't behave like animals; that would be a real insult to the animal world. They hid behind religion or custom as it gave them a convenient excuse to behave in ways that, in any civilised society, would see them sent to prison for years."

Silence descended on Bluebird. Harry knew that to speak of these horrors and relive them as the words spilt out must have been painful beyond belief but he realised too that it was not his place to comment or offer sympathy. He sensed he simply needed to be still and listen.

The eagles were riding the thermals in front of them now their wings barely moving, just the smallest adjustment at their tips as they glided with complete grace, one way and then the other.

"You know," continued Ana, staring up at the sky, "it's almost as though they contain the souls of those young women who never returned, somehow freed from their pain and torment. On the morning of the fifth day we could clearly hear gunfire getting closer and closer. Mortars fell near to where we were, leaving our ears ringing. Although still in darkness I was conscious that many of the girls didn't move or even cry out. It was as though a direct hit from a shell would be a release. In just those few days death seemed preferable to the lives they were living. The noise of battle faded but nobody came. Hours passed; the heat inside the container and lack of anything to drink was unbearable."

Ana paused, once again reaching for her own water almost as though to reassure herself that she could.

"Then we heard voices, but they were the voices of women. Those who could banged on the side of the container, shouting. Anything had to be better than this prison and whoever was out there, it wasn't those who had locked us in. The bolts scraped back and the doors opened, not partly but fully. And standing in that square of light were half a dozen women, guns sitting confidently in their hands as they peered in. They realised instantly that we were no threat and suspicion became concern and sympathy. We were led out blinking into the light and gratefully accepted some of their rations. The captives silently clung to one another. I realised that our rescuers were women from the YPJ, a Kurdish Women's Protection Unit. Strong, principled, determined but above all decent human beings, on a totally different level to everyone else fighting in this dreadful conflict. Nevertheless, they were at war and had no time for small talk. Leaving us with two of their number they joined the rest of their troop and moved off into the ruins. We never saw them again."

Harry reached across and took Ana's hand, squeezing it gently. For the first time in the story the tears were rolling down her cheeks. It was as though by its telling she had somehow laid bare some of those emotions that she had been suppressing.

"It turned out that I wasn't spared the fate of the others because I was a journalist, far from it. As an English woman I was being kept for the commander to enjoy first before the others had their turn. Fate Harry, the Kurds came before him!"

She roughly wiped away the tears. "I think I would like to go back to camp now. Thank you, not just for listening but for being the person you are. I have been unable to tell anyone else what I have just told you."

Harry eased Bluebird into gear. As he took one last glance in front of him, he saw that the eagles had gone.

He drove at an easy pace; at one spot he stopped completely and they watched a dung beetle roll a ball of dung far bigger than itself across the road, its head facing down, front legs on the tarmac as the back ones controlled the prize with remarkable skill until it reached the far side, when both toppled away dramatically into the drainage ditch. Having time to notice the smallest of things somehow made him more aware than ever of just how precious life was.

Chapter Eight

The next two weeks proved rather uneventful in that there was no evidence of poachers entering Uwingoni. Those who worked there and the small groups of tourists who came enjoyed the often simple pleasures that being in such a unique part of Africa bought.

Harry spent much of his time with the visitors. In many ways he had a foot in both camps. It wasn't so many months ago that he had been living in London so he was comfortably in touch with the positives and negatives of life in a large Western city. Despite his youth, that made him uniquely able to have an understanding of those who came, that the others in the reserve didn't necessarily have.

He saw the businessmen change in the shortest of times, without the daily responsibilities of their companies thousands of miles away; it was almost as though they found themselves and their youth again. Their wives laughed more and nagged their children far less and the children themselves were endlessly out swimming in the camp pool or inventing and playing games that their parents recognised from their own childhood. There wasn't an electronic device in sight. And of course highlights of the day were the game drives.

Harry would often accompany a group but always with

an experienced guide. He recognised that he had learnt a great deal in a comparatively short time and was quite knowledgeable about certain aspects of Uwingoni, but some in the Reserve had been there for more than twenty years and every time he was out he came back richer in facts he couldn't have imagined.

He spent time with Ana in the evenings but she was very into her writing during the day. Her journal had taken on an additional role. Wonderfully she used it far less as some form of support where she could write her darker thoughts. Instead it became somewhere she recorded the sights and sounds of each day and always there was a special space for the elephants. Whenever she could she took herself off, usually in Bluebird, while Harry was at work, and when she found a small family group she would sit for hours just watching them feed and socialise.

She brought her watercolours with her after a while and rediscovered her love of painting, something that had remained lost since her school days. Of course special to everything was the bond between Meru and Mara.

Sometimes she could go days without seeing them and her mind would start to itch with concern, nothing major but it was always there somewhere in her head. Then she would round a bend in the road and there they would be. They came to accept her presence easily. She never intruded into their space, happy to watch from a comfortable distance, often through her binoculars.

Despite the obvious connection between mother and daughter what surprised Ana was the part that the others played. They really were a family. There were eight of them and Kilifi had told her they were all related. When they did move a reasonable distance they often went in single file with Mara in the lead. It took Ana back to her childhood, watching *The Jungle Book*; Walt Disney wasn't far off when he had his elephants behaving in the same way. Sometimes the calves even wrapped their little trunks round their mothers' tails, almost like children holding their parents' hands. The older ones also kept the youngsters as protected as possible, putting themselves between them and possible danger.

She returned to camp one afternoon for some late lunch and found a blue police Land Rover in the spot where she usually parked.

There were no tourists there that weekend so she had a pretty good idea where she would find the police. Two officers were sitting at a table with Jim.

They all stood up as she came in. "This is Inspector Mwitu of the Kenyan police. Gentlemen this is Ana the daughter of one of my oldest friends who is staying with us at the moment."

"Pleased to meet you," said the Inspector. "Jim was just telling us about recent events in Uwingoni. He had mentioned you and your particular love of elephants."

Mwitu had a strong, honest face, the kind of policeman you could trust she thought. "Yes," she replied. "Just being near them seems to bring the most amazing peace and calm."

"My father is in KWS," replied Mwitu, "so I was brought up with a love and respect for wildlife and their habitat. He is proud that I am a police inspector but in his heart I know he would rather I had followed in his footsteps. We were passing Uwingoni main gate and I thought I would come in myself to update Jim with the latest news. Unfortunately there is one concerning piece you won't want to hear. I was just getting to that and of course you are welcome to stay."

"Thank you," she smiled.

"I am sure you will have heard about the Somali who was the only survivor of a poaching party that was here last month."

"Yes, Harry told me the story about the bees' nest and his capture."

"Well, we couldn't get anything out of him and so it was decided he was to be sent to Nairobi but the organisation of the transfer seemed to take forever. Anyway, yesterday morning the order came through and we sent him off in a special vehicle with a prisoner cage in the back, together with another well-known local criminal.

Mwitu's mood visibly darkened as he continued, "Well when they got to the steep bend on a thickly wooded stretch of road, where you really have to slow down, the vehicle was ambushed by at least half a dozen heavily armed men."

"I cannot believe anyone would have the nerve to do that to a police Land Rover," said Jim visibly shocked. "What's the world coming to?"

"They weren't ordinary criminals. We have every reason to believe that they were members of the Islamic jihadist group Al-Shabaab," Mwitu almost spat the final words out. "Everyone has heard of al-Qaeda and this revolting group operating out of Somalia is allied to them. I have had dealings with them before and like all decent people, despise everything they stand for."

"How do you know they were involved?"

"Fortunately Jim, Sergeant Jackson survived the attack. The driver was killed outright with the first burst of fire and the Land Rover crashed heavily into the barriers on the corner of the road. He smashed his head heavily against the door pillar and was knocked unconscious. As he had also been shot in the shoulder what they found was someone soaked in blood and not moving. I can only assume they were in a hurry to make their getaway and just assumed he was dead."

Ana felt her pulse quicken. A few weeks ago she knew the same reaction would have been because of concern that danger was so comparatively close, now it was almost a fury at yet another death and what this Somali's escape might mean.

Mwitu continued, "Although we have no proof I believe this particular individual might be a key player, one of the middle men who doesn't normally get involved in the poaching himself but gets others to do the killing for him. He then pays them per kilo of ivory, gets young men to transport it across the border to Somalia where it is then sold on at a large profit to others who will ship it to the Far East. That money, hundreds of thousands of dollars a month, is partly used to buy weapons for Al-Shabaab to help them continue their terrorist activities. These people are ruthless. They would be selling their own family members if they thought they would make a profit from it! I cannot imagine what hell it must be for all the decent people living in their country."

"How can you be sure it was Somalis who carried out this attack?" asked Jim.

"Well, before the police Land Rover actually crashed, Sergeant Jackson got a good look at the attackers and they all looked Somali rather than Kenyan. We also found the local criminal who had been travelling with him a few hundred yards further down the road. They had put a couple of bullets in his head. He was a pretty horrible individual but nobody deserves to die like that, his hands were still handcuffed behind his back, he had no chance."

"I can think of someone who deserves to die like that," said Ana, slowly and deliberately, "but by now he will probably be back over the border, crowing at his escape."

"I understand your feelings. For an ambush like this to have taken place, he has to be an important individual, which no doubt explains why we could get nothing out of him. But men like this are vain and he will be even more full of his own self-importance now so he'll be back, he's making too much from this white gold, as they now call ivory. Next time we will be ready for him."

"Thank you for coming to update us yourself. Between you, the KWS and our guys here, let's hope we get these bastards next time."

Mwitu rose to go. "I hope so too. Ana, nice to meet you." He gave a crisp salute and headed out of the mess tent, his highly polished shoes sounding as though they might crack the floor tiles as he went.

"Oh, for a police force full of Inspector Mwitus," smiled Jim rather sadly.

"Be positive," said Ana softly. At least we have individuals like him and Odika. Where good men lead others will follow. And of course you have some truly amazing people working with you in Uwingoni. When times are tough we must stay upbeat. And of course Jim we have you. There isn't a person here who doesn't look up to you and respect all that you stand for."

She moved across and gave him a short hug. "Perhaps it takes a woman to tell you something like that," she smiled.

Jim stood slightly awkwardly, unused to anyone speaking about him in that way. "That's very sweet of you Ana. I suppose the only woman in my life for a long time has been Uwingoni."

"Well there can't be anyone more special and magical to fall in love with. Now before I start getting too poetical we have arranged something special to show you but I'm starving, I haven't eaten since dawn and I doubt you have had any lunch either so let's go and get a bite to eat first."

"What is it you want me to see?"

"As I said Jim it's a surprise." Ana glance at her watch. "Ollie, the pilot is due to land in just over half an hour and he is carrying something which could prove a huge bonus in our fight to protect Uwingoni."

They couldn't have timed their arrival at the airstrip much better. As Jim parked under the limited shade of an old tree and looked east along the strip he could already make out the growing shape of the plane and hear the distant beat of its engine.

"Did you ever think of learning to fly?" inquired Ana.

"It is quite an expensive luxury. Getting a licence is one thing but then you have to both own a plane and more importantly pay for important regular checks and services. As far as I remember all planes have to go through quite a serious check after every fifty hours of flying and they aren't allowed to take to the air until that check has been signed off by a senior engineer and there are two much more serious inspections that come later on for the engine and body. The other thing is," he admitted with a half-smile, "that I don't really like flying; give me four wheels on the ground any day, unless I have no choice, of course."

The Cessna 206 came in low sending a family of warthogs that had been taking an afternoon stroll scampering for the comfort of the bush. The plane banked steeply, levelled out and landed neatly on the strip. It turned and made its way back to the waiting vehicles; Harry had timed his arrival almost exactly with the plane's touchdown. The single propeller on the nose stopped rotating; the flimsy looking door opened and out jumped Ollie, his white, short sleeved shirt as neatly pressed as ever.

He shook hands warmly with everyone and shared a joke with Harry as Bethwell supervised the loading of supplies onto the back of a Land Cruiser which then headed off back to camp.

"Are you ready for your surprise Jim?" asked Ollie as he reached across onto the co-pilots seat and brought out a medium sized box. "Well this is it. Inside is a drone."

Jim looked slightly bemused. "Before you take it out of

the box I thought we had agreed that the finances for anything like this must go through Aziz."

"Not this one," replied Ana trying to hide her smile. "You see I have paid for it. I did earn quite good money as a journalist and what's the good of that if it is just sitting in a bank." She put her hand up as if to stop any protest. "I talked to Ollie about this a couple of weeks ago. A friend of his has this exact model and he has flown it with him."

"Yes but Ollie is a pilot so of course he'll find it easy."

"You know Jim the great thing about this is that almost anyone can operate it. Early drones were quite tricky but this little beauty is something else." Ollie took the biro from his shirt pocket and ran it down the tape in the centre of the box and opening the flaps brought out something that almost looked like a model. It was shaped like a four-legged starfish and at the end of each limb was a small blade rather like that of a mini helicopter. There was a simple looking control panel in the centre and the whole thing was supported by four sturdy little legs.

"But it is barely two feet across. It looks so frail, I can't believe it would last an hour out in the wild!"

"Well you are wrong there Jim," said Harry. "Since I first mentioned this as an idea I have done much more research and this particular model is already used in a number of reserves in southern Africa with amazing results. That success is all to do with what you see hanging beneath it."

Jim peered at the small silver coloured camera slung underneath the body. "Are you telling me this can take worthwhile photographs that aren't just a blur?"

"Definitely, and far more besides. It's attached so something called a gimble which means even if it is windy and the drone is moving about a lot, the camera remains still. It can take videos as well as stills, close in or wide lens and can focus forward or straight down."

Ana could see that Jim was struggling and she felt uncomfortable for him. "I know this is a lot to take in. When you were our age you still had to take your film in to be developed and most cameras for wildlife photography had large, heavy lenses at the front. Technology is amazing and even most young people struggle to keep up with it. Instead of telling you more and more, can we just demonstrate and let this remarkable machine do the talking?"

Jim looked positively relieved, "Thank you Ana I would really appreciate that."

Ollie put the drone down on the strip and took out a small white box which had two control sticks, one on each side. To the left-hand side was a special bracket where he placed his mobile phone.

"There are special apps on my phone which link in with this control panel and the drone, so just give me a couple of minutes while I sync everything up. This is also linked in with GPS like all planes and your sat nav if you are driving, so it knows exactly where it is at any time. I must stress that what I am doing is not difficult. It obviously takes some practice but you will soon pick it up."

An angry buzzing sound like a number of large hornets began as the four propellers started to spin. Ollie brought one of the small levers back and the drone lifted off the ground and went vertically up. "What I want everyone to do is get behind me and look at my phone. It is linked in directly with the camera so we are seeing exactly what it does. Give a wave Jim and look at yourself doing it."

As they peered at the screen they saw their faces receding as it gained height. They were all grinning wildly, partly at the quality of the picture but also at the look of amazement on Jim's face as he waved into the sky.

"There are all sorts of remarkable things this little baby can do but I will try to keep my information simple. Firstly by using the GPS satellites we can program it to return to exactly the same spot it took off from. We can experiment with its range but just as you need fuel in the plane it is crucial to have a fully charged battery before you start. Once it is a few hundred feet up in the air there will obviously be winds that will either help or hinder it depending on their direction. And just like a plane too you have to be very careful about the height you fly, especially here where there are the valleys with streams running through them and the escarpment and high hills rising up above."

"Yes, I hadn't thought about that side too much," said Ana, "that could prove quite a problem."

"I hope I'm not sounding too much like a teacher," remarked Ollie, "but it's really just a matter of common sense. Here we are on a relatively flat, low area. If you wanted to operate from right up in the hills that would be the place to start and you can then instruct it not to drop below a particular height, which would probably be your starting point. Then there is little danger of it crashing into a hillside or tree top."

As they all looked at the screen they were amazed at the clarity of the images coming from the camera. Ollie switched modes so sometimes they had a panoramic view stretching for miles and then he swooped down on three giraffe, feeding off the top of acacias, their long, black tongues wrapping gently round the topmost foliage.

Ollie changed the photographic mode with a single touch and clear still images of the giraffes now appeared, so detailed they could even make out the fur on their stumpy little horns.

Even Harry seemed spellbound by the quality of the photographs. "I had no idea the images would be so clear. We should be able to pick out and identify specific animals we are looking for and if it picked up suspicious individuals in the reserve we might get a good record of their faces."

"Don't get too carried away," laughed Ollie. "It only has

a safe range of a couple of miles from the controller and it isn't really designed to be up for hours on end but I think it will prove a really useful asset for monitoring your animals and keeping them as safe as possible."

"So what do you think about my little gift to Uwingoni, Jim?"

"I am lost for words Ana. I think it will be a brilliant ally for us. I really had no clue it could give us such amazing pictures nor cover such wide views. Forgive me for being so old fashioned."

"Don't be silly," she smiled, "and remember, not everything new is great, some old-fashioned stuff is brilliant!"

"Just promise me one thing," replied Jim, "that you never ask me to fly it."

"I think that's a good call," laughed Ollie. "I've got some time before I have to head back to Wilson Airport, so I might just give these two their first drone flying lesson."

"Perfect. I have the delights of going through the accounts with Aziz in twenty minutes, even worse than going to the dentist! See you soon Ollie and thanks once again. And thank you too Ana for your huge generosity and to Harry for your endless belief in how technology can help us. With young minds like yours at work I really believe our wonderful reserve will be a safer place for everything we hold dear."

That evening after supper Harry found himself in deep conversation with Mike who seemed particularly interested in the features of the drone and was full of questions on everything from its range to the quality of the photographs. Harry, being the enthusiast he was, found himself talking as though he was an experienced pilot.

"It's a shame that the height of the eastern escarpment and its distance from camp will make it difficult to operate in that area," said Mike. "That is so often where the danger seems to come from."

"The best thing is for us to experiment, even in the more remote areas of the reserve," suggested Harry. "Something that worries me is GPS coverage. I know it is not the same as radio waves and that there are a surprising number of satellites up in the sky but we will need to check that there are no dead areas where we might end up losing the drone. That would be a disaster."

"Definitely," agreed Mike. "I think it would be very difficult, for example, to see the faces of poachers down in a deep valley."

"You are probably right but only trial and hopefully not too much error will tell us what we can and can't do."

"Of course but promise you will keep me up to date Harry."

"Absolutely. If you will excuse me, I need to hit the sack. My brain is a bit over tired: too much to take in during one day I expect."

On the way back to his tent he passed Ana's veranda. She was in her familiar position at the table with her journal open, pen in hand as a variety of insects threw themselves at the solar lamp by her side.

"Do you know Harry I haven't written a negative thought in here for ten days. That is some sort of record for me. Look I have even changed the front cover."

Somewhat bashfully she shut the book and there were two elephants set against the background of a hillside.

Harry was taken aback by the quality of the painting and it must have shown in his face.

"I know it's not that exciting but I enjoyed trying to capture them. I suppose you know who they are?"

"Oh, Ana I think it's incredible. I knew instantly that it was Mara and Meru. It is as though you have captured everything about them, their characters, even that special bond as they stand together."

"Can you really see it's them? You aren't just saying that to keep me happy are you?"

"Honestly, I think it's fantastic. I had no idea you could paint like this."

"Thanks Harry, that's very sweet of you. I used to be reasonable at art when I was at school but the subjects we had to draw and paint were a bit dull and predictable. Here there are images I can feel and breathe. It may sound daft but it's almost as though I don't have to think about it very much. I dip the brush into the little coloured pads in my box add a splash of water and paintings like this just seem to appear. Of course, this is my favourite. Some time when I feel a little braver I'll show others I have done."

"I'd love to see them but no rush, whenever you feel like it. Perhaps you could give me a painting lesson or two as well."

"Now that might be asking too much!"

"Look," continued Harry, "I don't want to spoil the good vibe but I just wanted to share something with you, if you don't mind."

"Of course, you know you can always chat to me about stuff. It's a funny thing because I have always been a talker more than a listener but I realised the power of listening when I came back from Syria. Those trying to help me listened for hours, yes they prompted me from time to time but they never made judgements on things I was telling them and I found that so reassuring."

"Thanks Ana. It may be nothing but I know it will help talking it through. I have just had the oddest experience with Mike. During supper I was chatting to him about the pluses of having a drone on the reserve. Now you know Mike, we all do, you are lucky to get more than a few sentences out of him at any one time. Well he asked me more questions while we were eating than he had asked me in a month."

"Perhaps he is just really interested in what it might be able to do for us."

"Yes, that was my first thought too but then after the meal I couldn't get away. It was like a barrage. One thing followed another, all about the drone's capabilities and how good the camera would be in particular landscapes. Goodness, we only got the thing today."

"Is it the questions that have made you uneasy?"

"Only partly, it is just so out of character. When we are here with quite a small number of people who we see every day we get to know them pretty well and when they don't behave as we expect, then I find myself asking why."

"But you don't necessarily know what to expect from me for example."

"But that's different because, well you know why."

"I know, that was probably unfair of me but I was just trying to make a point. Perhaps he has been so worried about our security that he really sees this as an exciting addition and just wanted to find out all he could about it."

"You are probably right. There was simply something strange about him which I cannot completely put my finger on."

"Then you know what I would do," suggested Ana. "Log your concerns away in your head but at the same time don't draw away from Mike, engage him further. That way you will either end up dismissing things or becoming more suspicious. If it is the second one, it's better to be in the loop than outside."

Harry's face visibly brightened. "That sounds a good plan. I knew you would have some sensible advice. It's so great having someone I trust completely to chat to?"

"Are you sure you can trust me Harry. Perhaps I met Chinese ivory traders in Damascus and I am going to make my fortune working for them."

Harry looked startled and then grinned broadly, "That had crossed my mind too," he laughed. "Oh, and by the way, keep a look out for snakes; one fell out of the thatch of the mess tent just as I was leaving. Be seeing you!"

Chapter Nine

It had been a restless night and Harry couldn't work out whether it was because his brain was overly active with his concerns about Mike or that there were a couple of particularly noisy mosquitoes that seemed to have spent hours somewhere near his head but at the same time irritatingly out of reach.

He knew they had no visitors for the next two days so it seemed the ideal opportunity to take himself off for a really early game drive before the rest of the camp woke up. It was a full moon and as he unzipped his tent flap he saw with satisfaction that there was a cloudless sky. Stepping quietly up the path he noticed the faint glow of light through Ana's tent flaps. He had intended to go alone, assuming everyone else would be dead to the world but knew that the company of a friend, especially if you are lucky enough to see something interesting, can make the whole experience more magical.

He tapped gently on the vertical wooden tent post in the centre of the veranda, announcing his arrival.

"Yes?" inquired a slightly irritable voice.

"Oh, hi Ana, it's me. Looks like you are having trouble sleeping too. I'm just off for an ultra-early drive, do you fancy coming along?"

"Sounds the perfect solution to lack of sleep, instead of trying to doze off, just do something practical. I'll see you up by the vehicles in five minutes."

Harry eased Bluebird gently down the main track, not even bothering to put the lights on. He fumbled under the dash board just to check that the hand held radio was there and then turning left out of the main entrance, headed east, navigating easily in the somewhat eerie, silver light.

The drive was uneventful. Every so often he cut the engine and they just sat and listened. Off in the distance they could hear the distinctive whooping call of spotted hyenas but sound travelled so well at night that they were probably well over a mile away.

Then as they levelled out onto a less rocky area where the track became dustier Ana caught the smallest of movements out of her right-hand eye.

"Harry stop here will you, I am sure something has just gone behind that termite mound but I only glanced a movement, I've no idea what it is."

They waited patiently but whatever it was didn't reappear. Ana was just about to tell him to move on, convinced that she must have been mistaken when from round the back came the strangest of shapes.

They were both transfixed. What they were looking at was something that seemed as though it belonged to a prehistoric age. It had a long snout almost like that of a thin pig and extremely large ears that would have made any rabbit jealous, together with a tail almost like that of a small kangaroo.

"I can't believe our luck; we're looking at an aardvark. I have seen photos of them but never one in real life, despite having passed this mound dozens of times. Bethwell told me something about them and obviously being solitary and nocturnal makes them difficult to spot. It must be searching for termites, its favourite food. Apparently they are amazing diggers and make many of the holes and burrows that other animals use, so without really knowing it they are doing a great service. Luckily for them they spend so much time in the earth that their bodies are almost always covered in a brown dust which means they leave very little scent, quite handy when you would make a tasty meal for lions or leopards. And talking of eating, these guys can get through up to fifty thousand termites in a single night. He is probably looking for his final course before bed time."

They sat transfixed for a while watching this secretive creature nuzzling into the base of the mound.

"Surely the termites have got something to say about this Harry?"

"They do get lots of bites which is hardly surprising but their skin is so tough that it's only a slight irritation. Wish I could say the same about mosquitoes and me!"

Leaving the aardvark to enjoy his meal in peace they drove on. Although they didn't speak of it both secretly hoped that if they came across some elephants it would be their favourite family.

After a further forty minutes they had seen nothing of real interest when suddenly on rounding a bend there right in front of them was a pair of young lions. Harry pulled to a halt and cut the engine.

"Wow what a piece of luck to find them up and about so early."

As they watched the larger of the two kept putting his head to the ground and scratched at his neck.

"I know I haven't seen that many lion Harry but the one on the right seems to be behaving very oddly."

"I agree, let's take a closer look." He reached into the door pocket and took out a pair of rather battered binoculars. Even without Bluebird's lights on he still got a remarkably clear image as he fine-tuned them, rotating the small circle on the eye lens."

"Oh my God, I don't believe it."

"Don't believe what Harry? Let me have a look."

"Round his neck, tell me what you see?"

Ana peered at the silver lion and immediately saw what had concerned Harry. "It looks like a wire. I would have said rope but there is about two feet sticking out rigidly at right angles. Poor thing now I understand his strange movements, he is trying to get it off."

"He will have no chance of that I'm afraid," said Harry. "My bet is that that is no ordinary wire but an animal snare. It's just like a hangman's noose, the more he pulls on it the tighter it becomes. I am sure those dark patches we can see under the straggly young mane will be blood."

"He will be in agony. We must do something," said Ana, feeling the helplessness of her statement almost as she said it.

"There is nothing you or I can do for him right now. He is a dangerous wild animal in pain, we can't possibly approach him. Our only chance is to get Jim here as soon as possible. I know he has a special dart gun and if the lion can be tranquilised then we would have a reasonable chance of cutting that snare off. Try the camp on the radio, the early birds are bound to be up by now."

Ana grabbed the radio, "Uwingoni camp this is Bluebird, do you read me?" She sat drumming her fingers impatiently on the set. "Uwingoni, come in please."

"Don't be too impatient, it's still ridiculously early."

"I know, I know but…"

"Bluebird this is Uwingoni. What's up I have just put the first coffee of the day on the stove."

"Oh Jim I can't believe it's you. Look we have a young lion on the track right in front of us and he's in a bad way. He's got a wire snare round his neck that he's been trying to get off. Please can you come down and help him. There is nothing we can do except watch, which is dreadful."

"OK, Ana just slow down a bit." His calm, unhurried voice helped them both to focus.

"I need an accurate idea of where you are now and more importantly, as much as possible, you will need to follow the lion from a sensible distance. He is unlikely to stay in the same spot unless his injuries are severe. In the meantime I'll look out my bush vet's kit and my dart gun and be with you as soon as I possibly can."

"Thanks Jim. We will do our best to stay close. What luck we came round the corner when we did. I can't imagine what sort of an end he would have met otherwise."

"We will do what we can Ana but sadly there is no guarantee that he will recover. It depends on how deep his neck wound is. Anyway enough chat, I need to get cracking."

They sat in silence watching the young lion in front of them, the only intrusion being the sound of some crickets warming themselves up in the chill. He made no attempt to run away but instead simply lay down on the side of the track, looking directly at them.

"Look at those yellow eyes Harry, it is almost as though they are pleading for help."

The early rays of the sun had just crept above the rocky horizon and now they could see the lion in greater detail. He was too young to have much of a mane but their early thoughts were confirmed in the light.

"Look under his throat Ana, it's covered in blood and he seems so thin. There is no way he would be able to hunt like this, he must literally be starving."

The other young lion moved off into the rocks a few hundred meters away and lay down watching. His sandy coat camouflaging him in such a way that, had they not been watching him, they would hardly have known he was there.

"I imagine they will be brothers and that's a strong bond between young lions, not just for company but for hunting together," said Harry. "He will have even more interest in what happens than us."

The sun continued to rise in the sky with the morning chorus from the birds accompanying it, but no other animals came their way.

After some forty minutes they were suddenly aware of the throb of a diesel engine drawing closer. The young lion lifted his head slowly but made no effort to move as the Land Cruiser appeared down the track behind them. Jim was at the wheel and had brought Kilifi with him. They drew up alongside Bluebird but didn't get out, exchanging conversation as they assessed the situation.

"Is this where you first saw him?" asked Jim.

"Yes, Ana and I were surprised that he made no effort to move away from us. It is almost as though he doesn't see us as a threat."

"Or he is literally on his last legs. Look at his ribs sticking out, poor fellow can't have eaten for days."

"I see his brother has stayed to keep him company," remarked Kilifi. "By the look of it I don't think he will be a danger to us."

"How on earth did you even spot him?" asked Ana. "I even made a note of exactly which rocks he was behind but I can't see him now. Kilifi just smiled and shrugged his shoulders.

"Give yourself another five years in the bush, Ana then you will notice more than you could think possible. Now let's get on with trying to help this young chap. Have you got the spare darts, Kilifi, just in case I miss first time?"

He brought out a container with the darts and opened it carefully on his lap.

"What I am going to fire," said Jim, " is really a syringe

which has an immobilising drug in it and a hypodermic needle at its tip, not much different from what you would find at your doctors. However the rest of it is quite clever. It has a tailpiece that keeps it on track in the air, a bit like a shuttlecock in badminton I suppose. Then right at the back is a steel ball so that when it strikes the animal the impact pushes the syringe plunger and so injects the sedative drug into the animal."

He picked up the tranquilliser gun and carefully loaded it. "You see this is much more like an air rifle than anything else and the gas in this canister by the trigger it what really helps to propel the dart. Some people use a crossbow but I much prefer this. Now let's see whether I am still a reasonable shot. Assuming it does hit home we will still probably have to wait half an hour for the drug to take effect."

Jim raised the gun to his shoulder and squinted down barrel, lining up the front and back sights with the lion's rear haunch. Breathing in to make himself as still as possible he gently squeezed the trigger. The dart fizzed out, imbedding itself exactly where he had aimed.

The lion was instantly on his feet, trying his best to look behind at the pink feathered dart in his flank. He moved off as quickly as he could into the light bush at the side of the track but even that sudden movement seemed to have exhausted him. He lay down in the shade of a large rock, trying to see what had stung him but unable to move his neck properly.

"Now all we have to do is wait for the drug to take effect. The plus of him being weakened is that it looks like we will not have to track him. If we are lucky he will just stay there. Sometimes after using the gun we have had to walk almost a couple of miles, following at a safe distance but often over really difficult terrain."

"Watch out," warned Kilifi, "here comes his brother."

The others had rather forgotten about him and everyone's focus changed direction. He moved cautiously down from his hiding place, his head swaying gently, small puffs of dust rising from the dry ground as his large paws hit the surface.

When he reached his brother he sniffed around then nuzzled him gently and lay down by his side.

"Oh my goodness, that is so moving," said Ana. "He can obviously sense something is not right, other than the snare I mean. It looks like more than just protection; it almost as though he feels he simply needs to be there for him."

"I agree," replied Jim. "But obviously this will be a problem for us unless he goes back up the hillside. Even having him relatively close certainly increases the danger for us." He checked his watch. "Another ten minutes and the tranquiliser will have done its job."

As Kilifi got out of the Land Cruiser, rifle in hand the other lion moved away much more quickly than expected, returning to his original look out spot behind the rocks. Nevertheless, Kilifi needed to keep a close eye on him and if necessary fire a warning shot to scare him away.

"If you are both happy to come with me it would help. Three pairs of hands are better than one but I quite understand if you would rather stay in the vehicle."

"I don't think either of us would want to miss out on helping all we can," said Harry.

"Right in that case can you bring that special toolkit in the back with those long-handled bolt cutters on the top? Ana there is a blue bag there too with a white cross on the side which has got all my emergency vet kit in. Both of you wait here to start with though, while I check out that the sedative has worked.

Jim moved cautiously towards the lion that remained motionless except for the rise and fall of his all too bony rib cage. He glanced across at Kilifi, standing under the shade of a tree, rifle in hand, who gave the thumbs up. "You two can come over now. With luck we will have about thirty minutes before the drug starts to lose its effectiveness but obviously we don't want anything sudden causing him to come round quickly."

Jim delved into his rucksack. "These are earplugs, might seem daft but if Kilifi had to use his rifle, for instance, that could have a dramatic effect on our patient."

Fortunately the lion was lying with his paws stretched out in front of him and his head resting on them in an upright position. His ears were rounded with quite shaggy fur and still sat proudly on his head.

Jim slipped the two extra large orange earplugs in place, pushing them down gently into the openings. "They are so remarkable when you are close up. By evolving rounded ears rather than pointed ones there is far less chance of them being noticed when they are hunting. You can see the colour almost matches the grass they are in too."

"I had never really noticed they had black fur on the back of their ears," remarked Ana.

"Even cleverer as the markings on each lion are different. You see when they are hunting in a pack the less experienced ones will nearly always be behind the leaders and they will be able to recognise the black markings in the long grass and know exactly who they are following. Anyway don't let me drone on, we've got work to do."

He placed a large cloth over the lion's eyes and then set about examining the snare. "You can see how heavy duty this wire is; he had no chance of getting this off by himself. However, in all this he has had one piece of luck. If you look at the rigid piece sticking out to the side you will see that has a smaller noose on it. That would have held a large wooden stake that would have been driven into the ground. My feeling is that because this wire is rusty the snare might well have been there for a long time and the wood probably rotted somewhat or got damaged by termites. When it ensnared his head and he fought to get free the stake would have broken and as he didn't have to pull repeatedly it might not have tightened as much as it could have done."

Jim felt carefully round the lion's neck, looking for an area where he could use the heavy duty cutters that would be needed to get through the snare.

"I am going to try underneath where the skin in his throat is not quite so tight. Harry can you see whether you can move some of this blood-matted fur out of the way?"

Harry bent down and tried his best but it was far from easy. The blood was thick but dried and there was red earth in there too. "The good news is that it doesn't seem to be bleeding at the moment but there must be dirt and muck in the wound."

"Here why don't you try these scissors I have just found at the bottom of the medibag."

"Thanks Ana they look like they might do the job." Carefully he sniped away the worst of it, exposing a line of angry looking pink flesh but remarkably right at the base, just as Jim had suggested there was a tiny bit of movement between the flesh and the wire.

"That's made a big difference, thanks Harry. Now comes the tricky bit. If you can get above his head, put your hands underneath his chin and pull upwards I think I'll be able to see just enough of the wire to cut it, but be as still as you can. The last thing I want to do is cut some major vein in his neck."

Harry could feel the sweat dripping down his nose, the lion's head was far heavier than he had expected. He pulled gently but firmly and as he did so Jim searched for the best place to try to cut the wire.

"Move your right hand round a bit Harry. Perfect. Try to

hold it right there. I might nick him a bit but I don't think I'll do much damage."

As carefully as he could he got the long-handled cutters round the wire.

"Right here goes." At first the wire didn't respond and Jim increased the pressure until he was pretty much using all his strength. Then without warning there was a sudden twang as he cut through and the tension on the wire was broken. Gently he pulled it away.

"I think we are in luck. There is quite a long cut but it is not nearly as deep as I'd feared. Ana can you please pass me some sterile wipes. I am not going to attempt to put stitches in it. I'll just have a go at cleaning it up as well as I can."

Harry continued to hold the lion's head while Jim worked his way round the whole extent of the neck. As he cleaned each section he sprayed a pink liquid that further sterilised the wound.

"Thanks Harry. You can let go now. Almost done. I am just going to give him an antibiotic jab and then an antidote to bring him round again. Although it doesn't work straight away, will you collect everything up now and put it back in the Land Cruiser. Then you can return to Bluebird and we can watch to see if he seems OK."

As they sat back in the cab Ana held the snare in her hand. "What sort of people put things like this out for animals? This really is a war we are fighting."

"Too true. When you look at what is happening to wildlife across the world I sometimes feel the tide of greed will just overwhelm those standing against it. But you know every day there will also be hundreds of small victories like this one. In themselves they might not seem that much but put them all together and it's a different story. I like to believe in the power of good."

"You're right Harry. I know we must take all the positives that life throws our way."

Jim was at their window. "The antidote should kick in pretty quickly but he will certainly feel a little groggy for a while. I know we've all got things to do but I want to stay here until I feel he's going to be all right."

"Oh, us too," said Ana. "I almost feel like we are watching a member of our family come round after an operation."

Kilifi came back down from the hillside and the four of them sat in their vehicles, and watched as the young lion began to stir.

To start with he lifted his head but almost instantly it dropped back to the ground but his eyes remained open as if trying to focus and make sense of his situation. After a few more attempts he finally managed to sit up but seemed reluctant to try to stand.

A short whistle from Kilifi alerted them to the second lion that was making his way cautiously down the hill, stopping periodically as if to assess both his brother and the two vehicles that remained close to him.

As he came forward the injured lion managed to stand, all be it in a very faltering manner, where his back legs looked as though they could give way at any moment. His companion walked past him, rubbing his left flank gently against his side several times. Turning to face him his long pink tongue licked across his brother's whiskers while he made a throaty sound somewhere between a gentle roar and a purr.

"That's amazing," whispered Ana. "There is such affection there. I can sense the bond between them so strongly. They have both been eying us up but it is as though they sense we are on their side."

After a few more minutes they started to move together slowly up the track with the uninjured brother remaining protectively on the outside. The patient walked with barely a wobble and on final turn where the pink of his neck contrasted dramatically with the deep yellow of his eyes he stared back, unblinking at them, before cutting off into the bush.

"Wow," said Harry. "I think that final image will remain with me for a long time. I only hope between them that they can find some breakfast and he can begin the road to recovery."

"Talking of breakfast," smiled Jim, "I'm starving and do you realise it is not even nine o'clock yet! I feel we've done enough for a day's work already."

Chapter Ten

"I told Aziz I would drive him into the local town this morning to collect a few supplies. It's a couple of hours each way and I will probably run out of conversation in five minutes. Please, please can you come with us Ana."

"Of course Harry. It will be good to see a little of the outside world."

Aziz was already waiting down by the garages and looked at his watch in rather a pointed way as they arrived.

"Sorry we are a little late," smiled Ana. "It's been a pretty full-on morning already."

Aziz's usual gruff manner seemed to melt somewhat. "That's fine Ana, no real hurry. I'm glad you are coming along for the ride." She squeezed in next to Harry and Aziz heaved himself up next to her, his lap awash with papers stuffed into a tattered notebook. "Think I'll leave the window up for a while if you don't mind. We don't want all our shopping lists blowing out down the track."

As the road began to level out, they started to see more plain's game. The dark shapes of the wildebeests dotted the area to their right, their long faces looking both sad and startled at the same time and their almost grey beards brushing the dry grass as they ate. Their presence startled one which sped off in a haphazard zigzag run, causing others to do the same.

"They haven't got too much in the way of brain power," grinned Harry, "Nevertheless, they are part of one of the greatest shows on earth when they move north from Tanzania into the Maasai Mara looking for fresh grass that comes with the rains. Jim was telling me that there are about one and a half million of them as well as hundreds of thousands of zebras and gazelle. I have only seen pictures in books but I would give anything to witness it first-hand."

"It's a sight you will never forget Harry," said Aziz. "It is ranked as one of the great wonders of the natural world and I have been lucky enough to see it twice."

Harry found himself speechless. He had never heard Aziz talk about wildlife with any enthusiasm.

"Most people only see me an accountant of course. All I seem to be interested in are figures and stores but as a young man, working in a dull office in Nairobi, I persuaded my boss to send me down to one of the camps in the Mara that the company owned. There were some issues that needed looking into. In fact I found a clerk working in the store who was selling some of our supplies to a crooked, local shopkeeper." He grimaced at the memory. "Well I soon put a stop to that! However, when I was sorting things out I got to go on early morning game drives before getting back to the accounts at my desk. They were happy memories."

"I haven't heard you share your love of wildlife since I have been in camp," commented Ana, looking at him with more curiosity than usual.

Aziz shrugged, "I suppose I am quite a private person and while it's quite true that I haven't gone on a game drive for ages it would also be fair to say that nobody has asked whether that's something I would like to do."

Just then Harry stopped the Land Cruiser. The side of the track was thick with wildebeest. "Just listen for a little while. We see game viewing as so visual but one of the things I have done more and more when I am alone is to cut the engine and just take in the sounds."

They were instantly aware of grunts all around, some of them surprisingly loud, almost like a bellow.

"Perhaps it is just because I like figures but the sound they make can be heard almost two kilometres away; I remember being told that by our guide in the Mara. Did you know too that once they are born the young can walk within five or six minutes? Rather puts us to shame eh?" said Aziz, looking positively animated.

As they watched Harry was aware of half a dozen vultures that had just settled on the branches of a bare tree in the near distance.

"Look at that," he said, pointing to his right. "Something is certainly up. Kilifi said that when they gather and watch from perches there has either just been a kill or they are watching lion or leopard hunt in the hope that they will be left with some tasty pickings."

They just sat listening and watching. A male impala, his magnificent antlers setting him apart from his nearby wives grazed just near the road side.

"Look on his back," exclaimed Ana. "What are those little birds?"

Several small brown birds with vibrant red and yellow beaks were strutting confidently on the back of the impala, their heads moving constantly up and down.

"Those are oxpeckers," replied Harry. "They love nothing better than the ticks that live on the impalas' backs, apart from a tasty bit of their earwax of course."

"Oh yuck, that's enough detail thank you," she winced, screwing up her nose somewhat.

"I don't want to be Mr Boring again," interjected Aziz, "but we do have a fair way to go for supplies and we really need to be back before dark."

It wasn't long before they reached the entrance to the reserve. A small brick building with a thatched roof marked the border with the outside world. The warden on duty gave a gap-toothed grin and raised the red and white barrier as they sped on their way.

These roads were of no interest to the Chinese and were worse than those in the reserve after years of neglect and the Land Cruiser rattled and bumped its way mile after mile, leaving a dusty cloud behind in the hot, still air. Children waved and those herding goats made some sort of effort to keep them off the track, the passing vehicle probably one of the only things of interest that had happened in their day.

After what seemed an age, dirt gave way to tarmac and despite the frequent potholes it certainly made for an easier journey.

Small shacks with mud-built walls changed to brick buildings, their corrugated iron roofs glinting in the sunshine. Traffic began to build up as they entered the outskirts of the town. Young men washed their motor bikes on the sides of the river and vastly overloaded three-wheeler tuk-tuks, a relatively new addition to the country, strained to carry huge bags of charcoal up comparatively small slopes.

"Can we head for the Make Good Hardware Store as our first stop please?" said Aziz. "We need to get some heavier stuff from there first which should then make loading the rest of the supplies somewhat easier."

Harry pulled up outside a well-built store, its freshly painted green walls advertising the advantages of the Safaricom mobile network.

"Come in with me," suggested Aziz. "It's good to learn all that is needed to make a business work. Without this side of things there would be no worthwhile game reserve to visit."

They blinked as their eyes adjusted to the gloom inside

the single room store, the open door behind them almost like a portal to another world.

A serious looking man wearing small round rimmed glasses and boasting a large tummy, barely kept in check by straining buttons, moved from behind the counter, hand outstretched towards Aziz.

"This is my friend Mr Kariuki who can usually get us anything we need, even if it isn't in his store at the moment."

Ana shook his outstretched hand and Harry greeted him with what he hoped was a cheery hello. He had been fascinated on his previous visits by this Aladdin's cave of a shop.

Aziz had his lists on the counter and as he read from them Mr Kariuki dispatched assistants who reappeared from the depths with bags of nails, canvas sheets, mops and buckets and even two smart-looking director's chairs that would replace the damaged ones on the veranda of one of the tents.

"Do you think you two could go to the bottle store up the road while Mr Kariuki and I discuss some more equipment that I'm after? We certainly need to stock up on beers for our guests, White Cap and Tusker, as well two dozen bottles of that new South African wine they promised they would have in. Take this list. I'll see you back here in about twenty minutes."

Ana and Harry headed out into the sunlight. "Let's leave the Land Cruiser here, order the drinks and then we can load them up after finishing in the hardware shop."

They walked down the street past the stalls selling vegetables and fruit and a young man cooking maize cobs.

Dusty crates of beer stood just inside the door. "How many of each do we need?" asked Ana as she scanned the shelves piled high with bottles of every description.

"It's on the list that Aziz gave us, I really can't remember."

"Well have a quick read Harry then we might have time for some of that good smelling maize on the way back."

Harry patted his pockets. “I can’t believe I left the wretched thing on the counter.”

Ana raised her eyebrows in mock irritation. “Look you make a start here, you must have a reasonable idea and I’ll pop back for the list.”

Before Harry could protest she was gone. The hardware store was only a few hundred metres back down the street.

When she entered the place seemed oddly deserted. There was an assistant behind the counter but no sign of Aziz, Mr Kariuki or indeed the list. “Where is everyone?”

“They have just gone into the office at the back to discuss something, I’m sure they will be out soon.”

Ana took a few steps towards the office door. “Oh I don’t think they want to be interrupted,” said the young man, his eyes widening somewhat.

“That’s fine, I just need the list from Mr Aziz. It won’t take a sec.”

As she opened the door she was surprised to see not just Aziz but another man sitting, back to her, at Mr Kariuki’s desk. All three looked up but the one that held her gaze was that of Mr Hu, his face expressionless but dark eyes seeming to bore into her.

“I am so sorry to disturb you,” said Ana, trying to sound as matter of fact as possible, “I just wanted the shopping list for the drinks store. We seem to have left it behind.”

Aziz got up from his seat, his face a mixture of irritation and concern. “I am sure I left it on the counter, but hang on just in case.” He opened the well-worn notebook and sifted through his papers. “How silly of me, I can’t believe I put in back in here.” He handed the crumpled paper to Ana.

“Many thanks, I’d better dash, Harry will be waiting.” She was shutting the office door behind her before anyone had the chance to say something else and striding back up the road, her mind whirling with questions.

Harry looked up from the counter, his light-hearted jest about shopping lists frozen on his lips. "What on earth is the matter? You look as though you've seen a ghost!"

"Worse than a ghost I'm afraid! I have just barged into a meeting in Mr Kariuki's office between him, Aziz and can you believe it, Mr Hu!"

"Mr Hu, are you sure? I mean of course you are but what in the world is he doing there?"

"What indeed? I have met a few men like him in my time, humourless, ruthless and almost inevitably bad news. But more to the point, what were they talking about? I wasn't even aware that Aziz and Mr Hu knew one another."

"Me neither," said Harry, "but let's just play dumb. If we start asking him questions he will only clam up."

"Agreed. I'll do my best but he must have seen the look on my face when I barged into the office."

They went through the list, putting the crates they needed on one side and making sure that the wine bottles were well wrapped for the bumpy journey back to camp.

When they returned to the Land Cruiser the last of the purchases were being loaded by Mr Kariuki's assistants.

"That's fine," said Aziz. "We'll pick up the drinks and there are a couple more visits for flour and rice and then the garage for some new suspension parts that have been ordered for a Land Rover."

Shopping over, they stopped at rather a shabby looking restaurant with outside tables that didn't look as though they had been wiped down for a few days. "Fried chicken and masala chips are a speciality here, I can recommend them," smiled Aziz.

It took a while to arrive. Breakfast seemed an age ago and their tummies were rumbling. Despite the dirty table and cracked plates that the food was served on, the smell was enticing and the taste even better.

"Well," said Ana, "as the old saying goes *never judge a book by its cover*. That is the tastiest meal I've had for ages."

"Indeed," said Aziz. "Things are often not what they appear."

How true thought Harry but then what a strange thing to say, bearing in mind the meeting Ana had disturbed. Was Aziz trying to be funny or give them a message?

The return journey was somewhat slower with Harry trying hard to avoid the worst of the potholes and taking it especially easy over the heavily ridged tracks. Nevertheless, their cargo seemed to bounce about rather alarmingly in the back.

"I hope we are going to enjoy the occasional cold beer once we're back," joked Ana.

"Don't worry about the beers," said Harry, "they are all in crates and the bottles are pretty thick."

"Agreed," added Aziz. "It's the wine at two thousand shillings a bottle that worries me. By the way is it getting colder or is it just my imagination?"

"Well the word according to Kilifi is that heavy rain is on the way. He was talking about that yesterday and the others were teasing him as there wasn't a cloud in the sky and this is not really the rainy season. However, somehow he seems to be in touch with nature in ways that leave the rest of us far behind."

"Well Harry, I think he might be right as usual. Having worked in dry areas of the world I learnt that you can smell the rain sometime way before you see it," said Ana. "If my nose is to be believed I would say his prediction is spot on."

As though on cue, the sky was visibly darkening in front of them. It wasn't that the sun had gone behind a few clouds; in a remarkably short time it was almost as though it was early evening. The darkness seemed to swallow the colour, the track appeared as a black strip leading unerringly towards the all too distant hills where the camp was.

They could see the rain now although it was still miles off.

In the vastness of Africa where your eyes were used to looking at faraway horizons this was not unusual. Individual storms could be picked out with ease but this was something different. There was only darkness.

All three of them were silent, and the sound of the Land Cruiser changed as Harry engaged a low gear to take on the first of the steep hills that led to the camp.

"I know I am pretty new to the country but this storm looks as though it means business," he said as he turned on the wipers in response to large blobs of rain that were striking the windscreen.

"It certainly looks a bit of a monster," agreed Aziz. "There isn't really anywhere between where we are and the camp that we can shelter and this looks as though it will go on for hours. I think we are better off just ploughing on slowly."

"Agreed," said Harry as he picked up the radio. "Uwingoni this is Harry, can you hear me? Over."

Mike's voice, somewhat distorted answered, "Hello Harry, yes can just about hear you over the noise of the rain. Where are you?"

"Just climbing up the first hill towards the base of the escarpment, Mike."

"Well take care the tracks can be treacherous on the hillsides, they almost turn into rivers but I would just keep going if you can. It looks like a long drawn out storm and there is nowhere for you to hole up."

"Thanks for the cheery advice Mike. We'll do our best."

"He wasn't kidding when he talked about rivers. I am just looking at the level of water down the left-hand side of the track. It's already washing away small rocks in its path and the wipers hardly seem to be making any difference at all," said Ana, as she gripped more firmly onto the seat.

When they reached the top of the first rise Harry stopped and engaged four-wheel drive.

"The brakes will be wet and by the look of it we will need all the control we can find. Luckily I have a fine teacher in Bethwell, but the truth is I wish he was behind the wheel, not me!"

The rain was relentless and the attack on the roof made it difficult for them to hear each other inside the cab. Harry had the head lights on but despite the fact that it was only late afternoon the darkness seemed physical and even with the other two beside him he felt strangely isolated.

They crawled down, the Land Cruiser sliding slightly now and again, especially when avoiding larger rocks that had been dislodged and on occasions branches and other debris that was being washed in from all angles.

When they reached the bottom Harry stopped short of the river crossing, peering intently at two steel girders that formed the new bridge.

"If we still had that old rickety wooden framework I suspect part of it would have been washed away. I know aspects of this new structure aren't quite finished yet but the girders form the base and I have crossed them several times without a problem."

Aziz looked positively pale in the gloom, his brow glistening slightly in the reflected light from the front of the vehicle. "I've changed my mind about driving on slowly to the camp! You aren't seriously going to try crossing over that now, are you? We can just wait here or try that river crossing further down."

"That crossing will be impassable, not just the volume of water which will be way up over the doors but the track on the far side is very steep and in these conditions, even with four-wheel drive, we would never get up. In fact we would have a good chance of slipping back into the water and possibly even getting washed downstream. We either try to cross here now or sit and wait for the storm to pass which could be hours and by then the track on the far side might well be impassable anyway!"

"What do you think Ana?" asked Aziz. "You have been very quiet for a while."

"Well, I can see where both of you are coming from but the prospect of staying here all night is seriously unappealing. I have confidence in Harry's driving so my vote is for the bridge but as an extra measure I suggest I walk across first and can help to direct you as you drive over the girders. You know, a little like the guys who show planes to their airport berths once they have landed. And before you say it, I know the girders are straight, but it is easy to get slightly disorientated in these conditions and you only need to be a little bit out to find yourself twenty-five feet down in the water. What do you say?"

"That sounds a good idea Ana. There is a lip on the inside of each girder which I should feel if the wheels go up against it but having you in front would be very reassuring."

"Not reassuring enough for me I'm afraid," countered Aziz. "I'm certainly not sitting in the cab with you. I'll make my own way across. I wish you luck of course but think you're mad."

Within seconds of getting out Ana was soaked, almost as though she had been thrown fully clothed into a swimming pool. Cautiously she made her way across the right-hand girder, the headlight beams lighting the way. The steel was absolutely smooth but with a top layer of water it was more treacherous than she had imagined. She did her best to look ahead and not down and found herself marvelling at the skill and courage of tightrope walkers as she slid one foot gently in front of the other.

Strangely the far side arrived faster than she had expected. She turned and gave the thumbs up and cupping her hands she shouted, "Dip your lights, it will make it easier for both of us."

With the beams not glaring in her eyes it was so much simpler to check that the wheels were lined up properly.

She signalled across to Harry and slowly the Land Cruiser edged towards the bridge. The first contact would be all important. Ana moved her right hand out slightly and there was a correspondingly small movement from the front wheels. That looks spot on she thought. She brought both her hands together and realised it looked as though she was praying. She smiled; that wasn't far from the truth.

Harry was looking both at her and the glinting steel ahead. He had decided to do his best to keep a gentle but constant pressure on the accelerator, thinking it was better to have a slow regular speed rather than stopping and starting. Already his foot felt achy. Vehicles like this weren't made for gentle, subtle movements.

Up ahead Ana had both her hands up; they were waving him forward in unison. This was not going to be so tough he thought, they were making good progress. He looked out through the side window to check his position and then almost instantly he felt a bump on the front wheels. He glanced up urgently to see Ana pointing strongly to the left and he realised straight away that the front wheels were up on the steel lip.

Trying to be slow in his movements he turned the wheel gently and felt the comforting bump as they came down onto the main girder again. He could feel the dampness in the back of his shirt and he knew it wasn't the rain. What an idiot he thought to himself, just concentrate.

Ana was moving both her hands together in a forward motion, resisting the temptation to wipe the streaming rain from her eyes. Harry kept his gaze fixed on her. He was so close now that he couldn't really see the bridge, only Ana. He felt his hands tighten on the wheel and resisted the temptation to put his foot down to clear the last seven or eight metres quickly.

He was aware that Ana was walking backwards slowly but still signalling in a calm unhurried manner. He felt a slight bump again and knew that the front wheels at least must be off the bridge but Ana was still ahead and the signals kept coming and then suddenly she put both her arms together in the sign of a cross.

Harry pulled hard on the handbrake and then rather than slumping in the seat he leapt out and holding his arms out wide put them round Ana and held her tight with both a mixture of relief and thanks.

She looked up at him and smiled broadly, "Just one little blip, otherwise pretty good going."

"Thanks to you too. It wasn't just that you were giving me direction and keeping me focused, it was a real comfort just to know you were there. It was almost as though you were somehow in the cab with me."

Harry put his arms down, suddenly feeling a little awkward at the length of time they had been wrapped round Ana's sopping sweatshirt.

They both looked up aware of shouting from the far side and there was Aziz waving his arms on the edge of the ravine. "I can't quite make out what he is saying, can you?"

"No but something is obviously up. He hasn't made any effort to cross over. You have just done the drive so sit back in the cab and chill out while I go and see what the matter is."

"OK," agreed Harry, secretly relieved that he didn't have to take on the crossing again, even if it was on foot.

Ana found the journey back so much easier but thought to herself that was often the way in life when you have done something you don't particularly want to do; the second time usually seemed a bit of a breeze in comparison.

Aziz seemed very agitated when she reached him. "Look, just slow down, take big breaths and tell me what's the matter."

"It's heights. I have never liked them but I thought I would be OK, until I got to the edge that is, then I just seemed to freeze. I've been like this for years I'm afraid but I hadn't thought it would be this bad here."

Aziz stood in silence for a moment and then taking a large breath he began, "It goes back to when I was a kid. I can still remember it so vividly. I climbed a tree with some friends, though I hated every second, but I couldn't be the pathetic one could I? You know what boys are like with each other. Well when we got to a large branch about half way the top I made the mistake of looking down and I just somehow felt trapped. I couldn't go up or down. Despite their taunts they eventually realised they had to do something."

He paused for a moment with a somewhat faraway look on his face. "Leaving a boy with me the others went and found one of their dads who returned with a long ladder. Even then he had trouble as I was so reluctant to let go. He was surprisingly patient and eventually I got both my feet and hands on it and step by slow step I made my way to the ground."

Ana saw his shoulders visibly drop as though he had just relived every second of that boyhood memory.

"It was a great story for them at school in the days to come. I felt very isolated for a while; it's miserable being the butt of everyone's jokes. Anyway I was a bit more careful about the friends I made after that and truth be told I have always tried to avoid doing anything that involved heights. The whole of that childhood experience can come rushing back so vividly it is as though I am actually up the same tree."

Ana reached out and took his hand. "Believe me when I tell you I know just how tough it is to overcome your fears when something really impacts your life, it doesn't matter what age you are or how long ago something happened. You need to learn to trust again, sounds so simple but I know it's not."

He was looking at the ground almost as though he was embarrassed to meet her eyes directly.

"I think that's the first time you have ever told someone that in your adult life."

"How did you know?" he replied looking up at her face again. "But, yes you're so right. I felt ashamed I suppose."

"I think that is fairly normal. We are usually much tougher on ourselves than we need to be. But just now we need to find a way across." The rain had completely stopped but they were absolutely soaked so it made little difference. The leaves continued to weep and they could sense the power of the water beneath them.

Ana took a deep breath and gently grasped Aziz's hand again. She looked and spoke with far more assurance than she felt inside. "Look we have to get to the other side but we will do it together. Do you trust me?"

He nodded, trying unsuccessfully to smile.

"Right now I want you to keep hold of my hand all the way. I will be in front and the single most important thing is that you do not look down. That's so crucial, just look at me all the time. We are going to go slowly but we want to avoid stopping. Does that all make sense?"

"Yes, look at you don't look down!"

As she edged towards the girder she felt his grip tighten uncomfortably but she didn't stop. Peering across it seemed a long way to the other side but she knew that was just in her head.

She placed both her feet on the glistening metal and looked back to Aziz. "Now you can feel the inner lip so as you take each step make sure your foot is against it, that way you will know your feet are in the right place and you won't need to look down to check."

Slowly they edged away from the comfort of the land. Ana turned back repeatedly, talking gently and holding his gaze. “You’re doing so well.”

“If you say so.”

“Yes, the water is directly below us now.” Immediately she felt his already tight grasp become vice like. He was standing rigidly looking straight down at the torrent under his feet. Ana cursed herself, realising her comment, meant to be encouraging was the worst thing she could possibly have said.

He stood rooted to the spot. “Look at me. Aziz look at me.” Every fibre of her wanted to shout the words out but to her surprise her voice sounded calm and in control.

“Slide your foot forward and feel that lip. Come on, we just have to repeat that movement. That’s all to need to think about. Now look at me and move that front foot.”

He remained rigid, as though he was incapable of a movement in any direction. Although he was staring straight ahead it was almost as though he was in a trance. His eyes, pupils bulging, had that faraway look in them.

Ana turned completely to face him and taking his other hand too, squeezed them as hard as she could, surprised at her own strength. “Look at me not anything else, not down, not at the far bank at me, right into my eyes. Come on Aziz focus!”

He suddenly went limp and for a heartbeat she thought he might actually fall as he wobbled to his left side.

She didn’t give him time and was straight in with the same repetitive instruction. “Slide that foot forward, head up, look at me.” Slowly, agonising step after agonising step the distance to the far bank shortened. Suddenly Ana was aware that the surface under her feet was no longer smooth but she didn’t look anywhere except into Aziz’s eyes holding his gaze until he too was standing on the sodden track.

He seemed to sag, aware his ordeal was over. "Thank you," he mouthed as he moved to sit on a fallen tree trunk, suddenly heavy legs barely getting him there.

Ana felt the energy drain out of her body as she stood arms now hanging loosely by her side. She was aware that Harry was there beside her, huge grin across his face. "You were just amazing. I wanted to help or shout encouragement, but in the end just stood here, living every step with you, frightened if I did anything I would break the spell."

"You make me sound like a witch," she laughed, easing the tension. "I only did what anyone in my position would have done."

"Oh, I don't think so," said Harry. "I really don't believe you realise the qualities you have. What you did took real guts. I don't know many who could have done what you have just done, certainly not me!"

The three of them squeezed back inside the cab. Nobody talked and with the heater working overtime to dry them out, the Land Cruiser bumped and slid its way to the top of the hill.

The welcome lights of the camp, now only a short drive away, greeted them like a long lost friend. Everywhere else darkness was king.

As they pulled into the garage area they bumped into a busy Bethwell, spanner in hand. "Good to see you back and in one piece, it has been just a little wet. You must have remembered some of those tips I gave you."

"Without them we probably wouldn't be here, and without Ana neither would Aziz," said Harry. "I'll tell you all about it at supper. Just remind me to check the weather forecast next time I'm away for the day. Only a fool would want to be out in a storm like that."

Bethwell's face suddenly showed concern, "Well, we're still waiting to hear from Samson. You know he's one of the most experienced rangers and I dropped him off this morning to patrol towards the far end of the escarpment. Of course we hadn't expected the storm either. He has a tent and supplies for a couple of days but he didn't do the standard radio check in this evening and he's not responding to our calls."

Chapter Eleven

There was a real stillness in the morning air as Harry followed in Jim's tracks. Luckily the top road was hard and stony, so despite all that the storm had thrown at it, the drive was comparatively easy. The wheels bounced along the surface, a pleasant change from the sinking black cotton soil of yesterday far below.

The fact that Samson still hadn't made contact by first light was the talk of the camp. He was a seasoned veteran and had his own mobile as well as a fully charged radio.

It was possible that he had fallen badly or even been attacked by a wild animal. The bush at night was a dangerous place even for those who knew it like the back of their hands. There were others who went further and thought he might have fallen foul of poachers

"Who in their right mind would be out in a storm like that?" Jim had asked when Harry had seen him on their return.

Harry had agreed with him in some ways but it was the wisdom of Kilifi that won the day. He had made a comment that in many ways was so obvious that nobody had considered it.

"Wild storms provide the perfect camouflage for those with evil intentions," he had said. "Only a madman or a poacher or both would be out in such weather!"

It was a point simply made and they had all gone to bed that night turning the thought over in their heads and hoping that all would be well in the morning.

Samson was a popular member of the Uwingoni family and there was no shortage of volunteers for a search party.

For the first time in many weeks, Jim and the men with him in the front Land Cruiser were carrying guns; that is with the exception of Kilifi who refused to ever touch a modern weapon, but instead relied on his trusty spear that he always carried with him at such times.

Harry well remembered when he had been allowed to hold it. He had felt very special, honoured almost. It had belonged to Kilifi's father and his grandfather before that.

It had a leaf-shaped blade, dark in the centre but gleaming and surprisingly sharp on the entire surface of the edge, not just the point. The aged brown wood of the shaft was totally smooth, there wasn't even the hint of a knot and was free of any pattern or decoration. What had surprised Harry most was the almost perfect balance. Kilifi had explained that although you could use this for stabbing your enemy it was very much a throwing spear, but of course that meant that you had to get very close to your target to use it effectively.

He also sometimes carried a bow and a small ancient leather quiver for the arrows, but as yet Harry hadn't been given an introduction to his archery skills.

Jim had stopped in front of them and Kilifi was out examining the track and the nearby undergrowth but he returned shaking his head and they continued. The animals they passed in the bush still looked somewhat bedraggled. There were far fewer trees and areas of cover on top of the escarpment and when the storm had hit many of them would simply have had to ride it out. A small group of Thomson's gazelle still stood close together for warmth, their eyes looking somewhat sad as the vehicles passed by, steam rising gently from their coats with the first heat of the day.

They drove much more slowly now. Kilifi was sitting on the front wing, his leather sandaled feet braced against the large, black, protective grill bolted to the bumper. This gave him a far better view of the track.

Every so often he would put his hand up in the air and the vehicles would stop as he jumped down to examine the ground. After a forty minute crawl even Harry was beginning to realise just how difficult it was to find one individual in such a huge area.

"I can't help thinking what might have happened under cover of the storm. I hate this negativity I have sometimes."

Ana gave him an understanding look. "Sometimes it's better to be realistic Harry. Then if things turn out badly, it's not so hard to deal with."

There was increasing warmth in the air now and they were conscious of more and more animals moving with purpose.

A family of warthogs shot out between the two vehicles, the father inclining his tusks slightly towards Bluebird. In the near distance the heads of two giraffes could be seen, taking the most succulent of the leaves at the tops of the trees for breakfast. It felt just like a normal morning in Uwingoni.

Again they stopped but instantly everyone was aware that Kilifi seemed far more animated. As he examined the ground he summoned the others to come over to where he was. At first Harry couldn't see anything out of the ordinary but then as Kilifi pointed he made out faint tyre marks but they made little sense to him because they were intermittent and far too close together to come from a vehicle.

"If you look carefully you can see that these tracks belong to three separate individuals. By examining the markings in detail you will actually make out the separate patterns."

Ana and Harry were both peering at the ground, trying to look intelligent but failing rather badly. Kilifi read their faces as easily as the tracks and smiled. "Two of the men are wearing million milers and if you look really closely you will see that in fact they have been made from not two but four different tyres."

Harry's expression suddenly lightened with understanding but Ana still looked perplexed. "It seems so simple now that he has pointed it out," he said, turning to her. "Many poorer people have their sandals made from old car tyres. They are cut, still with the bend of the tyre on, and then two simple canvas straps are attached across the top, you slip your foot between the two and off you go. The feeling is that they will never wear out, hence the name."

They all bent down looking at the individual tread marks in the ground and could just make out the subtle differences between them.

"The third set are certainly unusual," continued Kilifi. "My guess is they are hand-made boots of some sort, they have flat leather soles with no form of recognised manufacturing pattern."

"What do you suggest we do now Kilifi?" asked Jim. "You are the expert; we are in your hands."

"Well, we will need to go down this side of the escarpment, which is where these men have come from. You can see which way they were walking because the tread is a little clearer where their heel is, as that is the heaviest part of your footfall. However, just at the moment it is probably even more important to see where these tracks head. They are very recent; they have to have been made after yesterday's storm. We need to find out who they are and just what they were up to."

They all followed the hunched figure and even to the least skilled the million miler prints, in particular, were still visible, although much more difficult to identify on the hard track itself where they left little imprint. The road took a slight dip and within fifty metres Kilifi had stopped again.

He was down on his knees examining the ground almost scientifically. His face frowned in concentration, the eyes around the deep crow's feet peering intently at everything. He licked his fingers and rubbed them on the hard surface, then held them up to his nose as his eyes narrowed even further. Then he suddenly stepped back, almost as though he had been bitten. Nobody spoke as Kilifi stood stock still, making sense of the clues he had uncovered.

"I am afraid none of what I have to say is good news," he sighed. "Of course I can't be sure of everything but some of what I have seen can't be argued with. Last night the three poachers, for that is unquestionably what they were, stopped here for a rest and put down the tusks they were carrying. There are two vague semicircle marks here and just to the centre of one are some small traces of flesh. So I am pretty sure this is where they leant two freshly poached tusks and some of the gore from the right hand one rubbed off onto the track."

There was a stunned silence. "Are you sure?" asked Jim, knowing the answer almost before he asked the question.

"I'm afraid so," came the heavy reply, "but there is something else you need to know. They met a fourth man on this spot. You might not be able to make it out that clearly but to me the prints are obvious. This is a man who drags one foot slightly as he walks. Our Somali is back!"

Nobody spoke. This was a man they hardly knew and yet the knowledge they did have was enough to fill them with both anger and dread.

"Well, at least we know what we are up against," said Jim. "I will get in touch with KWS once we return camp. Men like this have one real weakness; they think they are untouchable. Well, we are going to prove otherwise."

As Ana looked at him she had no doubt that somehow they would get their man. The line of his mouth and the hardness in those normally kind eyes radiated purpose.

"We have one of those horrible choices now. Do we follow the tracks in front of us in the hope of catching up with them or head back down where they came from? My gut feeling that by doing that we are more likely to find the answer to Samson's disappearance."

Everyone waited silently for Jim to come to a decision. "Right, Kilifi, I'd like you to push on after these bastards with two of the rangers. If you spot them, even in the distance, don't take them on, but radio me back immediately. Matwapa, you're a great tracker too so you stay with us and we'll follow the trail back down the side of the slope and see what we can find."

Once they were off the road it was easier to follow the poachers' tracks than Harry had anticipated. They had been far from subtle in making their way to their meeting with the Somali and Matwapa barely paused, broken foliage often marking the way they had come.

Suddenly he was pointing up, rather than looking down and the others all saw the ominous signs of circling vultures. Their huge wings outstretched, individual feathers on the tips silhouetted against the light of the morning sky.

"Vultures mean only one thing," said Jim as he looked across at Ana. "They have that amazing knack of knowing when an animal is dead and before you know it, there they are, ready for the cleanup. Actually I have amazing respect for them. They may not look too attractive on the ground but they are majestic in the air and believe it or not just like the elephant we are bound to find, they too are under threat. What are we doing to this beautiful land?"

Ana didn't respond, she knew he hadn't expected an answer. She realised that in his final question he was simply speaking his thoughts aloud. She could see the pain in his expression and knew that to him these weren't just creatures to be protected and nurtured; it was almost as though they were part of his family.

They scrambled down the last steep part of the slope, loose stones from their descent rattling down in front of them. The small clearing they found themselves in displayed evidence that a number of elephants had been there. One of the trees had actually been pushed right over and on others it was easy to see where the tusks had ripped off the bark.

To one side of the clearing was a small waterhole. "Look," said Jim you can see where they have been digging up the salts in the ground round that hole. I didn't even know this place existed, how on earth the poachers found their way here is a mystery."

Matwapa was signalling to them from the far side and as they moved across it was instantly obvious what he had found. Lying on his side was a single elephant, back legs splayed out behind him.

As they approached the body Harry braced himself, seeing a dead elephant was bad enough but the brutality involved in gouging out the tusks was something else. The trunk was lying forlornly on its own as he had expected but as he looked at the face itself he felt almost instantly light-headed. There was no evidence of the vicious axe blows he has witnessed in the past, this was revoltingly clinical instead.

Even before he voiced his thoughts Jim exclaimed, "Oh my God, it looks like they have used a chainsaw here. That would explain why Kilifi saw the prints of neat semicircles where the poachers had rested and put the base of the tusks on the ground. It looks like we are up against an even more organised enemy than I had thought."

"I think you are right," said Matwapa. "If you look at the

elephant's side you will see just two bullet wounds. Whoever shot this animal was no amateur. These were shots directly to the heart by someone who knew just what they were doing. I'm sure this will be the man with the leather boots."

"That brings a really concerning new aspect to protecting our elephants," sighed Jim. "If they have recruited some form of professional hunter; who is he and where did he come from?"

"What is even stranger," chipped in Harry, "is what is he doing with the Somali? This couldn't be more different from the way his poachers were operating before. And also how does he have the knowledge to track this poor elephant to a remote waterhole and an unknown salt lick?"

Ana looked down at the young elephant, "I have been doing a little journalistic research recently. I know China has banned legal ivory imports, which is a huge step in the right direction but the illegal trade in wildlife is still massive. It's worth billions of dollars a year and now the same criminal gangs that deal with drug and people trafficking are moving into ivory, rhino horn, animal skins and anything else they can get their hands on. I know there are few big elephants left now but the tusks from a single one could be worth a hundred thousand dollars. That's megabucks by anybody's standards. So it seems as though we are dealing with professional criminals here and yes they might well be linked in with Somali terrorists but they might just be out for the biggest profit they can make."

She looked round at the others, "Sorry I didn't want to bore you. There's lots of interesting stuff I have found out about but this is hardly the time for me to be lecturing you, I just thought it might give a different angle to what we have discovered here."

Jim smiled weakly, "You are far from boring. Everyone has different talents and the best way to try to defeat this dreadful crime is for us all to use those to the full. Sometimes I get too bogged down with what's happening here and rather forget the bigger picture."

"Talking of a bigger picture, Ollie is due to fly in with some more guests later this morning. Can I suggest that we see whether his company might lend him to us for an hour or so again? We will gain a far better idea of possible danger points and anything suspicious from the air. There is nobody who knows Uwingoni better than Kilifi and I would like to think I have got the youngest and sharpest eyesight. If the two of us were to crisscross the reserve from the air I…"

Harry stopped, drawn by the large smile on Jim's face. "Give Kilifi a lion or leopard to track any day but don't ask him to go up in one of those little planes. He often tells me that if the gods had wanted us to fly they would have given us wings."

They all chuckled. "Nevertheless, I think your idea is a good one Harry. I will radio through to Ollie's boss. I am sure in the circumstances he will be happy to help. Talking of Kilifi, let's see what news there is from his end."

He listened intently to the radio and everyone waited eagerly for news. "It seems the four poachers cut off into the bush a couple of miles further down. I know the area vaguely. It's very thickly wooded, you could hide a small army in there! Far too dangerous for Kilifi and the others to continue so I've told them to come back and we'll meet again on the main track."

Jim let his glance skirt round the clearing once more and was suddenly aware that there was no sign of Ana. He was just about to ask Harry where she was when there was a shout from the far side. Immediately on edge he reached down towards his well-worn rifle. Matwapa too was instantly alert, his weapon at the ready.

Ana's voice rose through the bushes, more urgent this time. "Please I need help now, it's Samson."

The others rushed towards the area of low-lying shrub and there, not twenty metres in, was Ana kneeling next to a figure at the base of a tree.

"Has someone got a knife? His hands have been tied together round the back of the tree."

Harry took the Leatherman from the pouch on his belt. It contained a number of different tools including a sharp blade. The rope was surprisingly stubborn, not only tough but wet from the previous night's downpour. Eventually the last strands parted and Samson's body slumped forwards.

Ana cradled his head on her lap. "Someone give me some water."

Matwapa handed her a bottle and she poured a little gently into his half-open mouth. Almost immediately his body was convulsed with a fit of coughing and his eyes flickered open, wide and confused but as they focused on those round him his whole manner visibly relaxed.

"Try some more water. You might like to take the bottle yourself."

Shakily he took the water from her hand and gulped down a few mouthfuls. The change was almost instantaneous and he sat up rubbing his wrists as though trying to get some blood flow back into his hands.

"You've got a massive bump on the back of your head but it looks like you'll live," she smiled reassuringly. "Just take your time."

With a little help Samson got groggily to his feet.

"Are you up to telling us what happened?" asked Jim.

"Well, a few hours after Bethwell dropped me off yesterday I was walking along the top track when that very distinctive sound of a small herd of elephants enjoying themselves came drifting up from below. The tree cover is so dense that I decided to make my way down to investigate and came across this clearing where they were busy digging up the ground looking for all those minerals. They seemed very unconcerned by my presence and I suppose I lost myself a little in the magic of the moment."

Samson paused for a few more sips of water and taking a deep breath continued. "Suddenly out of the corner of my eye I saw two men on the far side who were obviously nothing to do with Uwingoni or KWS. I challenged them and the herd suddenly became very agitated and made off into the trees right across my path. In the noise and confusion I was totally unaware that there must have been a third man behind me. Before I could react there was a massive blow to the back of my head. I must have been unconscious for some time and when I came round I was tied to the tree and the dead elephant was where you see him now."

"Did you learn anything more about these men?" inquired Jim.

"Oh yes." Samson's normally easy-going expression was instantly full of loathing. "All were dressed in army type camouflage kit, two were obviously Somali but it was the third one who was in charge, who had a rifle rather than an AK-47. Certainly wasn't from anywhere round here but South Africa, Namibia, Zimbabwe maybe, his accent was from that region. It was his idea to leave me tied up here. They thought it would be much funnier than killing me straight away and joked about the hyenas and lions being drawn to the elephant carcass and finding me as a tasty snack on the side. However, luck was obviously on my side, especially with the storm. I drifted in and out of consciousness during the night and the first thing I was really aware of was Ana's voice somehow making it through the throbbing pain in my head."

"Thank you Samson. Each new thing I hear about these

people makes me more and more determined that when we catch up with them, any form of mercy will be the last thing on our minds. We will stamp the life out of this organisation. Now we need to get you back to camp. Sadly there is nothing more we can do here."

There were two couples from the UK on board the Cessna, saving themselves six hours of slow grind on the Kenyan roads by taking a flight that took a mere seventy-five minutes.

After they had clambered out of the narrow doorway and been whisked off to lunch by Bethwell, Ollie greeted Harry and Ana with his usual cheerful positivity.

"I gather I'm taking you for a quick flight over Uwingoni, or so my boss says. Happy to help out as always but even in a plane it's quite a large area so you need to give me a good idea of where in particular you want to look."

"Of course. Ana why don't you sit in the other pilot's seat and I'll slot in behind you guys. There is lots of room back here."

The doors were shut and the engine, warm that it was, started instantly. Ollie pushed the throttle forward and the little plane bounded down the strip. "We'll be airborne in just a sec," said Ollie. "With three rather than six of us she cannot wait to be off the ground."

"The open savannah areas down in this part of the reserve are not a problem but once we are up on the escarpment it is much more remote and the tree and vegetation cover is thick so if you don't mind Ollie I think we should look there first."

"Your shout Harry." Ollie pulled back on the stick and adjusted the throttle. Below them the little tracks were no more than ribbons and they were able to make out small clusters of animals grazing peacefully, unconcerned by the engine noise hundreds of feet above. "I'm going to level off soon but I'm reluctant to get too low. If anything were to happen, there isn't exactly anywhere we can land up here."

The midday sun made it extremely warm in the cockpit and the plane seemed to dance over the tops of the trees, dipping and rising every so often as it caught small air pockets.

Ana marvelled at the sheer size of the reserve; and how being so remote gave it a timelessness that was hard to put into words.

"We are nearing the area where that steep dip in the road is. It is down the slope to the left that we found the elephant earlier today." The circling buzzards and vultures pinpointed the position precisely.

"If you don't mind I'm not going to take the plane down there. Get one of those in the engine and we would be joining your elephant!"

They flew on until the road began to level off. "Look to the left down there boys, are my eyes playing tricks on me or are those fresh tyre marks?"

"I didn't get a proper look Ana. Give me a sec and we'll go round again." Ollie banked the plane steeply to port focusing on a tight manoeuvre.

"Good spot. I was looking on the other side but I agree. Let's wait until Ollie has the plane level again." The track marks were feint but they were definitely there, leading unerringly to the boundary of the reserve. "Can we follow them as far as we can Ollie?"

"Of course Harry. I expect they will come and go as there are some thickly wooded areas down here if I remember, but it shouldn't be too difficult. Do you know what I find most surprising is that apart from some obvious steep rocky areas this track hardly deviates so when they were coming in how on earth did they know where to go?"

"I was thinking much the same," responded Ollie. "Even Jim had no idea there was a salt lick down where the young bull was killed. You know that once elephants find something like that they will endlessly be drawn back to the same spot and that is a huge worry for the future. We haven't really got the manpower to have a ranger patrolling just that area, especially as our enemy could strike somewhere else."

As they reached the deep ditch that marked the northern boundary of the reserve they could make out where the poachers had driven parallel for almost a mile before they came to a spot where the ditch walls had collapsed, making it passable for a determined driver.

"I suppose Jim could get some guys to fix that," commented Ana, "but the border goes on for miles and there would soon be a new crossing point. Tough isn't it. You have no fence so as to allow the animals to be able to roam freely but that makes protecting them all the harder."

"I know," sighed Ollie, "but Jim would never be able to afford one anyway. It's the same in so many reserves, big hearts but limited resources."

"There's no way of following the tracks once they are on public roads. I think I will just turn the plane and head back. The only thing further up this road of any note is the Prosperity Dam project."

"And you know what Ollie, somewhere in there lies the answer to all this. I feel it in my bones but unfortunately we have no proof, as yet anyway."

"I share your frustration Harry but for now we will just retrace out steps. With luck perhaps we'll be able to pick out a couple of the smaller elephant herds and at least check that they are OK."

They flew back, in relative silence, the engine humming contentedly as they gained altitude.

"Down there," shouted Ana, "to the side of that small clearing there was something glinting I'm sure of it."

Even as she spoke Ollie banked the plane sharply. "It won't take a minute to go back over it, I'll drop down a little." As they crossed the clearing all three of them were aware of something reflecting unnaturally in the sunlight.

"I know exactly what that is," exclaimed Harry excitedly. "It's a windscreen. There is a vehicle down there, right below us."

"We are too directly above it to see properly so I'll take us out a little again and then back as we now know where it is," said Ollie.

As they flew back towards the clearing they were all aware of what they were looking for and as is so often the case, the vehicle, although well camouflaged seemed quite obvious. It was a green Land Rover with a variety of coloured paint splodges to help it blend in.

"That has to be what the poachers are using. There is no way a random vehicle is simply going to be sitting under the trees in this part of the reserve. The question is; where are the poachers, down there too or coming back later?"

The question was barely out of Harry's lips when they all became aware of movement on the other side of the clearing. "Ana try to get the camp on the radio and let them know what's going on. This is not an easy place to reach in a hurry but perhaps they can get a KWS response team up here quickly. I'll see whether I can fly a little closer so we can form an accurate picture of how many men are down there."

"Uwingoni Camp can you hear me? This is Ana, come in please. We have just spotted some poachers and their vehicle. This is urgent." They were answered only by the static on the radio. "Surely we are in radio range Ollie. This doesn't make sense, the radio there is always manned."

"Give it another go and I'll… Oh my God they're shooting at us!"

The unmistakable flash of gunfire from the shadows by the Land Rover galvanised Ollie into evasive action. Almost simultaneously there was the sound of bullets peppering the side of the fuselage and a loud scream. Immediately the plane lurched to one side and started to lose height.

"Quickly Ana, Ollie's been hit, pull the control stick towards you, not too strongly and turn it to the right." Harry's voice was surprisingly calm and as Ana followed the instructions they started to rise. To her left, slumped back in the seat, one side of his face already covered in blood, Ollie seemed lifeless.

"Now gently push the black throttle control in. That's the one to the side of the only red knob on the instrument panel." They were instantly aware of the increase in engine revs. There was the sound of further bullets striking but it seemed as though it must be at the rear as nothing further entered the cockpit. "That's brilliant, just get us away from the poachers and the escarpment and we might be fine."

Ana was only too conscious of how hard she was gripping the control stick and she tried to breathe as calmly as she could.

"Look Ana I'm obviously not a pilot but I have flown with Ollie on a couple of occasions and he has allowed me to take the controls and explained the basics. For the moment we are safe from the poachers, if you can just try to keep us at this sort of height and speed I will see what has happened to him. That's our immediate priority. We aren't about to fall out of the sky."

"I'll try; what more can I say."

The cabin was small and cramped but Harry was able to extract the first aid box from under his seat.

Working from behind someone is far from easy but there

was no way in a plane this size that he could even begin to clamber into the front and there was absolutely no space there anyway.

He had done some basic first aid training when he had worked as a lifeguard in a local swimming pool as a holiday job but that hardly equipped him to deal with someone who had been shot.

He placed his fingers on the side of Ollie's neck and was instantly relieved as he felt a strong pulse. He gently moved Ollie's head so that he could get a better idea of just where he had been hit. The blood was only on the left-hand side which was hardly surprising as that was where the bullet had come from. In fact as he checked round the cockpit he could see two bullet holes, one right at the back of the door that had passed behind Ollie's seat and, Harry realised with a sharp intake of breath, must have missed him in the second row by a frightening small margin; he could actually see the exit hole on the far side. The second hole was higher up in the toughened plastic of the widow.

He gently looked for the wound, following the course of the blood. There appeared to be nothing obvious on his neck or right cheek and then as his gaze moved to his forehead he could see where the bullet had struck. Just on the corner of Ollie's temple, pretty much on his hairline was a wound no more than a few centimetres long, still weeping a surprising amount of blood. Even as a complete amateur he realised that the bullet had only grazed Ollie's head, there was no bullet hole.

"Oh Ana, I think he is going to be alright, it only looks as though the bullet has clipped his forehead. I say only, but it is still a bullet; he must have lost consciousness with the shock of the impact."

As though on cue a groan came from the blood splattered lips and Ollie slumped forward leaning his body against the controls. Ana frantically pulled back on the stick as they started to lose height. "Grab him back towards you Harry quickly; I haven't got the strength to fight against his upper body weight."

Gently but firmly Harry pulled him towards the back of his seat; and the little plane positively leapt up with Ollie's weight suddenly gone. Ana tried to correct their flight and keep them on a level course.

"Ollie, can you hear me? Ollie, it's Harry; you have taken a bit of a knock but you are going to be OK."

Suddenly Ollie's eyes opened, not slowly but wide and staring in an instant. His lips parted but he didn't utter a sound.

Harry gripped both his shoulders, part reassurance but crucially to keep him away from the joystick. "We were fired at by the poachers; you've been unconscious for a few minutes. Just stay still for a moment and try to readjust. You're safe and that is what's important."

Ollie's breathing began to steady and his gaze to focus, ahead and then to the cabin of the plane. He looked across to Ana, "Oh I didn't know you could fly, what a piece of luck."

"I can't," she replied as lightly as she could and despite the situation they all smiled.

"Well you seem to be doing a pretty good job."

"I don't know where we are heading and until a moment ago I didn't know how we were ever going to be standing safely on mother earth again!"

"That's fine," said Ollie. "I can take control again now." As he reached forward he let out a groan, raising his left hand to the stickiness on his temple.

"Just take a few minutes to readjust. I can keep us up here happily for a while. You are going to have the mother of all headaches, but nothing compared to what would have come your way if I had tried to land the plane!" she grinned, trying to make light of the situation.

Harry reached forward for the radio, "Hello Uwingoni camp, can you hear me?"

Mike's voice came back, clear and precise, "Uwingoni here. What can we do for you Harry?"

"Oh, Mike thank goodness. I tried you a few minutes ago but there was nobody there."

"Well I have been manning the radio for a couple of hours as we are a bit stretched for manpower at the moment but I'm afraid I haven't heard anything from you. Perhaps you were in a dead area without reception."

"That's strange, but never mind now. Dead area is almost exactly what it was. We have just been shot at and Ollie has been hurt. There are poachers in a vehicle at the back of the escarpment. Please tell Jim straight away and see whether the police or KWS can do anything. I expect they will be long gone by the time anyone gets there but you never know."

Mike's voice sounded shaky, "Poachers you say, are you sure? Well yes, I suppose nobody else would shoot at you. I'll try to get hold of Jim."

"Mike this is urgent and so is a plane to get Ollie back to Nairobi for a medical check-up."

"Yes, yes, of course. Leave it to me."

"Roger Mike." Harry put the radio down. "He didn't sound very with it and I really can't understand how he didn't pick up our first transmission. Anyway let's hope there is some action now."

Ollie was still looking groggy. "Let's gain some height Ana and get comfortably above the hills and then we can get our bearings. Are you happy to stay at the controls, just for the moment?"

"Now I know I've got a first class instructor, no offence

Harry, that's no problem. In fact believe it or not I am quite enjoying being your pilot."

Despite its own wounds, the little plane responded comfortably.

"Right now, keep a close eye on the altimeter in front of you. Another five hundred feet and we should have a safe distance between us and the ground."

Ana watched the large hand turn slowly on the clock like altimeter. When it reached the five directly at the bottom of the dial she gently pushed the controls forward to level off.

"Excellent, you're a natural. Now I can see where we are. So turn the controls gently to your left. Watch the compass and try to go through sixty degrees. Perfect, now stay on this course, keep at the same height for the moment and in about ten minutes you will be able to make out the camp and the strip."

The land marks below them became more and more recognisable and the rough cut strip was soon visible, like a clean scar running through the scrub and bush.

"That's great I think I am up to the landing now although in different circumstances I would almost feel confident enough to talk you through it. However, my worry is that there is some damage to the plane that we won't be aware of until the moment the wheels touch the ground."

Ana felt a mixture of regret and relief as she took her hands off the controls and for the first time since she had been in a light aircraft she watched meticulously as Ollie prepared to land. He took the little plane away from the landing area to start with then turned and lined it up. After adjusting the fuel mixture he eased back on the throttle and spun a little wheel to his right explaining that this helped the plane to lose height at exactly the correct rate.

"We want to land on the first quarter of the strip. I am putting down the flaps and you will feel the drag immediately.

I'm going to come in at close to fifty knots. Then as soon as we're lined up and close, power off, pull back gently, glide in and the two large wheels will touch the ground and then the front will follow."

It was a textbook landing and as the plane trundled back to the parking area they could see a Land Cruiser already waiting.

Chapter Twelve

Sergeant Odika and Inspector Mwitu were sitting next to each other, talking earnestly and jotting assorted points down in small notebooks. There were quite a number of Uwingoni staff round the table too.

Everyone looked up as Jim came into the mess tent. “Sorry I’m a little late; I’ve just been in contact with Nairobi Hospital. I know you will all be relieved to hear that our young pilot Ollie is going to be fine.” The news brought instant smiles to the meeting. “The bullet actually left a crease mark on the front of his skull but after another day’s observation they should discharge him. A lucky, young man, if his head had been turned a few centimetres the other way, he wouldn’t be with us now.”

He sat down on a spare chair next to Kilifi. “You all know the Inspector and Sergeant and I would like to thank them for coming so quickly and hand over to them to brief us.”

Inspector Mwitu got to his feet and the tent fell silent. “As you know I have been here with some of my men since early yesterday afternoon. Unfortunately there is no sign of the vehicle. It was probably out of the Reserve before we even knew you had a problem. We obviously have an alert out for a green Land Rover. The camouflage patches make it somewhat unusual but at the moment there has been no sighting; it's obviously holed up somewhere but we will keep searching."

He looked across the table at Harry's raised hand. "What about the Prosperity Dam area? There are plenty of places to hide a vehicle in there and it's pretty much on a direct route using the back road out of the Reserve."

"It is a large area, you are quite right but even as the police we cannot just march in. We would have to have some concrete proof or evidence of wrongdoing. They have very powerful friends and if anyone there is involved we have to tread carefully. That may not be the answer you want but we have to deal with the reality of the situation."

Everyone round the table understood the Inspector's position. Corruption dug its ugly claws into even the smallest corner of the country.

"What we do have on our side though is the possible involvement of Al-Shabaab. It was extremely embarrassing for the Kenyan Police that the Somali poacher you captured here was freed after an ambush while he was being transferred to Nairobi. If we prove a definite link between poached ivory here generating funds for a terrorist organisation in Somalia then that makes our position much stronger. Those who fired on the plane tried to clear up all trace of having been there but they were in a hurry to get out and we found two AK-47 bullet casings that had gone unnoticed under some leaves. We are still going through the Cessna to see if we can find anything else that our forensic department might be able to match up with previous crimes."

"Thank you, Inspector. You have been very open with us and we appreciate that. Can I ask Sergeant Odika to update us from the KWS side?"

The ranger stood up, an imposing figure in his neatly pressed uniform, his expression determined as always. "As you all know we lost another elephant, a young bull, but although the poaching team involved the Somali, as the Inspector mentioned, there are worrying differences between this and most other kills. We have no doubt that he was shot by a professional marksman. This makes it a very different sort of operation. I was talking to Ana before this meeting because I know, as a journalist, she has done some research on this. Large international crime gangs are now involving themselves throughout the world in all manner of poaching as there is so much money to be made. Sometimes that links up with terrorist organisations as they then supply them with the weapons they need, but for us the tragic consequences are the same. Our wildlife is being decimated. We have to stop this particular network as they will only get bolder and bolder. He looked round the table and nobody could possible doubt the purpose in his expression. "Yes Jim, you have a question?"

"There are no professional hunters in Kenya any more so I was wondering whether you had any leads on where this individual might have come from."

"It's too early to tell in this particular case but this is not an isolated incident. Generally professional hunters come from South Africa and Namibia so we are working with colleagues from those two countries, but that is all I can tell you on that front at the moment."

"Thank you for that Sergeant Odika. I am sure you will all be pleased to know that KWS have kindly agreed to let us have a small number of their rangers, for this week anyway, but of course like everyone their resources are very stretched too. If you have any ideas or further thoughts I think it is better you just find me during the day. We still have a camp to run and visitors to look after."

Chairs scraped back from the table and there was a quiet, sombre mood as everyone filed out.

Harry fell in step beside Ana as they headed back to their

tents. "That was interesting but I still feel we need to be more modern and proactive in our fight. I am going to ask Jim whether he would let me spend a few days up in the escarpment area with the drone. I really don't think it is something we have used to good effect since we got it. If he agrees I was wondering whether you would be happy to come with me?"

"Would that mean taking supplies with us and camping out?"

"I hadn't thought about that too much but that would make sense. We might have more chance of seeing something late afternoon or early morning. Unless we have an incident like the plane spot, they just seem to melt away during the day."

Ana was silent for a while, mulling over the idea. "OK, I'll come if Jim agrees, but for three days max."

"I'll see him before lunch if I can. I suspect he is still talking to Mwitu and Odika. There will certainly be things he won't want to discuss with everyone."

In fact it wasn't till early afternoon that Harry was able to track his uncle down and put forward the idea. He was pleasantly surprised about how receptive Jim's response was.

"How will you keep your drone powered out there Harry? I seem to remember it doesn't have that long a battery life once it's in the air."

"Well you know we have a solar charger and because we have a spare battery we should be able to land it, change packs and get it up in the air again pretty quickly."

"Are you up to flying it in rough terrain like that? If it goes down in some thick trees you might well never see it again."

Harry did his best to maintain a calm expression as he knew Jim had a good point. "I won't pretend I haven't thought about that but I have been out working on my skills and am fairly confident. We will be flying it comfortably above the tree line, partly to get the widest angle view but also to disguise the sound of the motors."

"OK Harry but just for three days and promise me you will take care of Ana. She has settled in so well but never forget what she has been through. If there is any chance you are putting yourselves in danger you are to return to camp straight away."

"Of course Jim. Thank you and please don't worry, I'm sure we'll be fine."

Harry stopped by to see the camp chef Raymond on the way back to his tent. He was always happy to see everyone and his face broke into a huge grin when he saw who had entered his little kingdom.

"I know I'm being a pain but would you be able to put some basics in a cold box. Ana and I are off on the other side of the reserve for three days and we'll need something to keep us going. Nothing too fancy!"

"I'll be the judge of what's good for you Harry and I know what Ana likes too. No secrets from me in this place! I'll obviously put in the gas camping stove; you can't spend three days just with cold food and even worse no coffee in the morning."

"Thanks so much Raymond. You're a star as always. This is a bit rushed though so I was hoping I could come back in forty minutes."

"Forty minutes eh. You would think I had nothing else to do in here." The loud chuckle rang out across the kitchen. "Go on off you go now or I'll never get this done."

He found Ana in her usual veranda seat. "Jim has agreed to the idea. Better pack a few things quickly we need to be gone in under an hour."

"Journalists know how to throw the essentials into a bag in a few minutes. Don't worry about me, what can I do?"

"Can you meet me at the stores as soon as possible? I just need to get out one of the small camping tents, a couple of sleeping bags and a few other bits and pieces and we can be off. I want to make it to the site I have in mind so that we have an hour's daylight left to fly the drone today."

In under half an hour Bluebird was loaded and they had worked through a checklist together. They had done pretty well but Ana had sent Harry back for his toothbrush, reminding him that she wasn't prepared to sit in a small space for several days smelling his bad breath.

There was a final trip to the kitchen to be greeted by Raymond, a large cold box and a cardboard container with all their cooking gear in. "I managed to squeeze in a couple of bottles of wine for you Ana, but no room for beers on this trip Harry. Bad luck!"

They just managed to fit everything in, packing as tightly as possible so that they weren't driven mad by endless rattling from the back of the vehicle.

"I feel bad not telling Bethwell and Kilifi our current plan. I trust them completely but you never know, they might accidently let out what we are up to. You understand how people are round the campfire at night and the two of us being away for a few days will naturally have the guys asking questions."

"I agree Harry it's not ideal but as we know somehow crucial information seems to leak out of this place. Apart from Jim we're on our own and that's the way to be, for the moment anyway."

Bluebird seemed to positively fly along the track. Zebra they passed scampered off nervously into the bush and some giraffe, feeding serenely with only their heads and tops of their necks showing, looked down with mild curiosity, not even interrupting their gentle chew of the leaves.

It was a perfect afternoon. As so often happened, the severity of the recent storm seemed to have blown away even the hint of further rain. The sky was endlessly blue and they could make out the single silhouette of a bird of prey off to their right but it was too far away to identify.

"When I first came to Uwingoni I only took notice of the larger animals, then the smaller ones and now I'm getting into birds. Did you know that there are over a thousand different species of bird that have been recorded in Kenya? That puts it easily in the top twenty in the world. Six of the top seven countries are in central and South America which has given me a real desire to head off there with my binoculars one day but right now we are living in a bird watchers paradise."

"I feel they are something I could get into as well Harry. I used to love watching them on my parents' bird feeders in the garden when I was a girl but when I look back now I can't really remember the last time I took any serious note of the wildlife around me, until now that is. There always seemed more important things demanding my attention. Sadly I think I am typical of most of my generation. We love watching David Attenborough on the TV and then chatting about the show the next day but that seems to be our dose of wildlife, just something else on a screen."

"You are so right. Do you know I hardly ever use my mobile when I am here?"

"Strange, me too. It used to be almost glued to my hand, dealing with some deadline or another. Now I chat to my folks just to let them know I am OK but that's about it."

They fell into an easy silence, their minds drifting off to different places and situations, the sound of the hard-working engine occasionally bringing them back to the present.

They were reaching the furthest extremes of the spur road which was bumpier than usual as vehicles rarely came this far along the escarpment because there was no way down. The only way back was to retrace their steps.

"I haven't been up here in a while but there is one perfect little clearing on the left as far as I remember. We need both a decent campsite and somewhere we can safely fly the drone from."

Within a few minutes the bush seemed to open up and beyond, on the downward slope, they could make out an area surrounded by trees on one side but with quite an open view down to the lowlands at the bottom.

"This looks promising but there is no track so hang on, it will be pretty rocky in places." Bluebird bumped and crashed her way towards the edge and Harry pulled up just before it started to become too steep, jerked the handbrake on and bounded out of the door.

"Hey Ana this looks perfect for the drone. The edge drops away steeply here so we can take off and land with ease and be able to keep a good visual link for much of the time it is airborne."

"Agreed but we need to find somewhere really good to pitch the tent. I don't want to find myself rolling off down the side here in the middle of the night, nor do I relish the idea of trying to sleep on a bed of rocks."

They did a scout round the little clearing and found a fairly flat area under the shade of a large croton tree with its wonderful flat crown. Moving the more jagged rocks and stones out of the way left a thin area where they could pitch the tent and have the opening looking out to the far away horizon.

"Imagine tomorrow morning Harry as the first glow of the sun begins to light up those hills. Just before you fly the drone we will be able to put the flaps back and it will be almost as though we are the only people in the world. Do you think like that sometimes or is that my rather childish imagination at work?"

"Where would we be without our dreams and imagination? The short answer is yes but what I find odd is that when I look back at so much of my earlier life everything seems rather grey and dull. Somewhere like this unlocks your soul; does that sounds like a line from a bad film, sorry."

"Who cares? If you can say those words and mean it then that is more than special. Perhaps we should continue this conversation later tonight. We have the drone to launch and the tent to get up. Look, leave the tent to me. It shouldn't take long. You can get the drone unpacked and in the air and I'll come over once I've finished."

"You get the bum end of the deal but of course I'm more than happy, thanks. There isn't much more than a decent two hours of daylight to go anyway."

Leaving Ana emptying a little bag of tent pegs onto the ground, Harry carefully took the box with all the drone equipment off to the open side of the clearing. He gently put everything on an old rug from the Land Rover. He took the lens cap off the camera and checked that the throttle was set to zero before connecting the battery and then calibrated the sensors. With a final check that the GPS lock was activated so that the drone would return to the take-off spot, he placed it about ten feet away on the flattest piece of ground available. Standing back he slowly increased the throttle speed until it was hovering comfortably.

"She's airborne Ana come and have a look."

"I'll be with you in five minutes. I don't want to be doing the final tweaks to get the tent sorted out properly in the dark."

Harry sent the drone out, away from the ridge to start with and gave himself as good an overview as he could by selecting a wide-angle image. The magic of the camera was that when necessary it could zoom in close and examine anything of interest without having to lose altitude to do so.

Although the engines made quite an angry buzz when they were close by, he was pleasantly surprised that even though it was still not far away he couldn't hear it, so hopefully it wouldn't disturb animals or indeed poachers if there were any down there.

He realised almost immediately the limitations of using the drone in this sort of terrain. It was surprisingly difficult to make out what might be under the tree canopy. The leaf covering from above was far denser than he had realised. It seemed ridiculous, as he had looked down on it so many times, but then it hadn't really been with a specific aim other than perhaps seeing some interesting wildlife.

Harry tried his best to fly in a particular pattern rather than hover over an area he thought might be promising. He did a sweep to the right then took the drone a hundred metres or so away from him and brought it back to the left. From time to time he detected the movements of small animals as they went unhurriedly about their day but the flight was uneventful.

"How are you getting on, anything interesting?" He had been so intent on the screen that Ana's arrival took him completely by surprise.

"Everything looks pretty normal but I need to change the battery so as always you have come at a perfect time. Once I have landed it and killed the motors it would be great if you could be there to secure it as the ground is pretty rough almost everywhere."

The batteries were swapped easily and Ana put the used one onto the solar charger straight away in the hope that the last half hour of sunlight would help to give it some reasonable charge.

The second flight followed pretty much the same pattern but over a slightly different area. The clearest sighting had been of two tiny dik-dik on the edge of a clearing. They had stood absolutely still, allowing the camera to zoom in to such an extent that he could see them in amazing detail. Then suddenly they were gone, spooked by a noise or a scent on the wind.

As Harry brought the drone in Ana could sense his disappointment. The energy of the early afternoon seemed to have deserted him.

"Look Harry, we would have been ridiculously lucky to have anything really interesting on the first evening. Your expectations have to be realistic. We might not see anything but that doesn't mean this was a bad idea, far from it. Now let's get the drone stored away and we can see what Raymond has made for supper."

Everything in the cool box had been labelled and they dutifully followed the instructions. They had decided against a campfire, even though it was normally a key part of being out in the bush. In the total darkness that filled the night in this part of the world they didn't want to advertise their presence to anyone. They even put a small screen in front of the gas stove although that was also partly to shade it from the wind coming off the slope.

The smell of the chicken curry sizzling in the pan made both of them realise just how hungry they were. Using their naan bread to soak up the remnants of the sauce, left them with spotless plates, and as Harry pointed out saved on too much washing up.

"What is it about African nights?" sighed Ana as she sat back contentedly looking up at the heavens. "There is simply so much space and more stars than you could ever imagine. They even seem to twinkle far brighter than in any other sky I have ever seen."

"I ask myself stuff like that all the time. I can honestly say there isn't a day that goes by when I don't find myself marvelling at something or other out here."

Ana fumbled about in the bottom of the bag, looking for the cork screw. "I knew Raymond wouldn't let us down. I realise you are more of a beer man but do you fancy a glass of this? It's South African red, should be quite mellow."

He held out his glass and then took a couple of sips.

"Can I ask you a personal question Harry? Please don't feel you have to answer."

"Of course. I don't see any reason for secrets between us."

"Well your dad is Jim's brother, that is obvious just from the photo you have of him on your desk, they look very alike; and I assume that's your mum next to him..."

"And you wonder how come I am mixed race when neither of them are? I know because it's a question I've had many times before but strangely, since I've been in Kenya, you're the first person to mention it. Actually it's quite a simple story in many ways. That is Helen, my step mum in the photo; although in fairness she is the only mum I have ever really known. My dad met my actual mother in a night club in Nairobi just over twenty years ago when he spent a year over here with Jim. They fell in love and I was the result of what was, by my dad's account, a pretty tempestuous relationship."

Harry stopped for another slurp of wine. Somewhere in the far distance they heard the roar of a lion. Ana remained silent, giving him time to get his thoughts together. She knew better than many how difficult it can be to verbalise what you have often pushed deep down inside you.

"Mercy, that was my mum, had a real problem with booze. When she was sober she was lovely but once the vodka started to flow she became wild and very argumentative about almost everything. Anyway, one night they were taking the sleeper train to Mombasa with some friends. They played a stupid game of dare which meant getting up onto the roof on one side of the carriage crawling across and coming back in on the other side. It was a narrow gauge railway so the train didn't go that fast but somehow she lost her footing and fell off the roof onto the side of the track."

"That's dreadful Harry. What happened then?"

"One of the others pulled the alarm as quickly as he could and although the train stopped it wasn't instant, as you can imagine. As soon as it had slowed enough they jumped out of the carriage door and ran back up the railway line. It was pitch-black and they were in the middle of nowhere. They found her about half a mile from the train. She had broken her neck."

Ana leant across and laid her hand gently on his knee. She had always avoided saying the usual lines of sympathy. She knew they were well meant but somehow always seemed so inadequate.

Harry looked across at her, the small tears just under his eyes glinting mildly in the moonlight. "You are only the second person I have ever told the full story too. I don't really know why, probably didn't want to deal with all the questions that were likely to follow. And trust of course, even amongst friends trust is a special gift. It feels good to tell you, it has been lurking down inside me for far too long."

Ana met his gaze. "And then what?"

"Oh well, Mercy had never wanted my dad to know anything about her family. There is a story in there somewhere, perhaps that is why she drank, who knows. I was looked after by a nanny for a couple of months and then returned to the UK with my dad. He hitched up with Helen, his old girlfriend, got married and the rest as they say his history." There seemed nothing else to say, he certainly didn't want to get into emotional territory.

"Thank you for sharing that with me, I know it wasn't easy. Look I'm just going to wash the supper things up. You just stay put, gaze up at that sky and dream."

On the downward side of the tent she poured water from a large container into a small plastic bowl added a dash of washing up liquid and was amazed to see that the stars gave her enough light to work by. She had just finished with the frying pan when she was aware of a rustling in the leaves at the base of the tree almost in front of her. She reached for the torch she had brought with her and shone the beam towards the sounds of activity.

You certainly didn't have to be a wildlife expert to identify their visitor but what surprised her was how big it was, somehow she had always thought they were just large hedgehogs so she wasn't quite prepared for something over twice the size of her foot.

"Harry quick, there's a porcupine over here."

They both watched as it rummaged about unhurriedly, its surprisingly large claws digging and scraping the ground and the nose at the end of its bristly face twitching and snuffing all the time.

"How brilliant, just look at the size of some of those quills on his back, they must be over a foot long. There are some on his head and neck too. That is why they call this a crested porcupine." He laughed. "Just listen to me, the expert safari guide. This is actually the first one I have ever seen but I have been reading up as much information as I can on East African wildlife. When you see the light on late in my tent that's what I'm up to, exciting eh?"

After munching on something that seemed like a bulb, the porcupine looked at them with a questioning glance, as though to ask them what they were up to in his territory. He certainly wasn't going to be hurried by their presence but after a while, when the supply of bulbs seemed to have run out he headed off into the night, the striped dark and light quills moving from side to side on his back in a haphazard way, almost as though they had a life of their own.

Anything edible they put back in the cool box, making sure the top was firmly sealed. The supplies did have to stay fresh for several more days. Everything was then shut away in the back of Bluebird for the night, just in case.

Harry pointed out how well he was brushing his teeth, the tin mug he used for his morning coffee doubling up with water to rinse his mouth and the brush. "They will be positively gleaming in the starlight after this; just as well I remembered it!"

Ana chuckled, "Look why don't you crash out now; you've had a tiring day to put it mildly. I just want to stay out here and enjoy the space for a little longer."

"OK thanks but make sure you don't fall asleep in the open, just for your own safety. Good night."

Now that she sat alone Ana became aware of just how alive the night was with sounds of insects. Each seemed to have its own voice, a humming, ticking or other sounds that didn't even have words to describe them. She did recognise the distinctive sound of cicadas. She had never actually seen one but they were ever present in the trees, little crickets that rubbed their wings together with a sort of loud crackling sound to find a mate. That much she remembered from an evening chat with Bethwell.

Small dark shapes sped, fluttering overhead and she realised that they must be bats. There was so much which was new that she yearned to find out about.

Ana also knew too, just why she was here and not in the tent. It was small, enclosed, dark and claustrophobic. She more than anyone was aware of the fears she needed to overcome, but knowing and doing were two very different things.

She looked behind her with a start, aware of a sudden sound and smiled weakly as she saw Harry. "Are you alright? You've been out here on your own for over an hour."

The easy thing she knew would be to make some lame excuse but that wouldn't make the problem go away. "Look Harry, I have no idea what time it is but realise it must be late or even early, depending on which way you look at it. I know the hazards of being outside but I honestly don't think I can sleep in the tent. At the back of my mind I probably knew this but thought that somehow things would work out."

She leant forward, head in her hands doing her best to breathe in slowly through her nose and out through her mouth as she had been taught. Her heart rate seemed to steady and she took a breath, "Harry I talked to you a little about being imprisoned in that container in Syria. That still lives with me every day, not all the time of course, being out here gives me some freedom from my thoughts, but enough for it still to be dominant in my head. When I feel ready I will tell you more but just now I know that I can't get inside that tent."

"That's so horrible; you should have told me earlier."

She saw the concern etched on his face, "I realise that now. The problem is I've just been kidding myself."

He sat down next to her, not to talk but knowing that just his presence must somehow be a comfort.

"Do you listen to the news, or perhaps you see it on your laptop? It's a habit I can't get out of, I suppose that just goes with my job. When I was in Syria I wanted somehow to make everyone sitting in their comfortable, safe rooms in Europe or the States realise the living hell that so many decent people endure every day. And you know what happens, virtually nothing."

The tears were rolling down her face now and she impatiently wiped them away. "I'm sad, oh my God what sort of a word is that, such important issues barely scratch the surface. I am angry, sometimes so angry I feel my head will burst because our glorious, so-called civilised democracies wring their hands but do nothing. I don't think there's a politician I respect anywhere, self-centred, scheming and useless. Serving the people, what a joke they only serve themselves. There are a few amazing charities and individuals but they can't change things and so these atrocities just go on and on."

She stood up, stretched and drank in the cool night air. "Just the freedom to do something as simple as this is now beyond the dreams of millions. Yes that container was worse than any image I could ever have visualised of hell. I was convinced I would never see friends or family again, that I would be passed round a series of ISIS brothels and when enough of their brave fighters had showed this lying, Western whore of a journalist what real men were about they would put a bullet through my head because I wouldn't even be good for that any more, just a piece of worthless meat. And you know what's worse in a way is that I am safe now but how many containers, basements, hell holes in the rubble are there as I speak, all full of girls and young women, dreading the next footfall by the entrance and knowing that nobody will be coming to rescue them. I suppose I feel guilty being free."

Harry stood up gently, put his arms round her and held tight, as though he was trying to squeeze the misery from her.

"Thank you," she sighed. "I think I needed that." He stepped back searching for a tissue to dry her tears but they were long gone. The eyes he saw were strong and angry. "So what's being in a dark, little tent compared to that? If I can't do something this simple what does that say about me?"

"I've thought of something that might help anyway Ana. It's so obvious now I think of it. Inside the main flaps are an extra set made with a fine mesh to keep out mosquitoes and anything else that might bite. If we roll the outer ones back you will still be able to look out onto the night sky."

"All right Harry, I'll give it a go. If I don't do these things it's as though these bastards have won, but just leave me here with my thoughts for the moment."

He busied himself tying up the flaps and then wriggled back inside his sleeping bag, recognising that she would come in when she felt able. Much sooner than he expected he saw her shape at the entrance. "Putting things off only makes them more difficult; now where are the zips for these mesh flaps? No stay where you are. I've found them."

Ana pulled the zips until the entrance was secure and lay wearily on her sleeping bag. As she looked out she marvelled at how clear the sky still seemed, even through the netting. "Thank you, Harry. Strangely, now I am here it doesn't feel as bad as I had anticipated. We all have our fears. Do we let them rule us or confront them?"

"You're so right but how many people spend their lives in a dark place? Finding courage is the tough thing."

"And finding friends to help you unlock that courage too. You are a special person Harry. But you are still not going to get me into my sleeping bag. I want the freedom to be on top of it, and the night, what's left of it, isn't cold."

"Well, I hope you get some sleep anyway."

"You too." Even as she spoke she knew the chances were slim. She bunched up the small pillow keeping her head up so that the outside space remained a reality she could see. Harry's gentle breathing was all she could hear, even the insects had fallen silent.

Chapter Thirteen

Ana woke to some of the best smells in the world, fresh coffee and sizzling bacon. For a few seconds it took her time to get her bearings. She rubbed the back of her neck which felt uncomfortably stiff and realised that despite everything she must have fallen asleep, but bizarrely was still in exactly the same position with her head raised, looking out of the entrance. The sun was already glowing on the distant horizon and she could make out Harry's silhouette as he crouched over the small stove preparing breakfast.

At the sound of movement he turned round with a large grin on his face. "I just left you to sleep, figured you needed it. Might have known the prospect of breakfast would wake you up. Fresh coffee, Kenyan of course, and a bacon sandwich; just the way you like it I think, three rashers and a good dollop of ketchup."

"You're a wonder. Some woman is going to be lucky to have you in her life."

"Well that's you at the moment," he laughed, "and it's even my turn to do the washing up!"

They both sat back, enjoying the peace and letting the early heat melt away the stiffness of a night in the tent.

"Drone launch in ten minutes. This is such a great time

to see things. Like us, most animals are up and about looking for breakfast."

Harry was right. In contrast to the previous evening, within five minutes the camera picked up a small pride of lion in an open space, allowing the sun to work its morning magic on them too.

"I would love to stay with them but they'll probably take a while to get going and we have far more important business. I want to swing up further to the north."

He knew only too well the importance of keeping up his concentration, making sure he stuck to a flight pattern that covered all the areas he wanted. It helped enormously that there were two of them to look at the screen. He was very aware of what an eagle eye Ana had after her recent spots from the plane. They saw a few zebra, their stripes providing poor camouflage in amongst the greenery and on a rocky cliff face some baboons were squabbling and chasing each other, seemingly oblivious to the fall awaiting them, should they put just one foot in the wrong place.

Harry flew the drone back, quickly changed batteries and by the time Ana had put the old one on charge he had relaunched. However, the only excitement was when a bird of prey took an interest in the drone, swooping in fast but not making contact. When it continued its dive under the camera, they were able to get a decent image. It was grey with a particularly white rump and surprisingly long orange legs.

"Does your wildlife study tell you what that is?" grinned Ana. "I'm not being funny but if you can tell me after that two second flash what the bird was, not only will I be amazingly impressed but it will be worth a few cold White Caps when we get back to camp."

"Probably a fairly safe bet, though I'm reasonably confident with what we see on the ground, birds are a very different matter. There is a great Collins Field Guide in my rucksack so we can check at lunch. I am sticking my neck out. I think it's a goshawk but I don't know what kind."

"Let's wait and see then. That might be worth one beer and I would still be quite wowed." Ana looked at her watch, surprised at how quickly time had slipped away. "Oh, and when you bring the drone in for the morning, which will be pretty soon, please promise that you're not going to be in a grump if you haven't seen anything else interesting."

Ten minutes later with everything packed safely away they were walking back to the tent when Harry suddenly gripped Ana's shoulder really forcefully. "Stop right there, don't move." The urgency of the instruction was so unlike him that she instantly reacted and with a quick intake of breath stood stock still. "Right, now just gently take a few paces backwards. Look just to the side of that bush you were about to pass and tell me what you see."

"Oh my God how could I not have spotted that?" There partly under the shade of the leaves was quite a large light brown snake with much darker V-shaped chevrons running down its back. "That's the first snake I have ever seen, apart from in a little snake park somewhere near Twickenham when I was a girl."

"Well it might have been your last! That is a puff adder and a single bite can be enough to kill a person within a day. Luckily it's pretty lazy but if you spoil its doze in that nice warm spot you will be amazed at the speed of its strike. Strangely we don't see many snakes and most are more worried about you so will slide away, but not this guy. I think we will just let him get on with his morning nap in peace."

"Are we just going to leave him there? What happens if he slithers into camp later in the day or even tonight?"

"We'll just have to keep the tent tightly zipped and perhaps you won't want to spend so much of the night out under the stars."

Lunch was as good as supper and the salad tasted impossibly fresh. The camp had its own vegetable garden and everything was grown naturally, the only fertiliser being elephant dung that Eli the gardener was always keen on using.

"Do you know Harry I don't think I had a clue what vegetables really tasted like till I came here. Most supermarket fruit and veg is just a pale reflection of the real thing. Thanks for organising so much. I'll get my act together soon but I feel so drained. I'm going to experiment by seeing how well I can sleep in the tent in the day time. Perhaps the daylight will help me realise that small spaces are something I can live with. I'm sorry to leave you on your own but I'll be much better company when I wake up!"

Sometimes when you get unexpected time to yourself you do that one thing that has been niggling in the back of your head. For Harry that was mapmaking. He had realised recently that although he knew the main tracks, streams and waterholes, there was much of Uwingoni that still remained a mystery. Sweeping the drone backwards and forwards and examining what lay below the escarpment had made him determined to start putting something down on paper.

They had an A3 blank pad with them that Ana had brought in the hope of sketching anything interesting that caught her eye. He reckoned he would have a good four hours, so pencil and pad in hand he walked a mile or so along the top of the escarpment and then slowly retraced his steps, finding a large rock to sit on or even a sandy patch of ground where he could stretch out.

He soon realised that he was being too detailed and that this would make it totally impractical so he turned to a clean sheet and began again. His mind was also working on taking stills from the drone camera which he hadn't tried but knew couldn't be that difficult. When Ollie was back he hoped he could persuade him to fly a few circuits too.

After a couple of hours his initial enthusiasm had waned somewhat and he was sitting on the trunk of a fallen tree gazing rather aimlessly into the distance. From up here he could see way beyond the border of the reserve but there was little specific to look at. There were no villages or settlements in this particular area. The landscape was too rugged and more importantly too dry. On the far side of the range of hills it was very different, the river ran through the gorge and then into where the Prosperity Dam was being built.

The thought of that spoilt his mood and he got up and was just turning away when his eye was drawn to the tell-tale dust of a vehicle being driven down from the hills and along the track that led towards their far boundary. He couldn't see the vehicle itself, the distance was too great but there was no hiding its trail. He was wondering casually where it was going when it suddenly disappeared. Perhaps the driver has stopped for the call of nature he thought, but as the minutes ticked by there was no sign of it continuing its journey.

Am I going nuts thought Harry that I am now suspicious of an unknown vehicle using a dust track that just happens to be near our boundary. But he knew there could be little reason to stop there, it was in the middle of nowhere.

As he continued the walk back to their campsite his eyes were drawn constantly to the left and when he finally saw Bluebird and the tent there had been no distant dust plumes. The vehicle must still be in the same spot.

Ana was sitting in a canvas chair with the journal on her lap. "Just catching up with a few missing entries. It was a bit too hot in there and ironically too light to sleep!"

He joined her, a mug of hot tea in his hand. "How did you know to have the tea ready?"

"Actually I saw you coming from some distance back but it's been ready for a few minutes. You kept stopping to look at something. Is there interesting wildlife down there?

Harry told her about the strange vehicle and his concerns.

"I think we just have to be practical. Even if we contacted Jim and he sent someone to check things out over there, it would take them hours just to reach the place. The chances are they would only find a driver who has had too many lunchtime beers and is sleeping them off in the back seat."

"Yes I suppose you're right. OK let's get the drone up in the air and see what's out there."

The pattern followed that of the morning. They spotted a smattering of animals but nothing that interesting. Even the lions were long gone.

"You know Harry I just can't understand how so many people spend hours playing some game or other staring at a small screen. My eyes already feel strained after watching just a thirty minute flight."

He was just about to reply when they both let out a simultaneous shout. If there was one creature they couldn't be mistaken about, it was elephant. There they were, dark grey backs standing out boldly from their surroundings.

"What a piece of luck Ana. Now we just need to be patient, see how many there are, and whether we can identify just who they are too."

The elephants moved backwards and forwards under the trees. Sometimes they had a view of several, long trunks swaying gently and then they were gone again, grey shapes merging together and then melting away under the foliage.

"Is there any way you can get a better angle Harry? I'm amazed that animals of that size can disappear so quickly when we know almost exactly where they are.

"I'm doing my best but I don't want to come down any lower or spook them with the sound of the motors. If we stay with them I'm sure they will eventually move out of the tree line."

As always with wildlife things are unpredictable and they

stayed comfortably under cover and as the minutes ticked by Harry began to worry about the battery life. The little symbol was just short of blinking a warning and crucially they had to have enough power to fly the drone back safely. He knew they hadn't much more than a few minutes viewing time left.

And then almost as though they had read his thoughts the elephants came out into the open and immediately they knew this was Mara and her close-knit family group.

"I can count seven, but where is Meru?" Ana's face showed a mixture of excitement and concern. "Hang on look behind Mara's hind legs, between her and one of her sisters!"

And there was Meru, still small enough to get lost in amongst his family. He looked in their direction, his ears, which seemed far too big for his head, flapping and his tiny trunk moving backwards and forwards as he walked. Then before they knew it the trees swallowed them up again.

Harry couldn't stop himself smiling as he flew the drone back to camp. As it landed the battery on the screen indicated a minimal charge remaining; quite a close-run thing. "That's the first sighting of Mara's family in over four days. It is just so uplifting to see them all and know they are safe. However, I really wish they weren't on this side of the escarpment. They aren't that far from where that young male was killed. However, we can hardly redirect eight elephants to somewhere we want them to be! By the way, thinking about their safety, were you aware of any tell-tale dust signs from that mystery vehicle while the drone has been up?"

"Like you I suppose I was pretty glued to the screen but I didn't see anything out of the corner of my eye, for what that's worth."

"That's my take on it too. Look I know you probably think I'm neurotic but I just want to try one thing. If we put that battery you left on charge in the drone I would say we have enough power and daylight to do one quick flight out to that track. I have a pretty good idea where the vehicle stopped and that would ease my mind enormously to know that there's nothing to worry about."

"That's not such a daft idea. That's why we purchased the thing in the first place."

The motors were feeling quite warm as Harry placed it on the take-off area but the manual stated that it was well up to this much usage without a long break. It was an easy flight to the track, just a straight line with no pauses or detours and still just within range. Because of the rocky terrain what vegetation they could make out on the side was pretty sparse, certainly not thick enough to hide a vehicle. He flew a mile or so in each direction from where he remembered the dust trail stopping but there was nothing, just barren track. He didn't know whether to be relieved or not. He was just about to turn the drone on a homeward flight when Ana grabbed his arm.

"Harry just go back a bit. I hadn't really noticed before but the road goes over something that looks like a small concrete bridge, perhaps it is some sort of wash away from the hillside during heavy rains. Can you get a closer look?"

He flew the drone to one side and went into hover mode, angling the camera lens into the gloom under the bridge. "Oh God there is something in there for sure. Can you get any lower without giving away our position?"

He dropped by another few metres and there it was on the screen, there could be no doubting it, the front of a green Land Rover. "Look Ana you can even make out the camouflage paintwork on the front wings. I would swear this is the same vehicle that was in the reserve when they fired on the plane."

"Agreed and what's even better is that the drone will have

taken an image of the number plate. We can find out who owns it! Let's get it back as soon as we can. We've got a lot to do and not much time."

Fifteen minutes later with everything packed away they were still in conversation about the next step. The crucial problem being, that if there was someone in the main camp who was linked with the poachers, then using the radio would be an open broadcast of what they had discovered.

Suddenly Ana leapt up, rushed to the tent and returned with her rucksack. "I can't believe how dumb I have been, I'm sure my mobile phone is somewhere in the bottom of this bag. As you know I hardly use it in Uwingoni but it's just force of habit to take it when travelling."

Sure enough there it was nestling comfortably under a pair of socks. She pulled it out and turned it on. "Amazing, we have got some sort of a signal. I'll phone Jim directly."

"You can try but the chances of him even having his phone anywhere near him are seriously slim. Sorry to be pessimistic."

Harry's first thought was disappointingly accurate. He racked his brain. Who could he trust completely who might actually have a phone with them and a number he would know? His heart sank. Perhaps they would just have to risk the radio.

"Didn't you tell me that Kilifi's daughter was expecting her first baby any day now Harry."

"Definitely, she might have even had it."

"Well any potential grandfather I can think of would want to know the news straight away. Do you know his number?"

Harry smile vanished in an instant. "Who remembers anyone's number these days, it's just straight into your phone and that's it."

"I thought you told me you had phoned him sometimes

before we had the repeater masts up. Didn't he give you his number so that you could get advice about wildlife when you were out by yourself?"

"You're right!" Harry could hardly contain himself, rushing to Bluebird he flung the door open, rummaged on the shelf and with a triumphant shout held up The Pocket Guide to Mammals of East Africa. There on the inside cover, next to a large K was a ten-digit number. "Dial this now and fingers crossed. Come on Kilifi we need you."

Ana handed the phone to him. "If we get through you talk to him. You two have a special bond." The ringtone continued, monotonous and unhurried and then suddenly that familiar voice was there.

"Who is this? I don't know your number. Are you the hospital, is my daughter alright?"

"Hi Kilifi this is Harry, I'm on Ana's phone. I'm so sorry to contact you like this but we really need your help. But before that are you a grandfather yet?"

"Yes, yes. We are so excited but my daughter doesn't leave hospital till tomorrow. Of course I'll help. What can I do? We wondered where you two were, you haven't had an accident have you?"

"Brilliant news grandpa and we are fine thanks. I'll explain everything later but it is urgent that I speak to Jim. Can you see whether you can get him to phone me as soon as possible? Please don't tell anyone else about this call."

As they waited dusk began to fall and with the fading of the light Harry could feel himself becoming more agitated. What if Kilifi couldn't find him, did Jim even know where his own phone was? Negatives swirled round his head. This was such a remote part of the Reserve, even if he did make contact what could be done? He felt so powerless.

The phone buzzed in his hand, it was Kilifi again. "Yes Kilifi? Oh, Jim it's you." Despite the situation he almost smiled. Of course he had been unable to find his own mobile.

Harry explained the situation as well as he could, trying to be factual and keeping emotion out of things, as he knew that was Jim's way.

"Thank you Harry, that's good work. Luckily we still have some top KWS guys here so I am going to ask them whether they think there is anything they can do tonight. There is no obvious track to the area where Mara and her family are and that would even be in issue in daylight. I am also going to get in touch with Inspector Mwitu and give him details of where you saw the Land Rover, but the police are short of vehicles at the best of times so I don't hold out much hope of them driving miles down a dirt road in the dark, but you never know."

Harry felt despondent but knew in his heart that Jim was simply being practical and telling it the way he saw it. "Can we not get Bethwell and some of the guys along here now?"

"Look Harry, I need time to talk to the professionals and make a plan. We all feel equally strongly about the elephants but blundering into a dangerous situation would only make things worse. You are to promise me that you and Ana will stay put."

"But Jim…"

"No buts this is well outside your league. If they do come into Uwingoni tonight they will be heavily armed and extremely dangerous. You are not to do anything stupid. Now let me get those calls made. I'll talk to you later."

Harry handed Ana back her phone and told her what Jim had said. They both sat in glum silence. There was nothing worse than a feeling of impotence. The beauty of the African night for once was lost on them. The darkness would only offer comfort to their enemies.

"Well I'm certainly not going to be able to sleep anyway, I

don't know about you. I suggest we grab a quick supper and then keep watch from the side of the escarpment. We won't be able to see the elephants of course but if that Land Rover does come into the Reserve tonight they will have to use their lights. There is no way they can drive off road without them so we will be able to pinpoint their moves, perhaps even get back to Jim, who knows!"

For once Raymond's food failed to give its feel good factor. They made sure there was no sign of light visible in their camping spot and moved to where they could get the best view, found the least uncomfortable of the rocks and sat down to wait and watch.

Time seemed to crawl and although there was a sense of relief that all seemed quiet below there was always the realisation of the hours still to go. The ring of Ana's phone broke the stillness and there was Jim voice as calm as ever. "Just thought you needed an update before you turn in for the night. The inspector said he would do what he could but was not optimistic, as I had feared. We have made a plan with the KWS boys up here. Even they are unprepared to be out at night there, it's too dangerous and that's discounting the poachers. They will leave here with Bethwell and Kilifi before dawn, take the escarpment road until they are roughly above where you last saw the elephants late afternoon and try to establish where they have moved to. If they are lucky enough to do that they will be able to offer protection and hopefully by then the police will be on the move."

"Thanks for letting us know Jim. Please stay in touch early morning. You know we will do absolutely anything we can to help."

After three more hours they were stiff and tired and there was no sign of any activity. "Look Harry I don't want to seem a wimp but even if they do come now, how on earth are they going to be able to find the elephants? Wasn't it you who told me a herd can often walk twenty-five kilometres a day and only sleeps for a couple of hours a night? They could be anywhere, even on top of the escarpment by now."

Harry knew what she said made complete sense and that they wouldn't be much use in the morning if they had no sleep. However, somehow he felt responsible for them in a way he couldn't really understand himself; perhaps it was actually being there when Meru was born, he had given up trying to work it out.

"Look why don't you go to sleep if you feel alright in the tent and I'll stay up a little longer."

"I'm not a fool Harry and to be honest I don't trust you not to do something reckless. I am staying out as long as you. One thing I learnt over the years is how important it is to try to get into the heads of people you interview, and that's what you need to do with the poachers. Just like the KWS rangers, my bet is that they will move some time before dawn so as to be in a position to start their search for our family at first light."

Harry sighed, "You win, I'll turn in now as well but only on the understanding that we are up and ready an hour before sunrise."

Harry was asleep within minutes and Ana reflected on how strange it was that often people pumped full of adrenalin and purpose seem to exhaust themselves emotionally and are out like light as soon as their head hits the pillow.

As she lay there in the darkness she felt her heart racing but wonderfully not because of the fear of the darkness or the closeness of the sides of the tent but because of a strange peace that seemed to have settled in her. She felt an excitement, almost a breathlessness, because she no longer seemed to feel the fear that had dominated her nights for so long. Sleep seemed elusive but she didn't care, instead she drank in the sounds of the night and relished feeling alive.

It was pitch dark when she was aware of Harry struggling to find the tent zip. She was grumpy, deep colourful dreams, a forgotten magic, seemed to slip away in the chilly night air.

"Sorry Ana. It's a bit difficult to make a quiet exit from a small tent but those early rays will be creeping over the hills before we know it. Just stay cosy in there for a little longer while I get sorted."

When she realised that getting sorted involved fresh coffee she could almost forgive the intrusion. Her hands gripped the mug and she wondered how Harry was getting on with his morning scout. Pointless launching the drone, it was far too dark but he had disappeared ten minutes before.

"Quick Ana, come and look and tell me I'm not losing my marbles and bring your phone too!"

She peered down from the heights trying hard to focus on the area that Harry had pointed out. He was convinced that he had seen lights on a couple of occasions when he had been here earlier but they had come and gone so quickly that he doubted his own senses.

"There they are again. Did you see them?"

"Well I saw something but it just seemed a momentary flash, hardly Land Rover headlights."

"Shall I tell you what I think? It is them and they can get a fairly good idea of where they're going. Although the stars seem to be dimming, there are still millions up there. When they get to a tricky area they flash their lights on for a second just to work out the dangers and then continue. I know it's difficult with the wind coming off the side of the escarpment but I'm convinced I can hear a distant engine noise too. Please Ana really concentrate on where you thought you might have seen something and tell me this isn't just my imagination."

Looking into the blackness below, frightened to blink

and miss something required much more concentration than they realised, like a fisherman endlessly watching his float, feeling that the moment he looked away, the fish will bite.

"There Harry, at two o'clock from where we are, and again! Oh my goodness you are right. It must be them, who else would be here and driving like that? If we weren't right here on the edge we would never have seen those flashes. What do we do?"

"Try Jim's mobile. Let's see what he thinks. I thought last night how annoyingly right he can be about things. These guys will kill anyone who gets in their way and probably not lose a minute of sleep over it."

Armed with his own phone, Jim answered after the second ring. He listened carefully to their report and after confirming as accurately as possible the course the poachers were taking told them to keep an eye on any new developments and get back to him if they thought they had important news. He updated Ana from his end and hung up.

They continued to track the poachers from their vantage point. Every so often the headlights winked and now that they had a good idea of where they were, this became easy to spot. They seemed to be heading to roughly the same area where the young male had been killed.

"Do you know what I feel Ana, that the salt lick there is a real magnet and as there is one, there might well be others in the same area. We know so little about this part of the Reserve. Would you mind ringing Jim back and just tell him my thoughts. The KWS rangers and Kilifi will have to make a start somewhere."

In some ways time moved at a snail's pace because, as mere spectators, there was nothing they could do except watch. In other ways it positively sped by. Had the poachers got a sighting of the herd and how near were the rangers?

The vehicle had disappeared into thick tree cover and although this would probably slow them down they hadn't spotted the headlights for over fifteen minutes.

"I'm sure there is a faint lightness behind those eastern hills. I am going to get the drone ready and once those sun's rays show themselves I'm sending her up. Our little baby here could make all the difference.

She found him a few minutes later checking the battery connections for the drone. "Good news if your idea is right Harry, it looks as though Kilifi and the boys are pretty close to the salt lick."

African dawns in the bush are usually to be savoured but he could barely contain his impatience. Eyes in the sky could prove crucial for the elephants. And then there it was; the small line of distant clouds were a brilliant yellow and behind them the sky glowed orange.

"I'm launching now. By the time it gets over the salt lick area we should have enough light to get some good camera feedback."

Ana's phone rang again and this time it was Kilifi. They hadn't seen any elephants but they were definitely in the area as they could hear them. Anything of interest from the drone and they should contact him directly.

As it closed in on the thickly wooded area below, the leaves in the trees turned from black to a dark green. Harry was trying to work out their possible destination in his head. Then suddenly there they were, the unmistakable shapes of the elephants through the trees. He calculated they must be under a kilometre from the salt lick and that was certainly the direction they were heading in. They were closely bunched and Harry could feel the panic rising, a few well aimed bursts of gunfire and almost every elephant would be hit.

He kept on hover mode above them which was more

difficult than he imagined as the trees were so tightly packed. Then he realised his mistake, now he knew where they were he desperately needed to find the Land Rover. He tried gaining height in the hope that would help to spot it but the foliage was too dense and the camera lost definition. He tracked back towards where he knew they had been and flew parallel lines towards the elephants and back again, but there was nothing. They had to be there, had they abandoned the vehicle because of the trees? That was a very real possibility and if so they would just melt away and he would only discover them when it was too late.

Ana was in touch with Kilifi and the good news was that he reckoned they would be able to gain sight of the herd within five minutes. Even a small number in this sort of area made quite a noise and should be relatively easy to find.

Harry navigated back towards where he had last seen them. He dropped a little lower and then suddenly there was movement, not of a vehicle but definitely a number of dark shaped individuals, and then they were gone again.

"Ana quick, is Kilifi still on? Great. I'm sure I have their position, they can only be about seven or eight hundred meters away from the elephants. Tell him they are moving almost directly from the east towards the salt lick, the elephants are to the west of it but I don't know where he is."

Harry could hear his heart echoing through his head, thumping out a quickening beat in his ear drums. Indeed that was the only sound he could hear. The camera wasn't picking up an image of anything, just a blanket of green.

Then suddenly, the unmistakable sound of gunfire. He thought he picked out a few flashes but the sky was instantly full of birds, rising up from the trees, startled and scared by the noise beneath them.

The gunfire wasn't continuous but many of the bursts were prolonged. Were the poachers firing on the herd or at the rangers or had Kilifi and the squad from KWS been lying in wait for them and caught them off guard?

"I can't stand not knowing what's going on down there. Oh Ana; Meru, Mara and the family, how hard can a person pray that something will work out right?"

"I lost my faith in prayer a long time ago Harry. What will be will be."

The gunfire continued for around another five minutes and then there was silence, so intense in itself because they could hear nothing other than the squawking of the birds and the morning wind coming up the slope.

"Harry your battery warning is blinking red, for goodness sake get it back before it falls out of the sky."

There was no argument, they couldn't influence what had happened anyway. He flew it back low over the trees, thinking to himself that if power died it might be caught in the branches and suffer little or no damage. Somehow though, it managed to limp back to its launching site.

"Now we just have to be patient Harry. I'm certainly not trying Kilifi's phone. One ring at some crucial point and it might give away his position. Be practical, get the battery on charge, take a big breath and wait for a call."

But there was no call and no gunfire either, or even the distant trumpeting of elephants. It was as if nothing had happened.

"What has gone on down there?" Harry was pacing backwards and forwards, his hand over his eyes in the morning sunlight trying vainly to get some clue. And then, breaking the silence once again, the sound of gunshots, shorter bursts and fewer of them. They seemed more distant but it was so difficult to tell. He checked the charger once again but the sun was only just beginning to get to work on the solar panels, the drone was well and truly grounded; they had no eye in the sky to relieve their anxiety and tension.

"Harry please stop pacing, it doesn't help, in fact it probably does the reverse. Come here and sit on this rock next to me.

And then they both heard it, unmistakably the distant sound of the Land Rover. "Listen to the engine beat. It's not constant. It's down there somewhere on a non-existent track, that's why the revs are coming and going."

"Agreed Harry, it has to be them. I suggest we focus on the area where we last saw it. I'm sure they will retrace their steps."

They kept scanning the tree canopy but saw nothing. Then it was there, like a sprinter out of the blocks, bursting from the trees. Bucking and lurching over the rocky surface, there was no doubt it was their Land Rover, even at this distance the distinctive camouflaged markings that they had seen both from the plane and from camera images under the bridge the night before were clearly visible.

"Try Jim on the phone. I don't know what he can do but you never know."

He answered immediately and Ana gave him the most precise picture she could of what had happened in the last hour or so.

"He's going to try the Inspector again. Our only hope is that they have some vehicle out on that road beyond the Uwingoni boundary. Kilifi and the rangers are on foot down there so there is nothing more they can do. We only have to hope that they and the elephants are safe."

But there was no news from below and no amount of deep breathing or pacing made the situation any easier. Thoughts of breakfast or even coffee were long gone. Even if they could scramble down the steep sides into the trees it was a huge area and trying to find the salt lick without Kilifi would prove extremely difficult if not impossible.

In the distance the Land Rover had made it to the dirt

road and its course was still clearly visible as the dust cloud marked its passage back up the hill.

The phone rang, Kilifi's name blinking reassuringly in the screen.

"Is everyone alright?" Ana blurted out before she even knew for sure that she was speaking to Kilifi. His unhurried voice instantly proved a comfort. Harry watched her smile turn to a frown, followed by some serious nodding.

"And what do you all feel about the young elephant? OK that sounds positive and the ranger?" Despite the seriousness of the situation she couldn't help smiling. "Right so we will come back up the escarpment track to where the Land Cruiser is and see if there is anything we can do to help. See you soon."

Harry was fidgeting impatiently. "So what's the story?"

"Well they managed to get themselves between the elephants and the poachers so the herd is fine except for one of the two-year-old males who was hit by a stray bullet from the poachers. They have already called for a KWS vet but it is a leg wound so he should recover. One of the poachers was killed and another is wounded and in captivity. Unfortunately two of them made it back to the Land Rover. They followed them for a while but had to move slowly in the woods as it's too easy with so much cover around to be ambushed."

"Something in your chat with Kilifi made you smile."

"You know what he's like; he has a way of telling things sometimes even when situations are serious. One of the rangers is a Maasai and a bullet nicked him in the ear. You know how they often have large traditional holes in their ear lobes, well that is exactly where he was hit and that is what he found funny. However, it was seriously close for comfort!"

"That will be a good fireside tale for years to come. Let's

just leave the camp as it is for the moment and head back up the track and see how we might be able to help.

To say it was a busy morning would have been an understatement. Normal radio usage was resumed. It was now far too complicated to use mobiles. And if there was someone from Uwingoni in league with the poachers the story of the night was already out there, it had to be.

Ollie was coming in with supplies that morning and it had been agreed that two extra KWS personnel, including a vet would fly with him. They were stretched as usual with an ongoing situation in Tsavo East, so hitching a flight up was the fastest way for them to get to Uwingoni.

The poacher, with a bandaged arm, was brought up to the track by Kilifi and one of the rangers. Despite his wound he wore handcuffs but said nothing as he sat surly faced by the side of the track waiting to be taken away.

"As you can see," said Kilifi, almost spitting the words out, "He's not from round here. And neither was his boss. I would recognise that Somali's dragging footprint anywhere. But we'll get him and this piece of dung will be helping us." As the large KWS corporal dragged him to his feet the scowl had been replaced by eyes that darted fearfully from side to side as if expecting help to miraculously appear.

Unfortunately the police hadn't been able to get a vehicle on the road but Inspector Mwitu was on his way and according to the chit chat on the radio had some interesting news.

By the end of the day the young elephant had been darted, the bullet successfully removed and the wound cleaned. The vet was optimistic that all would be well. When he came round from the drug he headed off into the bush a little unsteadily with one of the large females who had been waiting for him at a cautious distance. Motherly bonds in elephants were unbelievably strong.

Harry and Ana packed their camp up. There was no point in flying drones with the changed situation. It was the general feeling that these particular poachers would not be back for a while.

As Jim said, perhaps this gave them a bit of a breathing space and an opportunity to go on the offensive for a change.

Chapter Fourteen

There was a real sense of optimism at the meeting. Everyone in the Reserve knew about the success of the previous morning's KWS operation and even the guys who worked in the kitchens had smiles on their faces. It wasn't just that their jobs depended on the wildlife being safe, everyone had come to love this remote little corner of the country and they were proud and protective about what they did.

Sergeant Odika was at one end of the table in deep conversation with Jim and it was he who stood up to speak first. "Good morning everyone. It is good to be back at Uwingoni, especially after the events of yesterday. I flew up early this morning to collect our wonderful vet George Okello whose services are always in great demand. But I bring good news too. It has been agreed that our small squad of rangers can remain stationed here for at least another two months."

There was spontaneous applause from everyone present. They were all aware how special this decision was.

"Thank you. I can also say it has been a pleasure to work with you. I would especially like to thank Kilifi. If there was a Tracker of the Year award I think we all know who would get it." Applause again, there wasn't a person there who didn't know how remarkable his talents were. "Now I know Inspector Mwitu has an update for you too."

"Thank you, Sergeant. Firstly apologies that we weren't able to help as much as we would have liked recently. We have a small number of old Land Rovers out here and our mechanics do an amazing job just keeping them driveable. Sadly even then we simply don't have enough fuel to use them as much as we would like. Despite what you read in the papers about the Kenyan police, and of course there are bad apples, there are many dedicated officers too, who want to make a difference."

The Inspector shuffled some papers on the table. "I would just like to say a big thank you to Harry and Ana. If I ever doubted technology, I've certainly had my mind changed. The photograph the drone took of the vehicle we know to have been used in this raid has given us the sort of proof we need to convince our superiors to let us take action. We have done a number plate licence check and it belongs to the Prosperity Dam Company."

You could hear the intake of breath from the room. Although there had been mistrust concerning Prosperity, this was the first confirmation of their involvement.

"Of course the crucial question is who up at the dam is actually involved and how do they fit in with Al-Shabaab and the Somalis? We have several theories but forgive me if I don't share them with you just at the moment. Our biggest problem, which sadly will come as no surprise, is that a company as rich as Cheng Pang has many friends in high places so we can't just go marching in there just yet. I have already spoken to my Superintendent and I know it has continued up the chain to the Assistant Commissioner of Police. The chances are that he will have to speak to a minister in the government and so it goes on. I do think there is far more drive to get rid of corruption. As you know there were some major arrests of both Chinese and Kenyan individuals accused of pocketing huge sums from the from the Nairobi Mombasa railway project so I am not without hope but my hands, sadly, are tied for the moment."

They all knew what an honest policeman he was and that there was little point in asking him questions he would be unable to answer.

"Many thanks both of you," said Jim. "We so appreciate the dedication of you and your men. I feel confident that good will triumph in the end. Let's all get back to running this wonderful Reserve and doing all we can to protect the remarkable animals within its borders."

Neither Harry nor Ana were as optimistic and upbeat as they would have liked.

They sat down on her veranda and poured out two cups of strong, black coffee from a thermos. Hands cupped round the mugs and taking in the aroma, each waited for the other to say speak first.

"What do you think the chances are of Inspector Mwitu being able to gain access to Prosperity? You have far more experience of life than me."

"Of course that's the question in my head too and I don't have an obvious answer," she sighed. "There are certainly good people in this government and I know they will worry about the huge amounts of money Kenya will owe to China in one way or another. However, the sums involved are so vast, just skimming a bit off the top can change people's financial security for ever and so buy their support."

"You know that if things don't work out I thought we might be able to do something." He saw the disbelief in her face. "I am sure Michael who showed us round would be able to help, perhaps he can speak to his uncle. He would probably be horrified to know what was really going on in his business up there."

She looked across the table at him and took a slow breath. "Harry what I have learnt in life is that there are very few people you can truly trust and when you get it wrong the results can be life changing, literally. We are up against some of the most ruthless people imaginable. They have no boundaries or decency or common values with the rest of us. Please promise me you will not head off on some madcap scheme on your own."

Harry couldn't look her in the eye. He knew in his heart that's exactly what he would try to do. He didn't want to give her assurances or promises that he might break. "You're probably right. Let's just keep our fingers crossed for the Inspector. Look I've got to dash. Catch up with you at lunch I expect." Pushing his chair back he was striding back up the path before she had a chance to say anything more.

The pattern of life in Uwingoni soon eased back into its familiar routine. The number of tourists was on the increase which was great news all round. The KWS rangers carried out patrols, including some night time ones in areas they considered most at risk. However, nothing remarkable came of them and there was no indication of the poachers returning.

One morning when Harry was out with some visitors from the UK before breakfast they came across Mara and her family. They were all at one of the smaller waterholes, lined up at the water's edge. The larger ones started drinking first with the smaller ones in amongst their feet. He spotted Meru straight away, the end of his trunk turning darker as he dipped it in the water. As he brought it up to his mouth probably half of it ended back where it had started. You could sense the happiness in them all. He had come to realise that they genuinely enjoyed playing just for the sheer fun of it rather than as some sort of learning process, like so many animals.

It was heart-warming to see that the young male who had been wounded by the bullet seemed to be moving surprisingly easily and was joining in with the others as they gently pushed and shoved each other. One of them made her way completely into the water and was simply kicking her rear legs backwards and forwards, splashing the other in the process. She then sat down in the shallows, scooping grey mud from the bottom up in her trunk and splattering it on her head and back.

Interestingly the visitors were so engrossed in the scene too that nobody asked questions and although there was a great deal of camera clicking to begin with, even that slowed right down as everyone enjoyed the simple pleasure of just sitting and watching.

Other animals had joined them, a small group of Grant's gazelles, their pink tongues and gentle lapping in complete contrast to their bigger neighbours. A pair of warthogs appeared on the far side. Interestingly they didn't get down on their front knees but waded a few feet out into the water. It was a remarkable thing Harry thought that when elephants were drinking other animals felt safer and more inclined to come down to the water. Kilifi had told him that he thought their presence made the others feel safe and that even lions tended to stay away.

Gradually when they had all had their fill they headed off in various directions to get on with their day. Harry too turned the Land Cruiser back towards the waiting breakfast at camp as the visitors in the rear excitedly chatted about their first game drive.

He would have joined in but was unusually quiet and, if he was honest with himself, had been for over a week, a week in which there had been no news from Inspector Mwitu. He couldn't get the situation out of his mind and it was beginning to gnaw away at him. The poachers and the thought that they would get away with this, and be able to continue seemed to be his last thought at night and his first in the morning. He had arranged to see Jim later in the day, not that he was really expecting anything to happen. But he knew he really needed to talk to someone and he understood that Ana was fed up listening to moans about it, even though he knew she agreed in principle with what he felt.

When he got to Jim's office, somewhat fortified by eggs and bacon, he found him in deep conversation with Mike but he was waved in anyway. Harry took a couple of files off one of the chairs by the desk putting them as neatly as he could on the floor.

It was strange he thought that he seemed to come across Mike so rarely.

Jim looked across at him with a slight twinkle in his eye, "Now before you get going, I've got a pretty good idea why you want to chat so hear me out before you start. I've asked Mike in too, for reasons that will become obvious in a minute."

Jim twirled an old Bic biro round in his hand but as always his gaze was steady and direct. "The Inspector and I are just as disappointed as you that no decision has yet been made about searching the Prosperity Dam property. Officially his hands are tied but of course he wants to get these bastards just as much as us. So I thought we might try to use Mr Pang's relationship with Mike to see whether we can pay another visit."

Mike sat bolt upright, the colour seeming to drain somewhat from his cheeks.

Harry could hardly believe what he was hearing. "If it was anyone other than you telling me this I would think they were winding me up!"

"Well Harry life is a learning experience for us all. You are a different person in so many ways to the young man who arrived on a flight from London, looking for, I can't think of the words, perhaps purpose and meaning in life.

I was someone totally set in my ways who, if I'm honest, didn't want to change and I just hoped that somehow the problems we are facing would magically disappear somewhere else."

"I wouldn't say that," chipped in Mike. "You love this place."

"True but perhaps that is a bit like loving a person. The core of what brought us together doesn't change but other things do and you need to adapt too otherwise you might lose what is most precious to you."

Harry smiled, "That's almost poetic but even as a young person I know how true that is."

Jim looked awkward for a moment and then grinned back. "Perhaps I'm changing in more ways than I realised. Being serious though we need to be proactive, if we don't this beautiful place will slowly die round us."

"What part can I play?" asked Mike his expression earnest as ever. "You know how much Uwingoni means to me as well."

"I'd like you to contact your old chum Mr Pang. Ask him whether he would like to come on safari with us again when he is next out but also see if you can get another invitation for Ana and Harry to visit Prosperity. I'm sure we will come up with a good reason."

Mike fiddled uncomfortably with his hands, "I'm not very good at that sort of thing. I always feel a bit awkward."

"I'm sure you'll be fine." The no nonsense tone was back in Jim's voice. "You, Ana and I will have to have a serious chat. If we get access to the dam perhaps your new pal Michael will be useful. Go and brief her and the three of us can meet once Mike has set something up. Right, lots to do as usual. See you later." Getting up and ignoring the pile of paperwork in which he had no interest, he was gone.

It's strange thought Harry as he headed off to find Ana.

This is something that he had been thinking about so much but now that there was a definite possibility of a return visit he felt a real stab of apprehension in the pit of his stomach.

It was one of those days where he seemed to have a host of small things to do, none of them that rewarding but all part of his varied job in the Reserve.

After an early supper he was deep in thought in his favourite canvas chair by the side of the dining area, wondering which way to broach the subject with Ana, uncertain of her reaction. He knew from experience how important it was to choose your moment when you need to talk about something important.

As it happened the decision was made for him. "What's up with you Harry? I recognise that look on your face."

He sighed deeply, "Look, unlikely though it seems Jim is keen for us to have a second look round Prosperity Dam."

"Your uncle? You must be joking! This has gone round and round your head endlessly and you know my feelings." He saw the obvious irritation in her face and the slight narrowing of the eyes which he knew to be a dangerous sign.

"You're right of course but this is honestly Jim's idea. He's already got Mike on the case with Mr Pang but we might not even get an invite."

"It doesn't change my feeling."

"I have made a firm promise to myself not to be stupid and put us in danger."

Ana's face softened, "I know you mean well and I really respect what you want to do but I'm honestly not sure I'm the person to go with you."

Even as she spoke she could feel her thoughts drifting back to the previous visit, to the suspicion and the expressionless faces she couldn't read and to the container she couldn't enter. Then further back again to Syria, to another dark hole and girls and young women clinging on to their lives and sanity with their fingertips. It was a place she tried desperately not to revisit. There was a frayed curtain across her mind that gave her glimpses of those times. She made such an effort to confront them but there was still so much that she pushed down, right into the depths of her being where it festered and gnawed in the darkness.

Ever since Harry had mentioned the idea she had a bad feeling about it. There was nothing she could put her finger on but it was real and terrified her.

"Are you OK Ana?" She refocused and saw the concerned young face looking at her.

"Sorry Harry just letting my thoughts wander. Look I'll give it serious consideration but I doubt Mr Pang will be sending an invite anyway. I'm weary so I'm going to turn in now. Sleep well." She smiled without warmth and headed off to her tent, half of her mind praying for sleep the other half dreading the dreams that waited, clawing at the leash.

It was an unremarkable morning when she woke yet unusually the sky had a dull greyness to it and even the birdsong sounded subdued; foreboding in the air. She had slept in bursts and the nightmares hadn't come. She had to get a grip. This was a beautiful place and she was surrounded by lovely people and more importantly she was safe.

Ana stared at herself in the mirror, almost as though she was trying to read her own thoughts. She tried that odd idea that one of the kind young doctors had suggested. "Look in the mirror every morning and say aloud, *I love you*. It's not easy but in time you will come to feel much more positive about yourself."

When he had asked on one of her future visits how she got on with that, she had lied convincingly about how it made her feel better but of course it didn't. For every positive she found and she acknowledged that there were good things, she always managed to discover a negative to knock it off its perch. The smile in the glass was beaten into a frown and her eyes glazed over, she could have said anything but it wouldn't have registered.

A cold shower proved the answer, for the moment anyway. The powerful needles of water almost seemed to burn. In the end everything else was forgotten, she was alive in that moment with no thoughts of the future or past.

Ana took herself off in Bluebird with binoculars, pencils and a sketchpad. She was beginning to learn where the smaller side tracks led to and despite the odd wrong call, rarely got lost by more than a single turning.

The morning was beginning to find its brightness, there was more blue in the sky and the warm fingers of sun seemed to massage the tightness in her shoulders. She stopped in a shady area beside the glinting waterhole and cut the engine. The approach of the vehicle would have frightened away any animals but it didn't matter. Perhaps it was the mixture of solitude and beauty that brought her here, she wasn't sure.

The first thing she noticed as always is that the African bush is never quiet. Often it was the sound that led her to the bird. Straight away she heard the call of the glossy starlings as she spotted a small flock in the treetops. She grinned as their chirping always made her think of R2D2's robotic voice from Star Wars. Their iridescent purply blue and bright yellow eyes made them stand out in the foliage. She was reminded, as she had been every day since arriving, that even the most ordinary of creatures in Kenya seemed so spectacular. Then she heard the giggling of a wood hoopoe, the latest bird that Kilifi had pointed out to her on a recent trip, and found herself smiling along with it.

There were no animals at the water's edge although the large variety of prints in the soft mud showed that it was well used. Ana took out her pad and began to sketch, relishing her new free style, realising that she had started to draw the feel of the places she visited and the movement of the animals, and that was so much more powerful. It was life not a photographic image.

Time passed, although how much she wouldn't have known, and then suddenly almost majestically, as though from nowhere came two giraffes. How could she not have seen the world's tallest animal making its way through the bush and then again as she looked more closely and her pencil glided over the paper, she realised just how magical their camouflage was. The large brown splodges of colour separated from each other by lighter lines almost made their coats jig-saw puzzle like. Yet it was exactly this that helped them to blend in so well with their surroundings.

She stopped drawing and just sat and watched as they cautiously made their way down to the water. Slow graceful movements, yet underneath she could almost sense their urge to run for cover too. Splaying her front legs wide apart the larger animal gently lowered her mouth to the surface and barely making a ripple started to drink and the younger one, perhaps her daughter, moved to her side, mirroring her movements. She glanced up, her deep, dark eyes surrounded by long eye lashes staring, almost knowingly in Ana's direction.

The morning seemed to float by. Animals, individually or in their families came and went. She felt that though they were aware of her presence they felt secure. She drew when the mood took her but mostly just sat and watched, letting her mind wander.

She hadn't even put a watch on and had no phone so if it hadn't been for the sun directly overhead in a now perfect sky and the slight rumbling of her tummy she would have had no idea how long she had been there.

Neatly folding the morning's drawings and with more purpose than she had felt for some time she started the engine. There was no doubt in her mind that the decision she had come to was the right one.

This was not just about the elephants; it was about so much more. None of these animals had a voice yet this was their home. When the poachers finally killed the last elephant she knew it wouldn't end there, some other beautiful creature would be next on their list until there were none left and Uwingoni would become a barren wilderness.

She wasn't great at remembering quotes but one that had jiggled about in her head since teenage years was her father's favourite, "All that is necessary for evil to succeed is for the good person to do nothing." Well she wasn't going to be that person. Yes she knew that there would be events and people ahead that would fit comfortably into the evil bracket but she was determined not to be the one who looked the other way and hoped that somehow everything would be alright. She understood enough of the world to know that never happened.

There were just the four of them in Jim's office the next morning.

"The good news is that Mr Pang seemed happy with another visit to the dam and has agreed to come and stay at Uwingoni on his next visit. Thanks to Mike for arranging that and for coming up with the idea that perhaps future guests here might visit the dam. Mr Pang seemed particularly keen on that. I imagine he likes the thought of showing off his engineering feats to wealthy tourists."

"Oh it was nothing," Mike smiled weakly. "He seems a good man and I am sure he has no knowledge of any wrongdoing there. He is based in China most of the time anyway."

"The invitation is for tomorrow. Harry and Ana you need to chat things through. You are just trying to find anything that might be useful to Inspector Mwitu in his attempt to be allowed onto the site. Ana you are not as headstrong so I rely on you to make sure nothing daft happens up there."

"Don't worry Jim. I'll keep Harry on his lead."

"I'll obviously be happy when you are back safe and sound. Good luck."

The rest of the day was very full-on and there was little time for them to think ahead, which was an obvious plus. Harry knew only too well that he had one of those minds that was overly imaginative and created a whole range of things that could happen but in reality were highly unlikely to.

As they headed off to their tents after an early supper, Ana stopped before turning in. "Look Harry, I know you too well already and I can sense those cogs whirling round in your head. I'm not looking forward to tomorrow, that's no secret but that doesn't mean I'm not as determined as you. If we can play a part in stopping these people that would be wonderful but we'll just take things as they come. Try to switch that brain of yours off, empty your head and get a good night's sleep; that will be more use to us than anything. I'll try to do the same." She leant across and gently kissed his cheek, "Sweet dreams." And with that she was gone, stepping inside and zipping up the flaps to keep the night out.

Harry lay in bed staring at the canvas roof and eventually drifted off, an image of Mara and Meru the last thing on his mind.

He didn't feel much like breakfast, that apprehensive twinge in his stomach gnawing away at his early morning hunger. Nevertheless, he ate a fry-up without really being aware of the individual tastes. Ana settled for a yoghurt and black coffee and neither spoke much, other than rather meaningless pleasantries.

It was almost as though Bluebird knew the way and

everything had a sense of déjà vu about it. When they pulled up at the yellow barrier there was even the same humourless guard. Knowing the drill they parked and waited for the some internal transport to pick them up.

They had barely stretched their legs when the jeep appeared dragging a dust cloud behind it and there at the wheel was Michael Cheng. He bounded across to them and despite that slightly stiff Chinese formality greeted them like long lost friends.

"It's so good to see you both again. My uncle tells me you have ideas to bring some tourists up here to see the fantastic dam project. He thinks that would be marvellous and has asked me to work out some plan with you as to the best way to do this.

They headed up the main track towards the dam itself. "He didn't think you needed to see Mr Zhang Wei. His main focus is the dam itself. Indeed he would probably not be happy with tourists looking round. He's rather old fashioned in that way."

The jeep halted on the high ground above the gorge. There seemed more workers than ever toiling away below and Harry was reminded of the harshness of their conditions. There wasn't a tree or an area of shade to be seen anywhere. It was still early in the day; he could only imagine what it must be like when the sun was at its highest point.

"I had thought we could have a viewing platform up here, perhaps serving cool drinks and some tasty bites to nibble. What do you think Ana?"

She was somewhat startled by the question as her mind had been dwelling on what hell it must be to work here and yet with few other jobs around, what choice did these men have if they wanted to feed their families. "Oh, good idea Michael. It's certainly a great spot to see how amazing the whole project is."

He smiled politely, pleased with her response. They toured round the site for the next hour stopping every now and then while Michael chatted about ideas he had.

Harry was beginning to find the whole experience extremely frustrating. They hadn't seen anything of interest that might help them on their quest; he was almost beginning to wish they had never come.

He was trying to get his bearings when they passed a familiar barrier and he realised that was where Mr Hu's base was. This is a bit more promising he thought. They were never going to learn anything of value round the dam itself.

Michael chatted on pleasantly and they continued to make small talk. Ana, as always, sensitive to peoples' moods had been surprised by Michael from the start. This wasn't the same person they had met before. He was chatty and pleasant but there seemed none of the previous uncertainty in him. It had been replaced by an underlying decisiveness. She couldn't put her finger on it but questions kept nibbling away in her mind.

Michael swung the jeep up a right fork. "This is where we kept the geological rock samples but we have expanded and developed it so I thought it would be nice to stop for coffee and wash the dust out of our throats."

The hut had been replaced by some much more sophisticated buildings and the line of containers certainly seemed longer than on their first visit.

Ana already felt apprehensive. She hadn't liked this place before but now that sense seemed stronger than ever. She told herself not to be silly. Was she going to feel like this every time she saw another container? She had to get a grip of herself.

"We can get some refreshments in that larger building on the right. If you need the restroom it is round the back."

"You go in with Michael. I'm just going to use the boys' room. I'll have a white coffee with no sugar thanks."

With his usual courtesy Michael opened the door for Ana and ushered her down an almost sterile corridor with a shiny, tiled floor and pristine white walls. Even though it was a bright morning outside, strip lights hummed overhead. The room at the far end was open and as they entered the two men inside turned towards them and smiled.

Ana felt her mouth go dry. She hadn't seen either of them before but she knew instantly that they were both Somalis and that alone rang terrible alarm bells. There could be very few reasons for two Somalis dressed in army fatigue uniforms to be sitting in an air-conditioned room at Prosperity Dam.

The larger man's face was expressionless and brutish. She had met his kind in other parts of the world; men to whom violence was simply a part of their everyday life. The other man's dark eyes swam with a mixture of hate and delight and as he moved towards her, his right foot dragged slightly across the tiles.

"It's good to meet you at last," he said with undisguised glee. As he took her hand she could smell the staleness of his breath and inadvertently flinched back. His lips parted showing the rotting teeth stained by years of chewing khat, a drug so loved by Somali men. "Look what the Prophet has sent us Abdul, so thoughtful don't you think?"

His grip tightened viciously on her hand, "Sit down there you Western slut and don't even think of opening your mouth."

Ana could feel the outward silence closing in on her yet at the same time the yelling inside her head leapt up like flames fanned by a biting wind. Despite that she heard the door open and shut in the corridor and footsteps that could only be Harry's walking easily and unsuspecting towards the room.

"Harry run, get out it's..." the force of the slap knocked her clean off the chair and with a clatter it fell across her as she tried to get up.

"Ana what's up?" She could hear him running, but towards her rather than away. She tried to raise herself to shout another warning.

For a big man Abdul moved remarkably fast and as Harry stepped through the doorway he had one arm round his neck and the other pressing his left arm up behind his back in an instant.

Harry's face was a mixture of fear and confusion and then he saw the Somali grinning broadly in front of him. He struggled but Abdul's strength was such that he felt if his arm moved any further up it would break. The punch jerked his head violently to the side and as sucked in a breath it came again, even harder. A third blow and he felt a mist swishing across his vision.

"Stop, stop! Michael make them stop." He was distantly aware of Ana's voice as he felt his knees buckle. The grip behind him loosened and he fell crumpled to the floor.

The Somali's voice registered no emotion. "Welcome Harry. I've so been looking forward to seeing you again. The little boy who's desperately trying to find out where he belongs in this world. But you know the good thing is that you aren't going to need to worry about that for much longer. I wonder if you can work out why."

Harry head swam, "You bastard," he croaked.

"Oh I think you'll find that's you. Never knew your mother did you, shame. A bit of a whore I'm told. Your father could have been any one of hundreds of men in those Nairobi bars. Oh yes Harry I know all about you and you too of course Ana but we'll save that for later." His coughing laugh grated across their ears as brown spittle ran down his chin.

Ana held Michael's gaze, "What's happening here?"

He smiled and she realised that he was actually enjoying what was unfolding. When he spoke though, his voice was as impassive as ever. "Oh, you Westerners, you think yourselves so superior to everyone. Well the world is changing. Your old decadent, liberal ways have made you soft. The days of you setting the rules for the rest of the world will soon be over. All your bleating about saving your precious animals and their habitats will end up in the dustbin of history. We are ready for a new world order and China will take the lead and with our African cousins we will justifiably take what this planet provides us with, just as you did for hundreds of years. But enough of that for now. Abdul make sure these two are securely locked up. We'll deal with them later. We have more important things to occupy us now."

Two more Somalis, who would easily have passed for Abdul's brothers, appeared at the door. As they were dragged out Harry looked across at Ana, "Don't worry we'll find a way out of this. They are bound to come looking for us once we don't return." Even as he spoke the words he realised their futility. By the time any help came they would be gone one way or another. As he looked back into the room the Somali and Michael were deep in conversation, almost as though the last few minutes had never happened.

The strength of the arm lock made him realise the futility of trying to break free. As they passed a doorway on the left he glanced in to see Ana sprawled on the floor, a leering guard standing over her. He tried to make eye contact but her face was expressionless, her eyes almost unseeing and then she was gone as he was half dragged, half marched out of the building and down towards the original hut. Inside a door was opened into a tiny, stuffy, windowless room that wasn't much more than a cupboard. He heard the locking bolt being drawn across and as the guard's footsteps receded absolute silence and darkness closed in on him.

For the first time he really felt the pain in his face where he had been struck and he tentatively moved his fingers over the skin. He was conscious of swellings already beginning under both eyes.

His mind raced away with thoughts of what would happen next and the Somali's sinister words repeated themselves over and over again in his head. He realised that whatever his fate was to be it would happen fairly quickly. Even the Kenyan authorities would have to act reasonably swiftly with the disappearance of two British citizens and Jim was a determined man. However, if Inspector Mwitu gained access to the place, it was a huge area to search and Harry had no doubt that he would not be left conveniently in a hut to be rescued.

Time seeped by and he assumed because of the chill the sun must already have set. Although he strained his ears he heard nothing except the muffled passing of a vehicle. Despite the darkness he didn't even try to sleep, his mind was too active. The hopelessness of his situation beat against his brain almost drowning out clear thought.

He had to focus so he sat as still as he could and tried to empty his head. If he didn't think clearly and as positively as he could there would be no hope and of course the hope wasn't just for him but for Ana too. Somehow it was that thought and the last image of her face that brought his mind into focus. Michael and the Somalis were overbearingly self-assured and just somehow that might provide a small glimmer of hope.

Chapter Fifteen

Harry was woken by footsteps in the corridor. As his hands moved to wipe the sleep from his eyes he winced at the pain in his face and the events of the previous day were brought back with stark suddenness.

The guard strode in and yanked him up by the collar, propelling him through the doorway. In the hours of darkness with nothing else to do Harry had decided on a plan, well you could hardly call it that, more of a strategy. He had made up his mind to be as docile and non-aggressive as possible. He thought that by doing that the Somalis might just drop their guard and allow him some sort of chance to get away. It wasn't very original but it was all he could come up with.

He was marched round to the line of containers and there waiting for him was a small group of men and in amongst them was Ana. She was deathly pale and looked as though she hadn't slept a wink during the night. Her body almost seemed to have shrunk and the same far away expression sat on her face, her eyes appearing to lack all focus.

Before he had time to even greet her he was taken to the front of a dirty looking, once purple container where the words Ching Pang were stencilled in white on the side. Michael was standing by the doors, half a smile on his face.

"Good morning Harry. I would hate you to have come all this way for nothing so I thought before we part company for good, I would show you what you have been looking for."

He signalled to a couple of the Somalis who opened the large rusting doors allowing the morning light to display the horror of what lay inside. "Oh my God," Harry couldn't contain himself. "How many elephants had to die for you to amass this much ivory?"

In front of him, neatly stacked were row upon row of elephant tusks. Some huge and yellowing, others stained almost black in places and yet others clean and white, particularly the smaller ones from elephants that were perhaps only four or five years old.

He could feel the warm tears running down his cheeks. He lunged at Michael, not a thought for the consequences of his actions, wanting only some sort of revenge for all the misery and pain that was shouting at him from the container. A hammer blow to his back sent him sprawling in the dirt and dust. Rough hands grabbed him and hauled him upright. Michael's expression remained unchanged. "You have much to learn about life Harry but unfortunately no time in which to do it."

There was a smattering of laughter from the guards which quietened as soon as the Somali stepped forward. "You see my little bastard today is your last pointless day on this planet of ours. We're doing you a favour really. It must be terrible never to fit in anywhere. Well, we've found just the spot for you so you'll never have to worry again."

Words started to form in his head but the butt of an AK-47 in his stomach left him on his knees gasping for breath.

"Bring the whore forward." Ana was almost dragged to the spot where Harry was curled up on the ground. "Stay down there where you belong." The Somali aimed a kick at his head but he managed to move enough so that it only glanced off his brow.

"I gather this slut is almost as precious to you as the ivory so it seems to make sense to keep all those valuable things together, don't you think. Throw her in."

Ana started to struggle desperately, the glazed expression gone, her eyes wide and staring as they pulled her towards the jaws of the container. The scream when it came, cut through all his pain. "No please I beg you. Not in there! Harry help me!"

"Oh, there is nothing this boy can do for you. I doubt there ever was. We have been very thoughtful though. There is food and water in that box in there. I thought it would be interesting for you. Keep yourself alive and wonder what delights will meet you at the other end or curl up and die. It will be seriously hot in there I should imagine. This container is heading for Mombasa port tonight." The smile disappeared from his face. "Shut and bolt those doors now."

"Believe in you. Never give in!" shouted Harry as he watched the giant doors close slowly on the small figure pushing valiantly but hopelessly against them from the darkness.

Even when she was gone he could hear the frantic banging of her fists against the unforgiving steel. He was hauled to his feet and Michael, face expressionless once again turned in his direction, "Bit out of your league all this Harry, rather a shame really I thought we got on quite well on your first visit. My uncle will be sad never to have had the chance to meet you." The mouth smiled but the eyes showed no emotion. "I'm going to leave you with my Somali friends now." He turned on his heels and walked briskly away.

"They'll get you for this. That precious Chinese luck you treasure will run out and when it does we'll see what sort of a man you are." The departing figure just kept walking, there was no break in his stride; it was as though he had never even heard the words.

"Get this boy into the back of that pick up. I'm tired of listening to his nonsense." The Somali limped into the cab and the old diesel grunted into life, belching fumes into the clean morning air.

Harry had one man on each side of him, squeezed so tightly his shoulders were actually pushed inwards. Their army issue trousers were filthy and both wore flip flops rather than boots but their rifles, lying casually on their laps, were spotless.

They drove down the steep slope past small groups of workers who kept their gaze fixed on the ground.

He couldn't get Ana out of his mind and he doubted he could even imagine the nightmare that was playing out in her head. Strangely his own predicament seemed almost of secondary importance but as they finally reached the bottom of the ravine and the river itself, thoughts, all of them grim in the extreme, bombarded his consciousness. Why had they taken him right down here and what did they intend to do with him?

Finally they came to a halt, the tyres skidding noisily in protest. Harry was hauled out of the back, the two guards glued to either side of him. An animated discussion followed between them and the Somali and he didn't even like to guess what was being said.

For the first time his eyes were drawn to the monstrous dam construction to his right. It rose up through the narrow ravine gully to a height it was hard to fathom. As he crooked his neck upwards he reckoned it must be at least two hundred meters high. Yet it seemed so out of place with its surroundings, the smooth lines of concrete blocks rising towards the sky in stark contrast to the ancient rock sides of the ravine.

Down here in the shade of so-called progress he could sense an evil as old as time itself. The Somali had just got off his phone and seemed impatient. He gestured to the guards and led the way towards some buildings where there were few workers, indeed this part of the project, in contrast to almost everywhere else, seemed almost deserted.

They stopped by what appeared to be some freshly dug foundations and the Somali's lips twisted up in what might have passed for a grin. "I'm afraid I've got more important business so can't spend time with you but I just wanted the pleasure of showing you your final resting place. At the end of the day a large concrete lorry will make its way down here to lay the first layer of foundations for this pumping station. Unfortunately you will have fallen into this deep area right here and they will not see your body. You will still be conscious of course; I wouldn't want you to miss the fun. They will bind and gag you and leave you under this ledge, probably a few hours before the lorry arrives so that you have a good amount of time to wonder what it will be like to be buried alive."

Harry felt faint, his breathing coming in short breaths. Life was worth so little to men like this and he knew the futility of pleading. Looking up from beside his grave he held the Somali's stare. "All this death and destruction in the name of Allah but you and I know it is only for greed and power. That's all scum like you understand. What I am sure of is that when your Judgement Day comes, and it will, the evil that defines you will consign you to a hell worse than anything you could ever dream of."

Rage was etched across the Somali's face and he launched himself at Harry, kicking and punching in a frenzy of blows but as Harry hit the ground, on the verge of unconsciousness, he strangely felt only pleasure that at last his words had got to this man and he had somehow reversed the tables in a small way on someone who had simply wanted to gloat about his death.

When he came to, he found himself curled up on a dirt floor. He only seemed to be able to open one eye and as he tried to move he let out an involuntary groan. Every part of his body was in pain, the like of which he had never known. He felt the open wounds on his face, and hoped the damage wasn't too bad. And then he realised how pointless that thought was. Before the day was done he would be a few metres under fast drying concrete.

He tried to focus on his surroundings. This must be some sort of store shed. Cracks between the wood that made up the walls let in some light to reveal an odd jumble of tools in the corner but nothing else. He got gingerly to his feet and limped to the door. It was obviously bolted firmly on the outside, it barely even moved when he put his shoulder against it.

He flopped back down on the floor, dejected. Despite the battering he had just been given it didn't actually feel as though any bones had been broken. He forced himself up again, this was no time for self-pity. Unless he did something and quickly his day was only going to end one way. Squinting out of the cracks in the wall he couldn't see anyone about.

He took a few steps over to the corner where the discarded tools were stacked by an upturned wheelbarrow that didn't even have a wheel. There were shovels with broken shafts and a few badly damaged rakes but that was about all. Then as he was about to turn away, tucked in behind everything else, he saw the outline of a pickaxe. He pulled it out, the other tools clattering to the floor. The wooden handle was broken but only half way up, just perhaps it might be useable.

It was much heavier than he had expected but he took it over to the wall where he had been able to peer out. The thick wooden planks it was made from were all firmly set in a concrete base which ran round the whole hut. Methodically he tested one plank after another with his weight looking for any sign of weakness. Everything seemed very solid and well-constructed. Feeling somewhat dejected he continued and then when he was almost back to his starting point there was movement, not much but it was definitely there. He leant against it again but harder this time; there was undoubtedly a creak. He knelt down examining the base and he could see thin cracks in the concrete. He pushed again, much harder and there was the sound again, that hint of weakness.

Grabbing the pickaxe he took a blow at the base below the wood but missed completely, hitting the floor. Cursing he tried again but was still well off target. He gripped further down the handle and swung with less force. The pickaxe head hit just in front of the wood and a small chip flew up from the base. He attacked the same spot again. His breathing soon became laboured. His body ached but he kept at it again and again. The flakes of concrete became larger and the cracks began to expand.

He rested for a minute and pushed his weight hard against the wood again. There was more movement, no doubt. Encouraged he returned to his task. Everything in him protested, his hands were already blistered and his arms leaden but he drove himself on, sheer willpower directing each stroke. Then a large piece fell away at the base, and then another! With each blow he felt his spirits rising. Harder and harder he hit the same spot, gasping now between each strike and then a piece of concrete the size of his fist rolled onto the floor and he got a glimpse of the base of the plank.

Five minutes more and he could see the whole thing. He

put the pickaxe down and leant again with all the force he could muster against the wood. It was moving. He stopped, took two steps back and slammed into it. His shoulder screamed in protest. Three steps back this time and summoning that extra strength from somewhere deep inside he hit the wall. There was a snapping wrenching noise as the wood began to splinter. He hit it over and over again, all pain forgotten, driven on by the widening gap and then suddenly, almost tamely the wood tore away from its mounting. Forcing it upwards he cautiously stuck his head out of the gap. Not a soul to be seen.

Turning himself completely on his side he began to push with his feet, trying to get a grip on the dusty floor. The coarseness of the wood on either side dug into his chest and back and then suddenly, miraculously his shoulders were completely through. Now using his arms too he pulled and pushed and then with one final twist he was free.

He stood shakily, his one good eye squinting in the sudden brightness of the light which seemed to bounce mercilessly off the rocks. He felt weak, drained of energy but knew he had to force himself on and quickly.

He was acutely aware that he had to put as much distance between himself and the Somalis as possible and the only option was to cross the river and make his way up the far escarpment. To head back towards the main camp with its hundreds of workers was certain death. There was little cover but there was no time to worry about that, every minute was precious.

Harry hobbled down towards the water's edge, the few figures visible, just distant specks on the top of the dam. The water was surprisingly fast flowing and it was obvious that getting in where he was would result in being swept down to the side of the dam wall itself. He had to make his way further upstream. Half jogging and repeatedly stumbling on the uneven surface he just managed to keep his balance. After ten minutes or so the river became noticeably wider so although there was further to swim the force of the current would be easier to deal with.

The water was colder than expected as he waded in which had a surprisingly positive effect. It was almost as though it was cleansing his body, washing away the trauma of the morning. The surface was deceptively calm as he struck out for the far bank and it was comparatively easy to reach the middle but then the swirls and eddies became suddenly stronger. He forced himself through the water but the only direction he was heading was downstream. The cold which only minutes before had seemed his ally now started to bite into his legs, sodden trousers clinging tightly to his skin slowing down his strokes. He tried to swim against the current but at best was staying in the same place. His strength began to drain. Then almost magically, just as despair started to creep in, he was through the main current, the water was peaceful again, circling in gentle ripples round his face. His mind didn't really register the strokes; arm movements became robotic, almost as though some primitive survival instinct had taken control.

His feet fumbled on the bottom and half crawling, half staggering he made his way up the bank. Lying on the rocky surface, his mouth wide open sucking in the air in harsh gasps he knew this was only the first hurdle. Looking up at the steep slopes above him Harry wondered how he would ever make it to the top. He forced himself up. Only one end awaited him if he didn't start the climb and it wasn't just his fate; starting upwards, one unsteady pace at a time, the vision of Ana's face as the container doors shut, stood out firmly in his head.

Metre by painful metre, his legs protesting at each step, he edged his way up. His mouth and throat seemed drier than he had ever recalled. Despite the temptation he hadn't let himself drink from the river, only too aware of the chemicals and human waste polluting the water.

The surface was very loose under his feet and time after time he felt he was about to lose his footing completely. The tips of his fingers were bleeding from endlessly scrambling for balance on the slopes. After what seemed like an age he reached a large outcrop of rocks about half way to the summit. He had to rest, even for five minutes, movement would be all the quicker for it afterwards. His clothes were drying out and the sun was peacefully warm across his body.

He woke with a start, chin on his chest. The sun was lower in the sky, how long had his five minutes turned into? His whole being seemed to protest as he got to his feet. Focusing on the peak of the ridge he scanned the slope ahead looking for the easiest path and then before starting the final climb glanced back at the way he had come. The adrenaline rush was instantaneous. There on the far river bank were several dark figures, their features were indeterminate but he was in no doubt who they were. They seemed to be looking up the side of the ravine and he suddenly realised that where just a minute ago there had only been rocks, now his silhouette would stand out like a beacon. As if to confirm that, three of them started to wade into the river.

Tiredness pushed to the back of his mind, Harry positively attacked the incline. There was a lone tree clinging to the top of the ridge and he set his sights on that to avoid weaving sideways too much and eating up crucial time. He made himself look ahead, glancing back would slow him down and wouldn't alter the speed of his pursuers. He could only see properly through one eye which made him uneasy, worried about not spotting something important just out of his vision until it was too late, so he developed a scanning technique moving his whole head from side to side, continuing ever upwards. His goal seemed so close now, the individual roots of the tree, like gnarled fingers grasping at life when there was barely anything to hang onto, were remarkably close.

He heard the shots and almost felt the impact of the bullets simultaneously as they hit the ground behind him. He sprang to the right and heard another burst of fire. Five, six steps and he was grasping at the tree roots, now miraculously helping hands as they offered him a lifeline to the crest of the ridge. Hauling himself over the last few metres and collapsing, momentarily safe at the top of the ravine, he allowed himself to peer over the edge to check on the progress of his would be killers. They were gaining, past the rocks where he had rested and striding powerfully, directly towards him.

Harry had no idea what was ahead but whatever it was it had to offer some chance. There was thick bush in front of him which was a blessing in many ways, as it would make him more difficult to follow. Not taking the most obvious path he ran for several hundred metres and spotted animal tracks leading into a small opening. Remembering Kilifi's advice he darted in between the thick shrubs, knowing that following the prints was likely to give him some sort of a pathway through. Low branches plucked at his clothes and whipped across his face but he barely felt them. Birds squawked out of their perches, flapping away, irritated at the intrusion below.

He dismissed the idea of hiding. There would be no dramatic rescue party arriving at the eleventh hour and given time the Somalis would find and follow his tracks and flush him out of whatever safe spot he thought he had found.

The vegetation started to thin and before Harry knew it he was standing at the edge of the green line looking down a gently sloping hill towards a dirt road with a few small farmsteads beyond. Would he put them in danger and was there anything they could do to help? Those weren't questions for now. He simply had to put as much of a gap between himself and his pursuers as possible. After breaking the cover of the trees he would be an easy spot, but there was no choice.

The gentle slope was a welcome change from the climb and despite everything Harry lengthened his stride. The road was further away than he had realised but gradually he ate up the dead ground between it and the slope. Then unbelievably there was the distinct dust cloud of an approaching vehicle. He didn't care where it was going but it was heading in his direction. Could he reach the road in time? His legs simply couldn't go on like this, his knees were burning, his vision blurring with the effort and then suddenly he was down. The blow of hitting the ground knocked all the air from his body and for a moment he lay there unmoving, looking up at the sky. Then glancing back he saw three figures emerge from the line of trees, further to the right than expected but they must have seen him straight away. How could they not, there was nothing else out here.

Getting to his feet he felt his left ankle protest and looking down realised that he must have caught the edge of an animal burrow. It didn't feel broken and he couldn't put much weight on it but still he forced himself on towards the fast approaching dust. His heart sank realising that he wouldn't make it; they would simply drive on without spotting him. Frantically he waved his arms, shouting, almost crying in desperation and then unbelievably the old white pickup truck began to slow and then finally it came to a halt. Two large men got out and slowly made their way towards him.

"Hurry, please hurry," he shouted. "We're all in danger." They increased their pace and as they got to him Harry pleaded, "Please no questions now. See those men coming down the hillside, well they are Somali bandits and if we don't move quickly they will do for us all."

They men looked up and then down at Harry but they didn't hesitate. There was no love lost between Somalis and Kenyans in this part of the country.

"Come, hold onto us," shouted the larger of the two and with his arms over their shoulders they part carried, part dragged him to the vehicle. "Squeeze into the middle quickly. They're closing on us."

Despite the heavy load of maize cobs in the back, they took off up the road at a surprising pace. They heard the sudden stutter of gunfire but the pickup didn't falter and as the needle crept up the speedometer dial the danger fast receded behind them.

"My friends call me David," said the driver. "Just as well we came along when we did, another minute later and you wouldn't be sitting here. What's happened to you, look at your face and hands? There's blood everywhere, and your eye!"

"I know it must look dreadful but I haven't the time to explain now. Just trust me. I work on the Uwingoni Game Reserve, does this road go anywhere near it?"

"Within about seven miles, I think," said David.

"Do either of you have a mobile phone I could use for an emergency call, please. It really is life or death."

"I don't doubt that." David dug into the side pocket his right hand on the wheel skilfully dodging the endless potholes on the road.

"Thank you so much." Harry dialled the now familiar number. Because of the nature of their visit to the dam, Jim had assured them that he would keep his phone on him at all times.

On the fourth ring his voice was there, no longer matter of

fact but full of concern and worry. "Harry, thank God. We have been so worried. What's happened? Are you alright?"

Harry gathered his thoughts. He just had to stick with what was important. The full story could be told later.

"I'll try to be brief. We ran foul of the Somali and his men who are in league with Michael and goodness knows what other Chinese up there. I managed to escape, but only just. Crucially, as we speak, Ana is on her way to Mombasa port, a prisoner, locked in a container full of poached ivory. We have to rescue her. And with her will come the ivory and the proof that even the most corrupt officials cannot sweep under the carpet, about what has been going on up there."

"Right Harry, I'll get onto the Inspector and Odika straight away. We'll need more details of course and quickly, where are you now?"

"In a pickup with my rescuers. I'll see whether they can take me to the main Uwingoni gate, hang on." Harry looked across at David who had heard enough of the conversation to nod his head in agreement. "That's fine."

"Good. Bethwell is down there now, by luck, so he'll bring you back to camp and by then we will have a plan in place I'm sure. See you as soon as possible."

"Chinese and Somalis eh!" David spat the words out. "They are ruining the lives of countless decent people, either with their mindless violence or their interference in our country. Anything I can do to help just ask."

"Thanks David. Just get us to that gate as fast as this old lady will move."

Two hours later Harry was back in the main camp, a cold compress over his right eye, trying to give a brief summary of the previous twenty-four hours.

Through luck Sergeant Odika had been visiting his team and was in the office with Jim and Mike. Inspector Mwitu was on the speaker phone, as he was down at police headquarters in Nairobi.

Harry tried to keep his account of what had happened as concise as possible, without leaving anything out and his listeners stopped him every so often to ask a question or clarify a point. Although physically exhausted, he was surprised at how alert his mind felt and knew he was driven both by fears about Ana's safety and his desire to see those responsible brought to justice.

When he had finished the Inspector spoke with a grave authority. "I am going straight from this call to see the Assistant Commissioner. He will have to act and swiftly, especially as a British national has been kidnapped and imprisoned. Jim you need to get onto the British High Commission down there immediately, tell them everything and they will also be able to bring considerable pressure to bear on the Kenyan government. Believe me, when this gets out, corrupt officials will be keeping their heads down. We will need to send a crack squad to Prosperity Dam today. Sergeant I am sure KWS will want some of their best guys in there too. If we act fast we might just catch the Somalis, they certainly won't have gone with the container lorry as that would arouse too much suspicion. And of course that container is key, both for Ana and the ivory. There are hundreds of containers on the roads every day but being purple with a Chinese name and symbol on the side gives us a lot to go on. I am sure we will be able to authorise a nationwide alert for it. Nevertheless, the driver will have a large wad of shillings to bribe himself out of trouble and that is a powerful weapon. Any questions?"

"Thank you, Inspector. The sooner we all get on with what we need to do the better. I look forward to hearing from you." Jim clicked the speaker off.

"I am going to talk to my boss at KWS right now. If we

can get a top anti-poaching squad sent up right away by plane I will be able to go with them to Prosperity. Speed is the key here." The sergeant got up to leave, stopping on his way out to give Harry a friendly slap across his shoulder. "Well done out there. We might make a ranger of you yet."

Jim turned his gaze on Harry, "Yes you did amazingly well. We're all very proud of you. But there is nothing more any of us can do at the moment. Go and get some well-earned rest and I'll let you know as soon as there are any developments."

Chapter Sixteen

Although the fear that gripped Ana as the doors had clanged shut was horribly real and instantaneous, she quickly realised the futility of banging against the metal walls of her prison. If anything that would give those who had locked her in even more satisfaction and that thought alone made her stop and stand away from the sides. She clasped her hands together in front of her, tried to breathe slowly and calmly and in her head repeatedly played back small chants that she had learnt in an effort to block out the terrible danger she knew herself to be in.

On opening her eyes she gave them time to adjust to the surroundings. Just as in Syria, small amounts of light forced their way through the cracks round the doors where the seal was far from perfect. She examined the cardboard box which had a few bottles of water and packets of crisps inside, but that was it. Behind her row upon row of tusks stood, a chilling testament to lives cut short for nothing more than cold profit. Strangely the anger that generated was so strong and the number of tusks so overwhelming that it actually began to replace the fear of her own immediate future.

She stepped across to the nearest ones. Although the lack of light made the inside of the container like a faded, black and white photo, she was able to make out the shapes reasonably well. It seemed as though the tusks had actually been paired up, perhaps so that the ivory from a single elephant could be sold as one lot. Those nearest her were generally smaller, progressing in size to the back where the largest ones reached up, half way to the ceiling. Every poached elephant represented dreadful pain and suffering but, as Ana tried to take it in, she couldn't help but think that at least those at the back had been able to lead their lives to the full. It didn't make their death any less horrendous but the ones at the front were not much more than children.

The image in her mind switched. The horrific pictures from 1945 of liberated concentration camps, the bodies of young and old piled one on top of the other; whole families dead on the streets of Rwanda in the year she was born; her own much clearer memories of Syria and another container etched forever into her very being. And now here, more death, wickedness eating into the very fabric of people's souls.

She took one of the smallest tusks in her hands and sat on the floor, her back to the others with her knees up high towards her chest. She started to caress the ivory, gentle, easy strokes almost as though she was running her fingers through a child's hair. Was she searching for some connection to that particular elephant, she simply didn't know but there was something in her actions that provided a form of release.

And then they came, slow at first and then quicker and more pronounced; huge sobs that seemed to wrack her entire body. Tears flowed freely as though bottled up behind a dam of guilt as her hands continued their futile attempt to stroke away the pain. But she was no longer in this container and the tusk was now a young girl's head like those who had come before and those yet to be thrown into this metal hell to be raped and violated as and when the mood took their captors.

She hadn't cried like this for ages, the tears buried somewhere deep inside, where emotion was kept under lock and key. She saw it now, the guilt that ate into her. All these young women, their lives ruined forever, nothing more than play things, but it had always been them and never her. Although she had tried her best to ease their pain when the remnants of the person they had been returned, what did she know? She thought she could picture how horrific their experiences were, but of course she couldn't really begin. And as the days had passed and she had felt outwardly whole at least, she had stroked their heads and tried to mutter soothing words in a language they couldn't understand as they lay curled up on the filth of the container floor.

Ana angrily wiped the hot tears from her cheeks, her breathing steadying. She couldn't save those women, just as she couldn't bring these elephants back to life but perhaps here, despite the huge vulnerability of her position she might be able to play a part in bringing these men to justice.

Guilt and despair banished for the moment anyway, she sat hard against the wall thinking and waiting, the unforgiving metal pressing into her back.

Despite everything she must have dozed off. Her head jerked up at the sound of voices and banging on the side of the container.

She heard the noise of a large engine and the crunching of tyres, shortly followed by the scraping of metal on metal as something was being fastened round the container. The engine revs increased, there was a loud creak and some of the tightly packed tusks moved very slightly towards her, then the floor levelled out and they were back where they started.

Ana realised that they were being lifted by a crane. There was further shouting and some gentle swaying followed by a rasping noise and then all was still again. The container was obviously on the back of a lorry. She hadn't uttered a sound, it would have been pointless. Only when she was out of here one way or another would she be presented with any opportunity. She didn't even have an idea of what she might be able to do but there would be hours if not days for her to sit, think and plan.

Harry felt a squeeze on his shoulder and tried hard to wake himself from the deepest of sleeps. Jim was standing beside his bed, concern still showing on his face. "Sorry to wake you. I know you really crave rest but needs must."

"That's fine." He winced at the pain in his side as he sat up in bed but realised that he was now seeing out of both eyes again, so progress of a sort. "What's up?"

"Well, Inspector Mwitu is up, at Prosperity Dam that is, or at least he will be in a couple of hours. With your story and Ana's disappearance his superiors had no choice but to give him the authority and the men to conduct a search of the place. As you are the main witness and know some of the layout, he wants you to meet him up there. I'm going to drive you up myself. Anything we can do to help find Ana must be our number one priority. I want to leave in five minutes I'm afraid. I've asked Raymond to wrap a few bacon sandwiches up for the journey."

When they arrived at the now familiar yellow barrier it was clear that Mwitu and his men were already there. The once surly guard on the gate almost tripped over in his attempt to let them through as quickly as possible.

They made their way down to the main offices where Harry had come on his first visit. Mr Zhang Wei seemed a shrunken version of the man he remembered. He was at his desk with the Inspector and another senior officer facing him.

"I am sure you remember Harry and of course his uncle Jim who has hosted your Chairman Mr Pang up at

Uwingoni. I think the young man's face tells a story before he even opens his mouth. He came here just two days ago with his friend Ana at the invitation of Mr Pang himself and the fact that he escaped with his life is only down to luck and bravery on his part."

"I know nothing of this," said Zhang Wei, sitting up straight and trying to regain some of his authority, "but I do know that the Chairman and his associates in government will be far from pleased with this intrusion today."

"I don't think you have any idea of the seriousness of the allegations against this organisation. Not only has a young woman been kidnapped but we believe her to be in a container full of poached elephant tusks. On top of that the Somalis operating under your protection are known members of Al-Shabaab, a terrorist group responsible for some of the most appalling terrorist attacks on our country."

"I haven't been protecting any Somalis. I've never even met a Somali," protested Zhang Wei.

"Time and our investigations will determine that. Now I'd like to interview Michael, I gather he's the Chairman's nephew. Please arrange for him to join us here as soon as possible."

Zhang Wei shifted uncomfortably in his seat, his eyes flicking nervously towards the window and the outside. "I'm afraid that will not be possible. He's not here at the moment."

"That's very convenient. Could you tell us where he is then? Something important like a doctor's appointment in Nairobi I imagine."

"Yes, yes. That's exactly it," stuttered the engineer. "How did you know?"

"Oh, just experience. Would you be good enough to get him on his mobile phone? He does have one of those I assume?"

Harry watched the charade unfolding. It wasn't his place to say anything unless asked but he could sense the nervousness. Just like some animals in the wild when they sense danger, Zhang Wei's tongue licked repeatedly round his lips.

"Ah Michael, sorry to disturb you on your way to the hospital but the police are with me at the moment and would like to speak to you. I wonder if… Michael, can you hear me, Michael? Oh dear, Inspector. We seem to have lost the signal."

"Indeed," said Mwitu. "One of my officers will be staying in here with you and when Michael rings back, which of course he is bound to do, he will let me know and I'll be able to talk to him. Meanwhile you are not to leave this office complex."

"But I've got…"

"I'm not really interested in what you have or have not got. I still don't think you really understand the potential charges that might well be brought against Ching Pang. You will remain here. Thank you."

The door opened and a sour-faced man stood glaring at the intruders. "Ah Mr Hu I assume. I am Inspector Mwitu of the Kenyan police. You timing is perfect. We were just about to take a look at all the containers you have just a short distance from here."

Hu's eyes darted momentarily towards his boss who shrugged helplessly and returned to brushing off some imaginary dirt on his computer keypad.

"Oh and Mr Hu, please make sure you have keys to them all. We'll be waiting for you outside."

By the time they reached the containers they had been joined by Sergeant Odika, who had just arrived with a squad of six very determined looking KWS rangers. Mr Hu carried a large bunch of keys and despite the situation he still walked with a swagger. Harry felt a quickening of his pulse as he looked at where he and Ana had been held.

"The purple container with the tusks was the last in the line and I can see already that it's no longer here."

The sergeant looked at the ground. "It must have been moved very recently you can clearly see the marks of its imprint in the earth. Tell me Mr Hu what was in this container and where is it bound for?"

"I believe some heavy machinery that was being returned to China as it was no longer needed here any longer."

Harry couldn't contain himself, "That's a complete lie and you know it. It was filled with elephant tusks and my friend Ana was imprisoned in there too, by those cowardly Somalis who work with you."

Hu almost sneered, "Somalis and elephant tusks. What sort of dream world do you live in young man? There are no elephants near here and Somalia is several hundred miles away."

Jim laid his hand on Harry's arm. "Leave it. Just let the professionals get on with their job."

Container after container was opened. There were engine parts, large amounts of rock samples and all manner of equipment used in dam construction but that was about it. As each one drew a blank, Hu's arrogance grew and grew. "Perhaps we might find some live lions in this last one Sergeant. You never know." That too was empty of anything incriminating.

Harry felt totally deflated. "Jim there just has to be something. They haven't had a chance to move any of these, other than the one with Ana in, and this man Hu is just too cocky."

Odika seemed to have disappeared and then they saw him again walking down the far side of the first container in the line. He ordered two of his men to clear a pathway down the inside and push the machinery to the centre. He then walked in, taking long slow steps until he reached the end. He repeated the process and then went outside and did the same thing.

"This may be wishful thinking," he said to one of his rangers, "but something doesn't feel quite right. Have you got a torch?"

The man searched unsuccessfully through the equipment bag.

"Sergeant please use my phone, it has a good torch on the back. Hang on I'll just switch it on."

Harry handed his phone over and Odika and a couple of his men entered the container. Those outside heard much knocking and tapping and some minutes later they reappeared. "Where's Mr Hu?"

"The last time I saw him he was over to the side those huts talking in earnest to two or three men."

"Thanks Jim. Corporal will you please go over there and ask Mr Hu if he would join us."

"Ah, Mr Hu. Please would you arrange straight away for someone from your garage to come up here with an oxy-acetylene cutting kit."

"They're all terribly busy at the moment. They've got a lot on."

"I don't think you understand Mr Hu. This is not a casual request. I want someone up here with that equipment within ten minutes."

After what seemed an age a filthy yellow pickup appeared, driven by a man in matching overalls. One of the rangers helped him unload a trolley on which were two gas cylinders, coloured hoses and dials, an assortment of welding nozzles and finally a metallic face mask with dark glass across the eyes. All this was wheeled inside the container and Odika issued instructions. While he and a couple of his men stayed inside the welder set to work.

Odika hoped his hunch was right but of course there was no guarantee, however, he had come to learn how devious those involved in poaching were. It had seemed to him with his rather crude method of measuring that the inside of the container was about a metre shorter than the outside. The wall at the back, despite some crude attempt to paint it the same colour didn't match with anything else. False walls were not uncommon and if his suspicions were right, what if anything lay behind it?

The welder seemed to be taking an age and every so often when he took a short break, Odika came up to have a look at what progress was being made. He had started about halfway up the vertical upright, working towards the floor. It soon became obvious that where there should have been daylight on the other side there was none to be seen. However, there was no way of telling what secrets might be hidden in the darkness.

A chair was fetched so that the welder could reach the roof. "Right," ordered Odika, "I want you to cut a metre along the top horizontally and the same at the bottom. With luck we should then be able to peel it back rather like some giant food tin."

Time crawled but eventually the man stepped back from the wall and removed his mask to reveal a face dripping with sweat. "That should be enough now I think."

"Go and get me that tyre lever I saw in the back of your pick up. Come on man, hurry up." When he returned Odika instructed him to start forcing the metal back but soon lost patience. "Stand aside and give me the lever."

The sound of tortured metal filled the container and with it the unmistakable smell of dead flesh. "Where is Musambi?" There was a shout from the corporal and the youngest of the rangers was summoned. "Go and get your camera. I want everything recorded as proof of what I fear we are about to discover today. I assume it has a flash on it?"

"Yes Sergeant I'll just get it." He was back in an instant. "Ready when you are. If this stench is anything to go by I don't think I'm looking forward to the images I'm going to be taking."

Odika switched the torchlight on again as he squeezed through the opening. The area to his right was crammed with various shapes covered by large canvas sheets.

"There's a lot in here," he shouted back through the opening. "I don't want to take it outside for the moment. Corporal will you get as much of the junk cleared out of the container as possible. We'll bring whatever is in here out bit by bit and examine it in as much privacy as this metal box provides us.

He cautiously pulled away the first canvas cover, and although half expecting what he might discover he still found himself recoiling from the both the sight and smell of what lay before him. There piled one on top of the other were the skins of leopards. As he lifted the top one off he could understand the assault on his nose. There had been no attempt to cure the skins and the fat and in some places the flesh of the animal still remained.

Musambi's camera flashed and the skin was passed out and then another followed and so it went on until the skins of twenty-three leopards lay stacked up in one corner of the container.

Even before he had fully pulled off the covering of the next pile he could see the lion's mane and the same sickening procession of skins followed. "Right, I've seen more than enough already. Let's get someone else in here now. I need to see the Inspector."

He eased himself through the opening and heading out into the sunlight found Jim and Mwitu in deep conversation.

"Look I have already found enough lion and leopard skins to suggest that this is a large-scale organisation that must range far and wide across the country and even over our borders into Tanzania and Uganda. Do you know what it must take to find twenty-three leopards, let alone successfully poach them? The lion skins are coming out now and we are far from finished."

"I suggest we put an immediate ban on anyone leaving the site," responded Mwitu. "I'll get reinforcements up here straight away. Nearly all the men who work here are dirt poor, just trying to scrape a living for themselves and their families and will be of no interest to us. However, anyone in authority or who seems better dressed than the average worker, we need to talk to. Inspector Kamau, would you be good enough to get back to Mr Zhang Wei's office straight away and tell him what's happening and ask him to gather all his managers together in the office. I shall want to speak to them in half an hour."

There was a shout from the container, "Sergeant, please come quickly." Odika strode back into the container and there in a large wooden box up against the wall was the unmistakable sight of three large rhino horns laid out neatly on top of a bed of straw. He picked one up, dark grey in colour it had a surprisingly thick base and he could see where the chainsaw cut with chilling accuracy between that and the rhino's nose, every extra piece of weight representing an extraordinary value. He knew that such was the demand in the Far East; a kilo was worth more than the same weight of gold or cocaine. "There are five identical boxes in there, we'll get them out now but I fear it's going to be grim news."

"Get me Headquarters straight away Corporal. This is far too big for us to deal with alone. I need to speak to the Deputy Director Security, even if he is in an important meeting. Oh and by the way where's Mr Hu?"

Everyone scanned round the containers and buildings but there was no sign of Hu or indeed the men he had been talking to. Everyone had been so intent on the container that he had slipped away unnoticed.

"Did anyone see in which direction he went?" asked the Inspector.

Harry was thinking back to their first visit. "This is only a hunch but further up the track there was another turning, also protected with a barrier and I remember Michael Cheng telling me that is where Hu's base was."

"Thanks Harry that's as good a guess as anything and there is nothing more we can do here right now. We'll leave that up to KWS although I will see whether I can borrow a couple of their heavily armed rangers, just in case. Can you come with us and direct the driver. That is of course providing you keep well out of the way should there be any trouble."

"I'll come too if I may," said Jim. "I feel such anguish just standing here. I simply need to be away from this place."

Ten minutes later two Land Rovers sat, engines idling at an unmanned barrier.

"I know nothing more than his base is up there and it is off limits to everyone except the chosen few."

"Thanks Harry. You and Jim stay here with one of my men and the vehicles. We don't want to advertise our arrival. We will see you soon. Jim, you have my number, call me if I haven't got back to you within half an hour."

Mwitu and his men disappeared round the corner fanning out as they went. The lone policeman left behind seemed understandably disgruntled and decided to base himself in the hut used by those who usually manned the barrier.

Harry and Jim sat in one of the vehicles. It was ironic that in many ways there was so much to say and talk about and yet the last day or so had overloaded their minds and it was difficult to know where to begin. Being silent, although painful, was an understandable place to be.

Strangely it was Jim who spoke first. "You know Harry, you devote your whole life to the wild animals of this beautiful country with all its wonder and magic and to see what came out of that container almost made me cry. We all know this goes on but the scale of killing now is truly horrifying. People wonder what might be left for their grandchildren, I seriously wonder what's going to be here, in even ten years' time!"

"I know Jim. I felt much the same and I'm a complete new boy. But just at the moment I simply can't get Ana out of my head. I know there's a nationwide alert out for that purple container but Kenya's a big place. If they only travel at night who's even going to see the colour? We're not the police so what can we do? Just being up here and thinking of her on her own in the dark, rattling down roads to goodness knows where, fills me with useless rage. Yes we assume she's heading to Mombasa but who knows? They might stop on some remote part of the coast and load her and the tusks into a couple of dhows. There are so many possibilities and all of them harrowing."

The sound of gunfire cut through their thoughts, not just individual shots but prolong bursts. "Fingers crossed that's us taking them by surprise Harry, not the other way round."

The policeman was out of the hut looking up the track and then they heard it, through the shots, the unmistakable sound of a vehicle being driven at speed. "Are the keys in the ignition Jim? I know this is a police Land Rover but if we can drive it across the barrier, there's no way anything can drive out of this narrow entrance."

They leapt forward, Jim's foot hard down on the accelerator and as he spun the wheel, they slid across the track just as the other vehicle sped round the corner. They recognised the blotchy camouflaged markings on the Land Rover immediately, as the driver tried desperately to alter course at the last second but the steep sides meant there was nowhere to go. The front wheel hit a large boulder and with the sound of tortured metal they were forced halfway up the bank, the vehicle flipping onto its side as it did so. Then slowly it slid back onto the road, its rear wheel stopping against the very boulder that had propelled it there in the first place.

Remarkably the passenger door opened up towards the sky and a familiar figure, AK-47 in hand seemed to propel himself out of the vehicle. Seeing Jim and Harry, his face twisted with loathing, he raised the gun as they crouched down behind the cover of the police Land Rover. Two shots rang out clearly and as they glanced nervously from their hiding place, they saw the man clutching his chest, as his weapon bounced drunkenly on the rocky surface.

The policeman advanced towards him, rifle raised but already it was obvious he would never be a threat to anyone again. Cautiously approaching the upturned vehicle, he pointed his gun through the open door and peered in. The driver, his head still bleeding from the impact of the crash, stared up at the gun barrel and groggily hauled himself out of the door. The policeman gestured for him to lie face down, his hands behind his back, face next to the ever-widening stain in the ground as his comrade's life slowly drained away.

Harry stood up and looking down at his would-be executioners with their filthy army trousers and feet that somehow still clung to flip flops, felt nothing but contempt.

Jim smiled at the policeman, "Thank you, we owe you our lives." The man shrugged as though it was just a part of everyday life.

"It was an absolute pleasure," he grinned, placing his boot on the man's back as he pulled out his radio.

Jim and Harry were suddenly aware of the almost complete silence that had descended. Whatever had gone on up the track must now be over, one way or the other.

The policeman was very animated as he talked, set pressed to his ear. "I have been asked to escort you up to Mr Hu's base. We can just leave the vehicles here."

"Thank you. I'll take the keys with us nevertheless." Jim grabbed the second set of keys from the other police vehicle and the three of them, prisoner in tow, walked up the track.

Police officers and KWS rangers were talking excitedly as they arrived and the smile on Inspector Mwitu's face told the story.

"Welcome my friends. This has been a highly successful operation, particularly as, apart from one of my men sustaining a bullet nick in his leg, there were no other injuries to our team. On the other hand those up here had been so intent on packing up and getting out as soon as possible that they hadn't even posted a guard. We took them completely by surprise."

As they walked towards a smart looking bungalow which was obviously the centre of this little complex, laid out on the ground in front of the steps was a line of eight bodies. Six of them were obviously Somalis, their facial features and similar scruffy uniforms putting that beyond doubt. However, the last two were Chinese.

"As you can see we were up against a bit of a mix here but perhaps the best of the news is just inside." As they walked up the steps Harry noticed the smattering of bullet marks across the pillars by the door. Once inside the smartly furnished building they turned left into a large office area and there sitting in a chair, handcuffs behind his back and police officer standing guard nearby was Mr

Hu. The cockiness was gone and he sat shoulders hunched staring at the floor.

"We found Mr Hu inside, hiding under a bed in fact, not even prepared to risk his skin fighting with his own men. I would say that rather sums him up wouldn't you. Hu looked up momentarily, his `eyes filled with a mixture of malice and fear. He spat at the floor in front of them and sank back into the chair, perhaps realising the futility of the gesture.

"I have no doubt we will be having some fruitful discussions with him back at police headquarters. Like so many bullies he is of course a weak man."

As they moved out onto the veranda there was much excitement from the police sergeant who had just been opening up some of the surrounding stores. "Sir this place is an arsenal of weapons and we have only just begun. Not just AK-47s, it would seem in their hundreds, but grenades, explosives and even rocket launchers. Enough to start a small war!"

"Or continue and expand a larger one I think sergeant. It is rewarding to have such undeniable proof of the link between poaching and terrorism. This is a bleak day for Al-Shabaab and no doubt their leaders will be wringing their hands when they hear the news, not just for their cause of course, but for the huge dent in their own bank accounts. At the moment continue your search of the extended premises, make brief notes of what you find and where. The new squad of police who are well on their way by now will be able to list it all and get it taken back to Nairobi. And thank you for all you have done today, you are a credit to our nation's police force."

Jim couldn't resist shaking the inspector by the hand. "I really feel this time what you and your men have achieved will make a real difference. Thank you for your support and believing in us even when there was pressure from some of your superiors to forget the whole thing and look the other way."

"Thank you, Jim. It's good for my men to be valued and appreciated. My only regret in all this is that our limping Somali, who is at the centre of the web, seems to have vanished into thin air. He will have friends and connections everywhere. We need to find him and find him quickly.

Chapter Seventeen

The journey was slower than Ana had expected. Even in the darkness she was aware that they had not been on a tarmac road for several hours. Not only did the tyres make a different sound but the endless potholes seemed less jarring on dirt roads as there wasn't that same sharp impact that the edges on a tarmac surface seemed to bring.

It was strange the small things you started to think about when you have lots of time on your hands she thought. Her mind wandered back to long childhood journeys with her parents and younger brother in an old green VW Estate that seemed to plough on year after year. It took them from the Highlands of Scotland to the beaches of the Mediterranean. And everywhere they went always seemed full of fun and laughter. Endless quizzes and squabbles over music choices and trips way off the normal tourist routes, down tiny roads where they stayed in beautiful old cottages and forged friendships with other children in communities so different from their own. Perhaps that was the seed of her desire to be a journalist, the excitement of new places and people.

Her poor family; what they had been through with her. Their endless support as she studied journalism and their unbelievable pride when she started to have articles published. Then, when she had begun foreign assignments she had returned full of stories, some heart-warming, others unbelievably sad. They had sat down as they always did over long meals washed down with a lovely smooth, red wine that her dad bought from some obscure little vineyard in the south of France.

And of course there had been the offer to go to Syria. She had known how they would feel. Everyone had held it together pretty well until Heathrow. When her dad had kissed her goodbye he could do nothing about the wetness of his cheeks and her mum, always the stronger of the two, had held her final hug for so long.

On her return she had felt so bad. They had always been such an open family, few if any secrets, even in those awkward teenage years. She had known how much they had wanted to help, always encouraging her in the gentlest of ways to open up. She had told them unimportant snippets to try to keep them happy but that was as far as she could go. Yes she had opened up to Harry a little but he wasn't family so that made it easier.

How strange that it had taken being back in the same sort of situation where her very life was on a thread for her to look deep inside, face some truths and start to really haul herself out of the darkness.

Her thoughts were interrupted as she felt a definite change in their motion and realised that the lorry was changing down gears. The movement in the back became slower but more pronounced and then stopped altogether.

She heard the sound of both cab doors opening so the driver wasn't alone. Putting her ear right up against the rear door she strained to see whether she could hear voices. Was this a roadside stop, might there be people around willing to help if she shouted out? It was so frustrating not knowing what to do.

A sudden bang on the outside of the container made her

jump back involuntarily. "How's our pretty, little whore enjoying the trip so far? Wondering where you're going to end up and whether some magic rescue is going to take place? Sadly for you that won't be happening, nobody is going to find us where we're going and there will be no knight in shining armour. Of course there will be many of my fellow liberation fighters at the other end who will be only too happy to get to know you better."

The Somali's grating voice seemed to eat into her like some corrosive liquid. She wanted to shout every obscenity she had ever learnt at him but knew the increased pleasure this would provide. Somehow remaining silent gave her a small amount of control over the situation and as he banged the door and the taunting about her fate increased she heard the anger in his voice for the first time.

She made her way back to the tusks that somehow gave her comfort and after a while the pounding and shouting stopped, the engine started and the lorry pulled away. It had been a small victory for her, but a victory nevertheless.

Inspector Mwitu had suggested Harry and Jim return to Uwingoni. There was nothing further they could do to be of help at the dam. Additional police and KWS units would soon be on site. It was obviously going to be quite an undertaking to carry out so many interviews and for the rangers to determine the full extent of the poached items. There was still more to be brought out of the container and plenty of other areas to be searched. A specialist antiterrorist squad had also been called up to deal with all the weapons and look into any other Al-Shabaab activities and links with individuals connected to Prosperity Dam.

Back in Jim's office Harry was pacing to and fro, incessantly checking his mobile. "They are doing all they can to find her. The Inspector assures us that even the smallest police post has a description of the container. I'm sure it's only a matter of time." Despite his reassurances, Jim's unaccustomed fiddling with various things on his desk gave away his own uncertainty and concern.

"With that many police on the main roads they must either have parked up during daylight hours and be travelling at night or, which I think is much more likely, be using obscure tracks and back roads despite the size of the lorry. Oh Jim time is so short. I know KWS have got a couple of planes scouting over some of the larger areas but I wanted to ask a favour. I know Ollie is due in with some new clients in an hour or so. Look, I appreciate we have been here before but please can you ask his boss, just one more time, and see whether he would let us do some scouting of our own this afternoon. I've got enough savings to pay for the fuel if it's a question of cost. I can't just sit here hoping everything will turn out right."

"Of course, I'll phone him right now." The conversation was surprisingly short. "That's all sorted and there is no question of payment. You will have to go back to Wilson to refuel but then you and Ollie have the plane for the rest of the afternoon. He's going to sort everything out with air traffic control."

Harry was already half out of the door, "Thank you so much Jim."

"When I say good luck to you I don't think I have ever meant it so much in my life. Oh, and I'll keep KWS and the police informed with what you're up to."

He was down at the airstrip way ahead of arrival time but even a few extra minutes on a day like this might prove vital. He had borrowed the best pair of binoculars he could find but hadn't bothered with anything else, not even a small overnight bag.

By the time the tourists and their luggage were in the

Land Cruiser with Bethwell, the plane was already airborne again. It was a cloudless day, the sun heating up the cockpit as Harry told the story of what had happened over the last couple of days. Apart from the odd question Ollie just concentrated on flying and listened, his pilot's mind already picturing the huge expanse of land between Nairobi and the coast.

"Time will be crucial for them Harry. That ivory is so valuable they have to get it to the coast as soon as possible. They'll know that there will be a huge search going on. For them Ana is just a little extra and I'm afraid they would dispose of her without a second thought if they needed to. We just have to think like them. It's possible they might try to make it over some unmanned road crossing into Somalia itself but there are a lot of different factions fighting there who would give anything for that haul. No, my guess is that they will have a safe haven somewhere along the coast where they operate their own vessels to take whatever the latest poaching haul is to their stronghold in Somalia. I have some ideas but we can have a closer look at the map when we reach Wilson."

As the fuel was being pumped into the wings of the little Cessna and they were standing over a table in a hanger examining possible options that the lorry might take on its way to the coast, they were interrupted by a small, wiry figure in a KWS uniform. He had a broad smile but few teeth and the wrinkles round his eyes spoke of hardship and experience.

"Sergeant Odika asked me to join you at Wilson. I am Corporal Chyulu and he thought I would be able to help you out. As you aren't the one in a pilot's uniform I assume you must be Harry," he smiled stretching out a hand which had a surprisingly powerful grip. "Your uncle and Odika have been talking about this afternoon's search and thought you would be concentrating on the area around Tsavo East National Park and then towards Malindi and north up the coast. Tsavo is a huge area, even with a plane, over thirteen and a half thousand square kilometres I think. It's a region I know quite well so he thought I would be more use to you than I would be doing some paperwork in an office at headquarters. Believe me I didn't need to be asked twice."

Ollie introduced himself, "Welcome on board, another set of eyes and local knowledge will be wonderful."

The three of them returned to the map and they listened with increasing respect as Chyulu talked to them about the vastness of their task. "Visitors to our country always talk about the Masai Mara and with good reason but you could fit the whole of that reserve into just the southern tip of Tsavo East. Tourists go for four-hour game drives here and come back not having even seen another vehicle. The enormous northern region was closed to the public for many years, distances are immense and there is hardly any infrastructure. Of course it is famous for its elephants, we think around ten thousand at the last count and because it's so huge it's an area some poachers feel more secure in because the very size of the place makes it incredibly difficult to protect. My hunch is that we should start our search there."

"We are so glad you are here Corporal Chyulu, if anyone can help us find Ana and that ivory, you're the man,"

"Thank you, Harry, and please just call me Chyulu."

The aircraft mechanics returned, "She's all fuelled up Captain and ready to go."

Harry clambered into the rear of the plane and Chyulu handed him a large rucksack which he placed on the only spare seat. "And this if you wouldn't mind. There simply isn't enough room for it in the front." Harry placed the rifle carefully along the side with the muzzle pointing up and back.

"We have got enough fuel to stay up till dusk, as long as I'm reasonably gentle with the throttle. Depending on how things go we can land at Malindi right on the coast, refuel and head back to Nairobi at first light.

The initial hour in the little plane seemed impossibly slow. Chyulu told them about some of his experiences with KWS and before that as a tracker which gave them some optimism but didn't make the hands of the clock travel any faster.

"I'm not going to fly too low. We are here for one main purpose and that's so see whether we can spot the container lorry. It would probably be on the border of the reserve but of course it might even be inside. I'll stay at about two thousand feet as that will give a wide view but we will hopefully be able to spot anything suspicious on the ground. Dust trails are the obvious give away and Tsavo has this amazing red dust that should make vehicles easier to spot."

The first three or four trails they saw caused excitement in the plane but as Ollie descended and they got a clearer picture, it was quickly obvious what they were looking at was far too small. Harry used the binoculars, scanning what he could from the rear windows, clambering across the rucksack to the starboard side of the plane if he thought there was even a hint of anything interesting.

It just seemed to be a sea of thorn bush littering the bare rust coloured earth and always the horizon seemed impossibly far away. Their sweep continued with Ollie trying to cover as great an area as possible but as one hour's searching blurred into two, their initial optimism began to drain away. Chyulu spotted some form of vehicle in thick cover but when they dropped down to take a closer look there was a blue tourist Land Cruiser in the bush and it was immediately obvious what they were watching as four large bull elephants crossed the track almost in front of them, one whose tusks almost touched the ground. "Did you see him when he reached the other side?" said Ollie. "He thrust his tusks into the undergrowth, almost as though he knew his ivory is what might get him killed."

They saw giraffe, a herd of upwards of four hundred buffalo and even some Oryx, their long horns like spears laid across their shoulders but the largest vehicle they spotted was an old green truck laden with people, heading, no doubt, for some remote village.

The sun was already beginning to sink towards the west casting a shadow of the plane on the arid ground as it flew up towards the contrasting lush strip of green and the muddy water of a large river.

"This is the Galana River Harry, it empties into the ocean about ten kilometres north of Malindi. My guess would be that if the lorry is anywhere in this area it would be on this side of the water."

"Thank you Chyulu, so what do you suggest?"

"Well perhaps follow this road towards the sea. If the lorry has made it this far it would be amazing but it would need to keep to this side if it's going to make it to Malindi. I'm sorry not to be more encouraging."

"That makes good sense. Our fuel is getting pretty low. As we aren't dealing with such a boundless area I'll drop down a bit so that we can get a better view of what's on the road. We'll certainly start to see more vehicles as we get nearer the town."

"Thanks Ollie. This flight seemed like a good idea at the time. At least we can say we gave it our best shot." Even as he spoke the words Harry could sense his voice breaking. Ana was still out there somewhere, swallowed up by the vastness of this land.

The road wasn't particularly busy, a few pickups and some matatus stopping to collect and drop off their passengers but that was about it.

"What's that huge wooded area up there on our right, Chyulu? Such a change from everything else we've seen this afternoon."

"That Harry is the most wonderful place. It's the Arabuko-Sokoke Forest. It is the largest area of costal forest left in the whole of East Africa."

Harry marvelled at its size. Even from the air it spread away into the far distance. The trees themselves came up close to the border of the road.

"I'll drop our altitude even more Harry and then you can get a better look, it's quite something."

The road was deserted so Harry just busied himself with the view. Then suddenly under a canopy of trees was the unmistakable white lettering of Cheng Pang, like an eye blinking out of the darkness.

"Oh my God Ollie that's the container it has to be, right up against the trees. I'm not imagining it. Please can you turn back so that we can have another look."

Ollie turned steeply and flew back down on the river side of the road. "There, the white writing is even more obvious and despite being in the shadows you can just make out the dark purple colour."

The other two saw it clearly now as well. "There is a man beside it looking up at us. You can just make him out by the front bumper of the truck," shouted Chyulu. Harry got the faintest glance before the figure melted into the trees. Was it the Somali? He honestly couldn't tell.

Ollie was already on the radio to the air traffic control giving them the location and asking them to inform the police straight away.

"We have got enough fuel to stay up a little longer. What do you think Chyulu, you have the experience with this sort of thing?"

"Well I think we should just fly straight to Malindi

now. If we buzz about overhead he will know for sure he's been spotted while at the moment it will just be a suspicion. He can't drive off into the forest with a lorry that size and we have to remember how valuable that ivory is. My guess is that he will have fellow Somalis somewhere in Malindi who will have a property where he will be able to hide and unload the container. We need to find them too then we will be breaking their whole network. I know your thoughts will be for Ana, Harry but you will just have to trust me on this. If we show our hand now they will more than likely just kill her and dump her body in the forest."

Harry could see the sense in this, even though he couldn't stop a huge feeling of guilt deep in his stomach, as Ollie set them on a course for Malindi airport.

Chyulu asked Ollie to get the airport tower on the radio and then in rapid Swahili he rattled off what seemed like a list of instructions. "I was just telling them to contact the KWS special unit we have down here. Hopefully they will be able to get onto that road reasonably quickly. Everyone has a description of the container."

Ollie landed with his usual ease, the wheels seeming to make an almost seamless contact with the tarmac of the runway. He motored across to the airport buildings and had barely cut the engine when Chyulu was out of the door. Harry passed out his rucksack and then somewhat more gently the rifle. Leaving Ollie to sort out the refuelling of the plane, they headed quickly up into the control tower.

Harry's Swahili was still somewhat limited but he could understand enough from Chyulu's tone and body language to know that he was far from happy. He turned to Harry. "Can you believe it? The police vehicle they sent to investigate broke down before it even got to the C103 which is the road they will almost definitely be on. The KWS unit has also been delayed by half an hour. I'm afraid there is nothing more we can do except sit and wait till they get here.

They sat up against the wall of the main building, feeling the helplessness of a situation over which they had no control. Harry rang Jim to update him although it was difficult to sound positive when he knew that dusk was closing in and darkness would only be the friend of the Somalis. He learnt that Inspector Mwitu was in the air as they spoke which was definitely good news. This situation needed his authority and organisational skills. By the look of things his plane would land at much the same time as Chyulu's KWS colleagues were due.

Harry's guess turned out to be more accurate than he could have imagined. Just a few minutes after Mwitu touched down, a large sandy coloured Land Cruiser with six armed KWS rangers in the back pulled up outside the airport and sitting in the front was Sergeant Odika.

The two were deep into discussion with Chyulu when a white police car with flashing lights appeared. At last things seemed to be moving quickly.

Mwitu came across to Harry. "Thank you for what you have done. We have roadblocks up, so we know the container lorry hasn't come into the heart of Malindi but it's probably had enough time to sneak into the surrounding sprawl of slums. The local police have informers on the ground so hopefully we will get some quick leads. I know you would love to come with is but I'm afraid that's out of the question. This will be a dangerous operation. We will do all we can to ensure Ana's safety, you have my word on that and I promise we will stay in touch."

Harry realised the futility of any plea about joining them. He wished the Inspector luck and went to find Ollie.

"Look Harry I have some friends down here in the aviation business. I'm going to spend the night with them. You must come too."

"Thought I'd have a look round the town first, I've never been here before."

"You have to get real. If you start playing some sort of amateur detective in dodgy areas of this place it might well be the last thing you do. There are a hundred and fifty thousand people who live here, far bigger than you think. Leave it to Mwitu and Odika, no matter what your heart says." Harry's shoulders slumped; he felt totally useless.

They took a taxi to one of the nicer areas of town where two other young pilots rented a house together. On any other night Harry would have really enjoyed their company. He knew the grilled red snapper was tasty, his beer was well chilled and also that they tried to make the conversation light-hearted for his sake. Nevertheless, he excused himself early and headed for bed. As he lay there under the mosquito net, the large fan churning overhead, he realised that Ana couldn't be more than a few miles away and yet he knew with absolute certainty that her night would be as different from his as it was possible to be.

Chapter Eighteen

Ana felt sore and bruised. To say the trip so far had been uncomfortable would not even have been close. The roads and tracks they had driven on had been appalling and at times the container tilted so much to one side or the other that she felt as though the whole thing might just slide off the side off the trailer.

She tried sitting wedged in a corner but then her back and shoulders were rubbed mercilessly by the walls. Standing up had seemed a good idea for a while but she learnt that having to keep your legs endlessly flexed, like some skier, was exhausting. In the end she settled for sitting against a section of wall, using the cardboard from the food box as some form of insulation.

They had barely stopped and then it was just for the Somali and the driver to relieve themselves. They had banged the door, making crude remarks about how her bladder was holding out and then the lorry had lurched on its way once more.

To add to her problems some of the ivory had worked itself lose and she had to cope with large tusks sliding across the steel floor. She had tried to make them secure again but with only limited success. On a particularly rough stretch one tusk had hit the wall with such force that a few large slithers of ivory actually broke off. The largest piece was almost as long as a ruler and as she ran her hands down the remarkable smoothness of its surface she couldn't but feel a connection with the wonderful creature it belonged to. She sensed her anger rise again but was also conscious of the sharpness of the end where it had sheared off. Just possibly it might serve a purpose she thought, as she tucked it inside her top.

Ana was suddenly aware that the lorry was travelling at a slower speed and the surface beneath them seemed far smoother, and before long, with a hiss of breaks they came to a halt. Somehow she knew this was different and focused on any sounds that would give her a clue as to what might be going on in the outside world. She could hear the murmur of several voices and the lorry seemed to edge forward then suddenly came to a jerky stop and the engine cut. It was strange but the silence seemed much more threatening than the noise of the journey. There was a loud metal clang behind them as though gates were being shut and then nothing.

She realised it must now be night time as there wasn't even the faintest rim of light round the doors, but what was happening? The humidity of her surroundings told her they must be somewhere near the coast. She had tried so hard to remain positive but the thought of that filled her with dread. Once on any sort of boat away from these shores then she knew with absolute certainty that she would never see her friends or family again.

After what seemed ages, Ana had rather lost the ability to track time, she heard voices again outside the container. Her mouth went dry as the rasping sound of the bolts being drawn back echoed through her prison. The doors opened slowly to reveal a starry sky and despite everything her spirits lifted momentarily as she breathed in clean salty air. However, as she glanced out they sank again just as fast.

The Somali stood there hands on hips, his supreme self-importance obvious even in the half light. "Well Ana, I hope you enjoyed our journey. I hadn't expected to see you so soon but regrettably we have had to make some new plans. Your little friend has caused us a few problems, otherwise you would be at sea now, heading for an exciting new life." The words were expressionless but the menace in them all too clear. "Anyway we have some fresh plans for you. Take her inside."

One of the men standing at the rear jumped nimbly into the container and grabbing her forcefully by the hair, pulled her towards the opening. As she stumbled slightly on one of the dislodged tusks he didn't lessen his grip and she found herself being virtually dragged the last few metres. The other young Somali reached up and gripped her belt pulling her off with such force that she spiralled onto the ground, smacking the side of her head on the brick-lined courtyard. The half-formed insults she had been preparing to shout were crushed from her lips. She could already taste the sweetness of the blood as it trickled down her cheek into the corner of her mouth.

"Careful now," came the rasping voice, "we don't want to damage the goods so early on." They all laughed and she was scraped up off the driveway like some plaything.

Take her to the first room on the right of the corridor. There's a basin in there so she can get herself cleaned up. And don't hang about we have all this ivory to sort out tonight."

Ana sank to the floor as she heard the door being locked. Her head throbbed dreadfully and as she slowly got to her feet it positively swam in various directions. She ran a basin full of water, drinking thirstily from the tap as it filled. Gently she washed the blood from her forehead and examined it in the mirror. The wound looked angry but it wasn't that deep.

She sat on the corner of the bed trying to formulate a plan, close to tears with the vulnerability of her situation. The intentions of her captors were obvious but her determination to resist even if it cost her life, somehow gave her fresh courage and determination. She felt for the slither of ivory, it was still there. However badly the odds stacked up against her there was always a chance, she just had to be ready to take it.

Lurking in the shadows of a half built new property on the opposite side of the road Mike pondered his options. He had never visited the Somali house before but he knew some of the details of the Malindi side of the operation.

He tried to make himself as inconspicuous as possible. It was strange, he thought that when he was out in the African bush that was rarely a problem. Here was so very different. He had always hated towns ever since he had been a boy, the noise and bustle of people was never his thing. His parents had scraped the money together to send him to a decent Nairobi school but even there he stuck out, tall and gangly with an inability to make friends easily, he was usually the outsider. The only time he had felt happy was in the game parks and reserves. He simply fell in love with the places themselves, the endless space and huge skies and of course the wildlife of every shape and size. Animals had even learnt to trust him over the years when they realised that the ancient Land Rover and its lanky occupant, so often in the same place, presented no threat. That he had betrayed their trust in the most unimaginable way ate into every corner of his being.

He had always gambled a bit, outside wildlife that was his only real enjoyment. He lost more than he won, that was common but every so often there was a win that allowed him small luxuries he would never normally consider; he wasn't a man who spent money on himself.

When the casino changed hands he hadn't liked it at first, too glitzy, almost like something from show-business, with young women endlessly offering him top ups of whatever he happened to be drinking. However, he got to know the Chinese manager and they had shared stories about their lives and ambitions as people often do in the early hours of the morning, when they have had too much to drink. They became friends, or so he thought, and his visits became more regular, the girl who topped up his drink always seemed to be the prettiest and even better he started to win, not just small amounts but enough to allow him to travel to other parts of Africa in his time off. His last memorable visit had been to see the mountain gorillas in Rwanda's Volcanoes National Park. He had felt so privileged, there were only about a thousand of those wonderful animals left anywhere in the world.

In time had even met Mr Pang, whose company owned the casino, and taken him up to Uwingoni on safari. Life had never been better.

Then his luck changed, his winning streak came to an end. He still won small amounts but his losses grew larger and larger. The casino was generous and repeatedly extended his credit. Just one big win again and he would be able to repay everything, but his losses had spiralled out of control.

When they had called him in the friendly smiles were gone and even he was horrified at the amount he owed. His world was falling apart, what would happen, perhaps even a spell in prison, he couldn't stand enclosed spaces and the thought of a cell was beyond terrifying.

Mr Pang's nephew, Michael, had been at the second of these meetings. He had suggested a way out of this situation. All they needed was information about the whereabouts of certain animals in Uwingoni and some other useful news from time to time and the casino debt could be written off.

He had flatly refused but then they had produced photos of him with various casino girls in embarrassing positions. He had no recollection of anything but the threat of those being posted across the newspapers and online, together with formal complaints to the police about his behaviour broke him.

To start with their demands hadn't been too serious but then more and more of the elephants, his elephants had been killed. He had seriously considered taking his own life on several occasions, but didn't even have the courage for that.

The last few days, the scale the slaughter of so much he loved, and then what had happened to Harry and Ana had somehow helped him to find part of his old self. His own life was dispensable, he had come to terms with that but perhaps he might be able to do something to make up for his terrible betrayal.

He had just left a note for Jim, too many questions otherwise, and hitched a couple of flights down here. Mike knew this place was the centre of their costal operations but little more than that, so he couldn't believe his luck when the container lorry had arrived only about twenty minutes after him. He had heard snatches of conversation from inside the compound but not enough to determine with any real certainty what was going on. Of course he knew he should tell the authorities and he would, but first he had to play his part. His life for Ana's seemed a fair trade as he realised with unusual clarity that he was not afraid to face these men.

The lights shone brightly inside the compound and Mike was aware of some form of major activity taking place. While he was deliberating his next move a small lorry arrived at the gates. This was such a quiet under populated area of town, chosen deliberately no doubt, so they seemed unconcerned about opening up to the new arrival and as he glanced inside it became obvious what was happening. Tusks were neatly stacked against the outside of the container lorry, obviously ready for transfer to the smaller vehicle. There was no sign of Ana so that must mean she was inside the house. The Somali was already issuing instructions to the new driver and he assumed everyone would be involved in transferring the ivory as quickly as possible. They wouldn't be sparing someone to sit outside a locked room containing a young woman.

As the gates shut Mike made his way cautiously from the shadows, up to the outside of the compound wall. It was high but then few men were as tall as him. The glow of the compound courtyard faded as he moved level with the side of the house. Crouching down by a supporting pillar he took out his phone. "Jim, yes it's me but no questions please just listen. As soon as I hang up contact Inspector Mwitu and give him this address in Malindi. It's where the container lorry is. Ana wouldn't survive a police siege, the Somali would never allow it so I'm going over the wall now; just perhaps I can do something. I'm so sorry for everything. You've been a true friend. Look after Uwingoni."

He put the phone back in his jacket, feeling the weight of the old handgun in the lower pocket. It was a relic of his father's time in the police reserve. It had been in his bottom drawer for years and was loaded but that was all he knew. He had never even attempted to fire it.

Taking a couple of strides back he took a run at the wall, got his fingertips onto the top and with difficulty hauled himself up until he was looking down at the passage way that ran along the side of the house. He eased both legs over and lowered himself down.

There were bars on the outside of all the windows and shutters or curtains inside; it was difficult to tell as everything on this side of the house was in darkness. Cautiously he moved round to the back where a light from one of the rooms shone on a tiled yard. There was a table on which plates from what he assumed was an early evening meal still sat rather forlornly, but that was all.

Edging round the corner it became obvious that the light was coming from the kitchen. Hiding as much of himself as he could he surveyed the inside. It was surprisingly clean and uncluttered and far more importantly, empty. This was a time for caution, yes, but definitely not for being timid. In four strides he was at the door. Quietly but firmly he pushed the handle down and holding his breath, pulled it slowly towards him. With the faintest of a creak it swung open. He could hear nothing, even the loading of tusks in the front yard didn't register.

There were no lights in the corridor ahead but he could make things out well enough from the kitchen glow. There were three doors on each side. It was unlikely they would all be bedrooms. If he was to find Ana, he was just going to have to try them one door at a time and pray there was nobody else inside one of the rooms.

His heart pounding he eased open the first door on the left hand side. There was a stale smell but no sign of life. He tried the opposite door. There was the same unpleasant sweaty odour and clothes were strewn round the floor. On the bed were two AK-47s. He was tempted to take one but rejected the idea. He didn't even know how the safety mechanism worked. Next there was a bathroom and Mike didn't bother to open the door fully, it was clearly empty. The room on the other side simply mirrored it. Then he came to the furthest door on the left-hand side. The handle turned but as he pushed it the door refused to move. He tried again a little harder, it protested but didn't budge and was clearly locked.

It could only be locked for two reasons, because there was something or someone important inside. He was conscious of the activity at the front of the house now and could clearly hear the rise and fall of men's voices. He tapped lightly on the door but there was no response. He tried again a little louder with the same result and was just about to turn away when he heard movement inside.

"Ana is that you?" he whispered. "It's Mike here."

There was no response so he tried again, but louder. "Ana, it's Mike."

"Mike?" There was uncertainty in the voice but there was no doubting who it belonged to.

"How did you get here? Who's with you?"

"There's no time to talk. I'm on my own and there's one chance only to get you out of here. There is no key on the outside so I'll have to use brute force but as soon as I do the noise will bring them running. Are you in good enough shape to run?"

"Yes Mike but..."

"Right just stand back and be prepared to move as quickly as you can."

Although tall and rather gangly he had spent his life outside in the bush. There was no fat on him, only muscle. He stepped back to the opposite wall and in the limited space took two steps forward as powerfully as he could and hammered into the door with his right shoulder. Pain swept down his arm but he didn't give it a second thought and hit the door hard again. There was a splintering of wood and the door sagged inwards but it needed one more hit.

As it flew open he immediately made out Ana's silhouette in the middle of the room.

"Come quickly," he shouted, all pretence at silence now futile.

They ran down the corridor towards the light of the kitchen and as they reached it they heard the front door opening and the sound of shouting behind them.

Half pulling her with him Mike strode outside to the table, dragging it to the wall, plates and glasses smashing all around; he knew this would give Ana the height she needed to get over the top.

"Stay just where you are," grated the familiar voice from behind. "You're going nowhere." The Somali made a lunge for Ana, moving with surprising speed despite his limp.

"No you stay just where you are!" shouted Mike, the old revolver pointing unhesitatingly at the man he had come to loathe. But the Somali didn't pause and Mike pulled the trigger.

There was a loud click but that was all and as the Somali reached Ana, he was positively smiling. She was half on the table and kicked out as hard as she could, aiming for his head but he caught her foot and pulled, bringing her crashing to the ground. Yanking her up with animal force he held her directly in front of him, one arm up almost to breaking point behind her back.

"Do you fancy your chances at another shot?" he laughed without humour. "Come on, you've failed at everything else, perhaps this is something you might get right."

"Just shoot Mike, we're as good as dead anyway. Might as well go down fighting!"

Mike's face was a picture of indecision. He was not a trained shot with a revolver and with Ana as a shield there were few places he could even aim for. And of course it might misfire again anyway. Yet he knew she was right, if he put down the gun they could expect no mercy. The advantage was that he was close, even a poor marksman had a chance.

He kept the gun up, his back to the wall. The Somali was trying to pull Ana back to the house and he followed them with the barrel of the gun but he simply couldn't risk hitting her, not after getting this far.

Ana could feel the ivory blade. It lay nestled in her right forearm under the sleeve of her shirt but although she shook her arm vigorously it wouldn't move, the point stuck under one of the African bracelets she wore round her wrist. She raised her arm up high as though to reach for the face of the man who held her in such an iron grip and as she did so the blade fell back into her elbow. He shoved her forward violently and in that movement she suddenly felt the cool of the ivory in her hand. The pain everywhere else seemed to evaporate. This man, this excuse for a human being, symbolised everything she detested. And with a strength she didn't even know she possessed she stabbed down into his thigh, the ivory cutting through trousers and flesh like a knife in fresh mango.

With a roar he let her go, his hand scrabbling frantically at the white skewer of ivory sticking out of his leg. Two loud shots rang out, echoing round the rear courtyard. The look on the Somali's face registered only surprise as he stared down at his chest, his shirt already dark with blood. His knees buckled as he toppled sideways, his head striking the brick surface heavily.

"Over the wall now Ana! No arguments just go. Now, otherwise all this has been for nothing!"

She hobbled onto the table once more and reaching up heaved her body onto the top as two other Somalis entered the yard, AK-47s in their hands. As she let herself fall, legs ill prepared for the sudden impact of the ground, she heard the single, distinctive sound of a revolver shot followed by a long burst of machine gun fire. Then as she lay there in the Malindi dust she heard the unmistakable wail of several police sirens coming out of the night, growing in strength as they sped ever nearer.

Chapter Nineteen

Ana played with the curry on her plate, half-heartedly chasing the few remaining prawns round the rim with a fork. She hadn't been particularly hungry, just as she didn't really feel tired, even though there had now been a number of days with little or no sleep. A grey fog seemed to swirl permanently round her head and although she craved being able to break out, one monotonous day followed another.

Across the table Harry felt equally listless. More than anything else he wanted to reach out to her, to be reassuring that all would be well, but despite his efforts Ana had remained distant and unresponsive.

Inspector Mwitu had been instructed to make sure they remained at the coast until the bulk of the investigations had been completed. He had explained, rather apologetically, that because they were such important witnesses to what had happened, it wasn't realistic for them to return to Uwingoni just yet.

Ollie's friends had kindly offered them rooms in their home but it hadn't been thought sensible to remain in Malindi itself. It didn't seem that they would be in any immediate danger but Jim had a friend with a secluded house just up the coast in Watamu that seemed a sensible option. At any other time it would have been idyllic, a pretty garden sloped gently down to a small coral built wall with a rickety gate and beyond was the most beautiful of white beaches, with the Indian Ocean lapping gently at its edge.

Each morning they were on the shore line before even the first rays of the sun peaked over the horizon to silhouette the fishing boats anchored within wading distance of the beach. Crabs scuttled in and out of an array of holes leaving their delicate prints in the virgin sand. Although both of them appreciated the beauty of their surroundings they longed for the familiarity of Uwingoni.

On the fifth day Inspector Mwitu arrived just after lunch and much to their delight and surprise he was accompanied by Jim.

"I know you two must be bored by this beautiful scenery and to be honest everyone is missing you too. So the long and short of it is that I have persuaded the Inspector to let you return with me so you had better get your bags."

"Oh Jim, you're a star." Ana positively threw herself at him, her arms locked round his back in a long squeeze. "That is the best of all news. Thank you so much for agreeing to this Inspector. You're very understanding."

"Well I had to call in a few favours and it's not as though we won't know where to find you. For the moment you have given us all the possible assistance you can and your statements are wonderfully detailed which will help enormously."

Harry could feel his heart leap, not just because they were heading back to the Reserve but because in those few seconds he has seen a sudden glimpse of the old Ana.

"We have made quite a number of arrests, not just in Malindi, but up country too. The tentacles of this poaching network stretched into areas you wouldn't believe. Even Mr Kariuki is now in a cell in Nairobi so you might be getting your supplies from somewhere else in future.

"Oh goodness," exclaimed Harry. "I suppose we did see him with Mr Hu on one occasion."

"Yes. He was too greedy for his own good. His type can never resist the chance of making some extra cash, especially if they think they are well protected. Fortunately you have someone in your organisation who has been a great help to us over the years. As it's only the three of you here, I'm sure Mr Aziz wouldn't mind you knowing that."

"Aziz, well who would have thought it?" grinned Jim. "Always considered there was more to him than met the eye."

Harry looked uncomfortable, shifting his feet restlessly on the floor. "I know he's not your favourite person Harry but you can never judge a book by its cover." Ana gave him a slap on the back, "Now where did we last hear that expression? I'm only pulling your leg."

Jim and the Inspector looked a little confused. "Oh, just a private joke between us," she smiled.

"Well, let's get packed now." Harry was keen to change the subject and at the same time the picture of Uwingoni was ever large in his head.

The engine of the six-seater Cessna hummed contentedly and Ana chatted about all manner of things with their young pilot. Charlie could only have been in her early twenties yet she flew the plane with an easy confidence, her hands on the controls always seeming totally relaxed. Ana realised that it was ages since she had talked for any length of time to another young woman. Charlie's knowledge of East Africa was wide ranging, despite her youth, and Ana found herself asking a whole array of questions about subjects she hadn't really given much thought to. The frenzy of social media with much of its shallowness was something she was glad to be away from; so much that filled the thoughts of millions seemed trite and unimportant. However, talking face to face with someone who criss-crossed this huge area on a daily basis and saw the reality of people's lives, was both revealing and refreshing. Whether it was the never-ending curse of corruption that kept so many in grinding poverty, the aspirations of young women allowed a proper education at last, or the unhealthy influence of other nations, Charlie had well informed opinions on it all.

As Ana gazed out of the side window they were passing over a town, typical of many she had seen, where the huge increase in population was pushing ever outwards into the wild of Africa. It wasn't just that people needed land for their crops and businesses, that was understandable but there rarely seemed to be a plan. Trees and habitats were destroyed and the wildlife killed or driven off. What was the matter with the world? Everywhere there seemed to be conflict, if people weren't fighting each other then they seemed at war with nature.

"Are you alright Ana?" She was aware of the concern in Charlie's voice and glancing across she could feel the wetness of the tears on her cheeks.

"I'm fine thanks. Just letting my thoughts get the better of me."

Bethwell was there to pick them up at the strip and they couldn't help but smile at the warmth of his greeting. As they made their way up towards the camp he was full of stories and as usual all the characters were people who worked in the Reserve. Of course they were exaggerated, but that was part of the magic of being back.

Uwingoni slowly began to work its special charm and as the days turned into weeks both Ana and Harry started to enjoy the pleasure of simply living in the present. The past would always be part of who they were and they couldn't undo that but learning to live in the moment became an easier way of dealing with each day.

Ana wrote and painted more than ever but gradually became less solitary and evenings were spent chatting round the fire once more. Harry and Kilifi became more like father and son, tracking and observing wildlife of all descriptions whenever they could.

Inspector Mwitu kept Jim updated when possible. There had been further arrests up at Prosperity Dam. Mr Pang had flown over from China to deal with the crisis personally and had toured the project with two Government ministers and replaced most of the management team. However, the building of the dam was continuing almost as though nothing had happened. Of his nephew Michael, there appeared no sign. The whispers behind the scene were that he had been spirited back to China. Of course they would never really know but that seemed a pretty good bet.

On the day of the funeral it was a perfect Uwingoni morning. There were some delicate white clouds on the far horizon but everywhere else was an unspoilt blue. A pair of eagles rode the invisible air currents overhead, making minute alterations to their flight with effortless ease.

The sounds of Africa were all around them. Birdsong seemed to echo off the branches and the gentlest of winds caressed the dry grass; in the background the sound of crickets merged with the grunting of distant wildebeest.

It was a morning Mike would have loved and so it seemed fitting that so many were there to say their goodbyes.

They had gathered, not long after dawn, at his favourite waterhole. For a man who considered he had few friends he would have been surprised at the number of people who came to pay their final respects. Those he had taken on amazing safaris, friends going back to his childhood days in

Nairobi and of course so many of the wonderful people who worked at Uwingoni.

There was no bitterness, only forgiveness for a man whose soul must have been tortured beyond belief in the final months of his life.

Everyone knew of his sacrifice in Malindi. Indeed it had been splashed over the front page of the national newspapers. The poaching ring had been completely broken, and Al-Shabaab dealt a serious blow.

The several tons of ivory that had been recovered had been taken away by KWS to be safely stockpiled, and no doubt it would be publicly burnt as had happened to the staggering one hundred and five tons back in 2016.

Jim had said some moving words and displayed emotion nobody had witnessed before as Mike's ashes had been scattered around the water's edge. Then gradually everyone had drifted off back to camp, no doubt despite the hour, to toast the health of a man with White Cap, his favourite beer.

Only Bluebird remained. Harry and Ana sat silently on the old canvas seats, the physical scars now gone but united in ways they couldn't really put into words.

"How do you see your future now Ana?"

"Well, I'd love to stay, if Jim will put up with me. I want to start writing again. That journalist is always there inside me and there are so many stories to tell from this remarkable country."

She looked across at him and smiled, "And you?"

"We've touched on some of these subjects before but the last couple of months have brought everything into focus for me. All my life I have really wanted to belong. That's hard to explain to those who have never felt that sense of always being a little lost. My parents are lovely people and I know they understand. Uwingoni has become my home in ways that nowhere else ever has."

Even as he spoke they both became aware of movement in the far trees and with an ease and grace they had learnt to love, a small herd of elephants emerged from the bush for their morning drink. In the lead was Mara and close on her heels Meru who scampered forward to be the first to the water.

Lightning Source UK Ltd.
Milton Keynes UK
UKHW040633070420
361440UK00001B/42